Dear Reader,

I have four great *Scarlet* books to get you in the holiday mood this month! To start with, Judy Jackson's Canadian heroine suddenly finds her life whirling *Out of Control*. Then Stella Whitelaw takes *her* heroine to Barbados where nothing (and no one) is quite as it seems! In Kay Gregory's novel, Iain and Phaedra play out their involving story against a dramatic Cornish backdrop. And, last (but by no means least!) *will* Jocasta be *Betrayed* in Angela Drake's latest *Scarlet* romance?

You will notice that each of these authors has been published in *Scarlet* before and we are delighted to see their names back on our list. One of the things that makes *Scarlet* so special, I believe, is the very individual style each of our authors brings to her writing. And, of course, they also offer us a wonderful variety of settings for their books. It's lovely, isn't it, to be able to enjoy visiting a different country without having to leave home?

So, whether you're reading this book on a train, a bus or a plane, sitting at home or having a well earned vacation – I hope you'll enjoy *all* the *Scarlet* titles I have chosen for you this month.
Till next month,

Sally Cooper

SALLY COOPER,
Editor-in-Chief – *Scarlet*

Judy Jackson's first *Scarlet* novel, *The Marriage Plan*, was published early in 1997 and we are now delighted to bring you her second compelling romance.

Judy spent her childhood in Alberta before her family moved to the coast of British Columbia. She married her highschool sweetheart and they live with their two terrific sons in the Vancouver area.

All through school, Judy could never decide on her future. Since then she's worked at so many jobs she can't remember them all, though they must have involved bookkeeping. At age thirty she threw a 'what-do-you-want-to-be-when-you-grow-up costume party.' Judy, of course, couldn't make up *her* mind so printed 50 different jobs on slips of paper and pinned them to her maternity smock! Now she lives vicariously through her characters' professions.

With hindsight, Judy knows her career began as a child, entertaining her friends with imaginative stories, Telling 'stories' was so much fun, Judy never stopped. Thanks to *Scarlet*, she can continue to entertain people with her stories and get paid for it!

Other *Scarlet* titles available this month:

JUDY JACKSON

OUT OF CONTROL

SCARLET

Enquiries to:
Robinson Publishing Ltd
7 Kensington Church Court
London W8 4SP

First published in the UK by Scarlet, 1997

A copy of the British Library Cataloguing in
Publication data is available from the British Library

ISBN 1-85487-963-4

Printed and bound in the EC

10 9 8 7 6 5 4 3 2 1

To my sister, Wendy Spencer, and my friend, Peggy Johnson, for their help and applause. To my friends Susan Thomson, Barbara Briggs, and Bonnie Spidle, who read, critiqued, advised, and encouraged. And to my friends in RWA, the Greater Vancouver Chapter, and the Vancouver Island Chapter. Thank you all.

CHAPTER 1

After standing in line in the rain for half an hour, Rand Tremayne pushed open the battered door to The Kicking Horse, a privilege for which he reluctantly paid five dollars. Once inside, rock'n'roll beat at his ears, drifting smoke stung his eyes, and the combined stench of sweat and alcohol made him wish he didn't have to breathe.

Within moments the heat created by a room full of bodies enveloped him and he removed his overcoat, shaking off the sparkling raindrops that still clung to the fabric before draping it across his arm.

The door swung shut behind him, cutting off the wet but clean night air. As he waited for his vision to adjust to the gloom, the music built to a resounding climax, then died abruptly. When the lights brightened enough for him to see the busy bar on his left, he made his way through the mass of whistling, foot-stomping patrons.

'What'll you have?'

He leaned over the brass rail in order to hear the bartender's question, then grimaced as he realized too late the metal was sticky. Now a streak of cherry juice decorated the front of the suit delivered by his tailor only last week.

'Nothing, thank you. I'm looking for an employee named Margaret Forster.'

The huge woman frowned, plucked out the cigarette that dangled from one corner of her mouth, and stabbed it out in the overflowing ashtray. 'No one here by that name.'

'Are you sure? I'm reliably informed that she's been employed here for eight months.'

'Hey, Roggo!' Her shout rose shrilly over the din. A man who looked more like a stick figure drawing than a living person waved and then twisted his way back through the crowd, a heavily laden tray of empties balanced high over his head on the fingertips of one hand.

'Yeah?'

'You know anyone by the name of . . .'

'Margaret Forster,' Rand supplied when the bartender glanced his way.

'Nope.' The waiter grabbed another tray of drinks and the mass of bodies swallowed him up again.

'Can't help you,' she said.

Rand frowned and opened his mouth to reason with the bartender when total darkness dropped over the room like a shroud and the myriad conversations around him ceased abruptly.

'What the . . .' His voice was drowned out as two hundred-odd hands began to beat a slow rhythm on tables, increasing gradually until the entire room rocked with a giant heartbeat, then it faded away.

Words rang out of the blackness.

'Hello. Would you like me to sing for you tonight?'

Her low voice rasped across his senses; anticipation rolled down his spine and settled deep in his gut.

The whispered 'yes' came from several hundred throats, and he was startled to realize it included his.

'Then will you do something for me?'

The whistles and cheering broke out again, louder than ever, as the audience responded enthusiastically. At one man's shouted offer to do anything and everything the woman chuckled, a low-pitched gurgle of amusement that ruffled the neatly clipped hair on the nape of his neck.

'I don't have my guitar with me today so I need you to lay your hands together like this . . .' The light slap of flesh on flesh echoed through the microphone until her audience picked up the beat.

A glow slowly suffused the stage behind the singer until he could see her silhouette, black against the stark white light. The woman was alone, centre stage, one hip propped on a high stool, one foot hooked in the bottom rung, the other planted on the stage.

As her body began to sway to the music's beat her slender curves were as clearly delineated against the white curtains behind her as if she were a cameo. A cameo that had taken on flesh and blood and emotion and life. The tiny part of his consciousness not caught up in the enchantment she wove wondered what type of clothing could display her so explicitly. If she wore any garment at all, wouldn't its folds obscure the exquisite curve of breast, waist and hip?

The cynic in him wondered how her vocal performance could meet, much less match, the sheer sensuousness of this dramatic beginning.

And then she began to sing. A cappella.

He stood enthralled through three songs, then leaned back over the brass rail, aware of but indifferent to the streak of orange juice he was acquiring down his sleeve.

'What's the singer's name?'

He thought he had pitched his voice low enough so only the bartender could hear, but a burly man seated at a nearby table twisted around, his mutter as fierce as the glares on his companions' faces. 'Shaddup! Nobody talks while Zara sings. Get it?'

Zara? He beckoned the woman behind the bar closer, then whispered, 'What's the performer's name?'

'Zara Lindsey.'

'Thank you. Thank you very much.' Rand slowly pivoted to face the stage again. Margaret Zara Lindsey Forster.

He crossed his arms on his chest and prepared himself for a long wait. He'd come to the bar to keep a promise to a dead man. But, even if he hadn't had a reason to stay, he was damned if he would've left before he knew how the devil a billionaire's granddaughter had ended up performing in a seedy honky tonk.

Zara felt the music absorb her anger and she deliberately used the emotion to sing about cheatin' and hurtin'.

The catharsis left her lighter if not free. She slid into a love song, wondering if she would ever receive the kind of love that gave without taking. She must have once. Proof existed in the portrait of her family that had hung in her mother's sitting room all through Zara's childhood. Every night she prayed the portrait was still there. It wasn't in her possession but she needed to hope, to believe it still existed.

The song ended on a long note. She shrugged off the unaccustomed brooding and smiled at the audience's wild applause and shouted requests. So what if her own special man never came along? The kids at the Centre loved her, no demands, no rules. All she had to do was show up with a smile and a willing heart.

5

Damn her grandfather, she thought as she bowed toward the shadows that held her audience. Why couldn't the old villain have said yes, just this once? She could still hear his creaky voice as he refused to donate as much as a nickel. Unless of course she was willing to let him run her life again. If she would 'behave' herself he might be persuaded to help them out.

She knew better. He'd expect her to perform her part of their bargain first, then he'd keep coming up with reasons why he couldn't give any money right at that moment. Next week, next month, next year for sure.

Following her thoughts from the Children's Centre, so desperately in need of funding to keep its doors open, to her grandfather, who had refused to provide the necessary money unless she bartered away her soul, her song segued to one of wrongs done and revenge taken.

As the words slid smoothly from her mouth and heart she thought about Roggo's demand that she use back-lighting tonight to hide the bruises. She wore the clinging leotard because he'd insisted the men in the audience came to see her as well as hear her. He was probably correct; a performer's appearance and sex appeal sold tickets and albums.

She didn't have to like that basic show business fact even though she was practical enough to exploit it. There was something very extraordinary about performing for an audience she couldn't see and who could barely see her.

A few songs later, as she exchanged light-hearted patter with her audience the door at the back opened. The shaft of neon light from outside acted like a spotlight on the tall man who stood so stiffly beside Doris' bar. For an instant she had an impression of grey-clad elegance before the closing door cut off the light. Who was that? He was definitely in the wrong place, judging by the business suit.

A man down front whistled, the flash of curiosity faded, and once more she immersed her emotions in her music.

A stick of eyeliner and a bottle of nail polish rattled to the floor, knocked aside when Zara plunked her elbows down on the cluttered surface of the dressing table. She rolled her neck, deliberately averting her gaze from the reflection in the mirror. She carefully flexed the fingers of her left hand which she'd bruised with a hammer, the reason she hadn't been able to perform with her guitar.

The cramped, stifling dressing room used by every performer at The Kicking Horse was unusually quiet. Her shoulders slumped as she slid the icy surface of a large glass across her forehead. This was no substitute for a long, cool shower in her own bathroom at home, she thought, especially when she had very little of her twenty minute break left before the next set. At least on Tuesday nights she had the place to herself.

She contemplated the glass of gin and tonic, tempted to take a long swallow of the drink Doris had plunked down in front of her. She sighed as she held it against her neck instead. No matter what Doris guaranteed about alcohol's restorative properties, she knew it would be stupid to drink when she was so tired.

Maybe she should have stayed on the road, she thought. Touring hadn't been all bad. At least there had been an occasional air-conditioned dressing room. Maybe she could have learned to tolerate feeling like an alien visiting in the real world of the towns she passed through. Yeah, sure, she thought, and tomorrow her grandfather would come through with the money for the Children's Centre.

No, it was time to settle down. She propped her chin in her palm and thought longingly of her bed. She was bushed. Next time Roggo got stuck he would have to ask someone else because this was the last time she would agree to work ten nights in a row.

If only she could rest. Even for a few minutes . . .

Zara's eyelids fluttered shut, her head sank down, making a pillow of the arm angled on the table top, though her sore hand still cradled the cool glass. The canned music from out front

8

faded away as she drifted into the oblivion of exhaustion.

'Excuse me.'

'Huh?' More than half asleep, not really aware of her surroundings, Zara barely stirred but when her glass tipped over she woke up. Fast. Gin, tonic and half-melted ice cubes dribbled down her neck and between her breasts. The glass landed on her lap, where it emptied the rest of its contents.

'Darn! Who the . . .' Her head snapped up and in the mirror she recognized the grey suit with the rigidly perfect posture she'd noticed out front at the beginning of the set. He was also the most gorgeous man she'd seen since . . . since . . . She couldn't remember seeing anyone quite like him before.

Taking his features one by one he was perfect. Combining the total picture with that stand-offish attitude left her with a devastating temptation to see what he was like without both the attitude and the clothes. Too bad. He might as well have worn an 'ALL BUSINESS' sign on his chest.

'I am sorry if I startled you.'

'Not half as sorry as me,' she answered as she grabbed a threadbare hand towel and started patting her neck dry beneath the curtain of dark brown hair that hung to her waist. 'I'm going to be sticky and stink of gin all night now. Just wonderful. Everyone who comes near me is going to think I'm a drunk.'

'You're exaggerating.' Rand tried not to stare as she dipped the towel beneath the elastic neckline of the black garment clinging to her body. As she shoved the material aside he noticed an old scar, close to seven inches long, that followed her collarbone to the base of her throat. It was too jagged, too messy to have been cut by a surgeon. Judging by the mottled scar tissue it must have come close to claiming her life.

'Why? Ever smelled a drunk?'

'Yes.' He winced and his lips tightened. 'I have known a few in my time.'

'Oh.' Zara glimpsed the grief in his eyes before he shielded it. The flicker of pain he'd felt surprised her almost as much as the fact that he'd revealed it. She sneaked quick looks at his image in the mirror while she rubbed the towel across her stomach and thighs. In her experience his type did not allow themselves the weakness of emotion. 'They're not a pretty sight or smell.'

Although he was, she thought. The tang of his spicy cologne was detectable through the stink of the spilled drink. The slacks clinging to his muscular thighs were pressed to a knife edge, his black hair was firmly combed straight back from a high forehead, the knot in his tie was precisely centred beneath a well-shaped jaw. Only the stains on his jacket marred his immaculate image. Why and how

10

someone like him had found his way to The Kicking Horse was a mystery.

'No. They're not.' Rand swallowed past the pulse throbbing in his throat. Watching her rub the towel over her body was as erotic as anything he'd ever seen. An errant wish for her to turn around so he could see her face more clearly was firmly suppressed as soon as his sterner side recognized the stirring physical attraction. Damn it, this woman was strictly off limits, he reminded himself as he forcibly dragged his gaze away.

A faded poster of men wearing little more than bow-ties and bathing suits hung on one discoloured wall. On the other rows of rusty hooks held scraps of fabric studded with sequins, rhinestones, and dangling feathers. He didn't want to stare at half-naked men or imagine her wearing the skimpy costumes so he looked away, hoping she'd finished using the towel.

'Were you looking for someone?' Her hands stopped moving and she turned around.

'Yes, I was looking for . . . What the heck happened to you?' His heavy black brows snapped together in a frown. No wonder she had performed without a spotlight, he thought. Her jaw and cheek were marred with green and yellow bruises.

Zara self-consciously put one hand up to her face. 'Bad luck.'

The sensation of being naked to him was so disturbing she bent over, scrubbing the towel

11

down one leg, allowing her hair to fall forward to hide the disfiguring bruises. It was his eyes, she decided. Not their deep emerald colour nor the faint laugh lines that hinted at age and experience. It was the way they looked into her, searching for her secrets. As if he already knew everything she had to hide and only looked for outward evidence of who and what she was.

'Bad luck doesn't do that to a woman's face.'

'In my case, it does.'

'You don't belong in this kind of place, or in this part of town.'

'Where I belong is not your concern.' She recognized the stubborn determination on his face and decided an answer might get rid of him. 'I had an argument with a ladder and lost, okay? Patrons aren't allowed backstage, mister, so state your business and get out.'

'I want to know how someone like you ended up in a dump like this.'

'Oh, my, will you listen to the clever line.' She rolled her eyes. 'It's none of your business where –' At that moment she put together the phrase 'someone like you' with the intensity, the knowledge, in his eyes. She flipped her hair back and looked up. 'Who are you?'

'Rand Tremayne.'

She thought for a moment, then shrugged when she didn't recognize the name. Stupid woman, she chastised herself. This man was not a messenger

12

from her grandfather as she'd both feared and hoped. 'Never heard of you. And if you don't mind, I have to get back out front.' She dropped the towel and picked up a brush which she dragged quickly through her hair.

'Don't change the subject. What happened?' he demanded, as if he had a right to know the answer.

'I have no intention of telling you anything. Why would you care?'

'You are Margaret Forster, aren't you?'

She forgot to be careful and winced when her hands clenched on the brush. 'What's it to you?'

'Your grandfather asked me to talk to you.'

'How did you find me?' She shivered as a chill swept up her spine. She hadn't told her grandfather where she worked.

'Heinrich hired a private detective. I knew Margaret Zara Lindsey Forster was your full name. If you really wanted to remain hidden you should have chosen to perform under a more obscure stage name.' Rand came all the way into the dressing room and shut the door behind him, which he immediately decided was a mistake when she stood up. 'I have a message from your grandfather.'

The already cramped quarters shrank when they stood practically chest to chest, with hers faithfully outlined by clinging, damp, thin fabric. Too thin, he decided as he dragged his gaze away from her breasts.

13

'I wasn't hiding. I prefer the names my mother gave me. Why would he . . .' She bit the tip of one finger as she studied his face. 'Unless it's about the Centre's money?'

'The Centre?'

'I didn't think so. He's never changed his mind before, he wouldn't start now. If you'll excuse me,' she stepped forward, hoping he'd get the hint and leave, 'I need to get to work.'

'I have to talk to you.'

'But I don't have to talk to you. And if I don't get up on that stage, Roggo is going to dock my salary for every minute I'm late.'

'Heinrich asked me to . . .'

'Look,' she glared up at him and jabbed one finger into his chest, deliberately pushing the edge of a mother-of-pearl button into his flesh, 'I told you to buzz off. And, quite frankly, if I have to wait a hundred years to hear what my grandfather said, it will be a hundred and one years too soon.'

'Will you stop that?' When he snared her fingers she cried out in pain. Immediately he relaxed his hold and looked down at the hand he held. The index finger on her left hand was swollen, the scabs on the knuckles red and ugly. No wonder she wasn't playing her guitar tonight. 'More bad luck?'

'Yes!' She tugged free but his warmth still lingered on her skin. Furiously she scrubbed her good hand down her thigh. 'I had a stupid accident

14

with a hammer. Now, do I have to ask the bouncer to escort you out?'

'After I deliver a message, I'll leave.'

'No thanks.'

'Dammit!' Frustrated, he swept his fingers through his hair and she was diverted by what had to be an unusual disarray, judging by the precision of his hair cut and clothing. But the amusement only lasted a second until she absorbed what he said next.

'Your grandfather is dead. He died early this morning.'

'Dea . . . dead?' She groped for the edge of the table behind her and used its support to lower herself to the bench.

'Are you all right? I'm sorry I broke it to you so bluntly but you wouldn't listen!' He jerked forward one short step, as if he intended to comfort her, then stopped. 'I'm sorry.'

She sucked in a deep breath. So it was over. Damn that old man, she wasn't finished with him! Why did he have to go and die on her?

'Can I get you something?'

'The only thing you can get me is a little privacy.'

Simmering irritation was visible in his eyes when he spoke. 'The memorial service will be held Friday, two o'clock, at the estate. The reading of the will is scheduled to follow immediately. Your grandfather asked me to pass on his request that you attend.'

15

'His request? My grandfather never "requested" anything in his life, especially from his rebellious grandchild. He ordered. He commanded. I've known for years what he thought of me, you didn't have to pretty it up.'

He shrugged. 'Shall I send a car for you?'

'No. I won't be "attending".'

'Why not?'

'Why should I?' She crossed her arms at her waist. 'Business always came first with my grandfather. Anyone who didn't live, breathe and bleed for the bottom line was wasting time. "You shall not expend time, emotion, or effort unless you earn enormous profit" was the basic tenet of his faith. I guess it took a few years, but he'd be pleased I finally learned. I know there is no "profit" for me in his will so I'll pass on the event.'

'Heinrich was a very successful man.'

'That's a matter of opinion and depends on how you measure success.'

'He was your grandfather.'

'So?' Zara lurched to her feet, still holding her arms tight to her body, and paced in the confined and cluttered space. 'He was a beastly grandfather. When I wouldn't behave exactly as ordered, he kicked me out of his life.'

'You were young and a lucrative career in the entertainment industry is extremely difficult to achieve. He saw you making a mistake and took

16

what he felt were the necessary steps to rectify the situation.'

'Rectify the situation! Pretty words for kicking your granddaughter out of the only home she'd ever known. How could you possibly know what happened, anyway? You weren't around ten years ago, were you?'

'No. Heinrich told me about the disagreement over your unsuitable career choice.'

'You agree with him, don't you?' She dropped back onto the bench. 'I bet you bow down to the god of commerce, just like he did all his life.'

'Choices have to be made, some of them unpleasant.' Rand's eyes flashed at her insult. 'Profit is not a dirty word. Money is what keeps all businesses running smoothly, even yours.'

'Yeah, I'll agree that there is big money to be made in the music industry. But don't you see, that's what irked my grandfather more than anything. I wasn't in it for the money.'

'How admirable.' The mockery in his voice made his true feelings clear. 'Any commercial enterprise that is not profitable is soon out of business, as I'm sure the recording companies are very aware. Even a place like this one would close down if people weren't spending their money on alcohol.'

'What do you mean, *even* a place like this?'

'It is not exactly Carnegie Hall, is it?'

'I want you to leave. Now.' She had to work hard to control the urge to throw something at him,

17

preferably something that would mess his beautiful suit. 'And I will not be at the service on Friday.'

Damn, but the woman was obstinate, Rand thought. How on earth did she infuriate him so easily? God of commerce! He bit back a curse as he reviewed this fiasco of an interview. Had he been in control of even one minute in the last ten?

So she would not attend, hmmm? Well, he had promised Heinrich and Rand Tremayne kept his word. He'd compromised his honour once in his life. No way was he going to do it again for a honky-tonk singer, no matter how sexy.

'Heinrich wanted you at the reading of the will.'

'Why, for God's sake? He disinherited me a long time ago. And he made damn sure I knew it, along with everyone else in my family. I was the example that kept them in line.'

'And since you don't expect any monetary reward for your time and effort, you'll ignore your grandfather's last request?' He let the accusation dangle in the air between them, a carrot to her indignation.

'How dare you say that to me? I've never cared about his money —'

'Step on it, girl. I got a business to run, ya know?'

Zara looked behind the tall man looming over her. Both of them had been so engrossed in each other that neither had heard Roggo open the dressing room door.

'I was just coming.'

'Yeah, sure looked like it. You know the rules. No boyfriends backstage.'

'He's no friend of mine.' She didn't look at Rand on her way out. The thought that he was no boy, either, ran through her mind before she squashed it.

So darned silly. Why couldn't she have simply ignored him?

Why hadn't she forgotten all about that man the moment she was back on stage? After a normal working night the only thing she could think about was getting out of here and going home to her pillow. Tonight Rand Tremayne was still on her mind.

Her hands paused on the perfume bottles, tubes of lipstick, and jars of cold cream she was rearranging. Several times early on during the last set she had caught a glimpse of his tall grey form at the back of the big room, watching her. He didn't sit, or lean against the wall, or even allow his shoulders to slouch. It wasn't until she was half a dozen songs into the set that she had figured out why his presence disturbed her.

It was as if he observed from a distance, as if he wasn't a part of the life around him. She'd seen the same attitude often when she took the children from the Centre to visit the zoo. They always watched the animals in that same way, fascinated by the cautious glimpse into another world.

She had thought he would hang around to hassle her some more but about halfway through the set she'd seen him leave.

It bothered her that she'd cared enough to notice. What was the matter with her?

'You staying here all night?' Doris said as she stuck her head in the door. 'Roggo wants to lock up.'

'No, I was tidying up a bit.'

'You're what?'

When Zara recognized the amazement in the big woman's eyes she knew she'd been dawdling, waiting for Rand to come back and argue with her again. She'd even rushed backstage to freshen her make-up and comb her hair at the end of her performance. 'I couldn't stand the mess another day, all right?'

'Okay, okay.' Doris backed away. 'Don't bite my head off.'

'I'm sorry. Could you call me a cab? My car's dead again.'

'Sure. See you tomorrow.'

Zara fussed around for a while longer then shrugged on her jacket, picked up her purse, and clicked off the light.

She didn't really care, she told herself. However, it did annoy her that the really caustic brush-off she'd prepared would be wasted because he hadn't shown up.

Outside the side door she buttoned her jacket against the chill in the air, then stepped carefully down the stairs to the paved alley. She wrinkled her nose against the odour of rotting food and wet garbage that always lingered in this dark tunnel between the tall buildings.

With the clouds hiding the moon, the alley was black beyond the circle of light cast around the bar's staff exit.

It might have been smarter to leave with everyone else, she thought as she glanced around. No matter how much she loved her job, the years of travelling had taught her not to take stupid risks. Tonight she had forgotten that basic lesson which proved how distracted she was.

It was all that man's fault, she decided as she headed up the alley to the relative safety of street lights and passing cars. He'd made her think about the life she'd left, the big house, the bottomless bank accounts, the lavish lifestyle that would have been hers if she'd been willing to pay the price.

Her childhood had been happy, living on her grandfather's estate with her parents, taking for granted everything he provided. Then, when she was five, her mother had died and life had changed.

Her father had buried himself in business and her grandfather had decreed a small child needed a woman's influence. Within a week her widowed aunt, Lucy Bendan, had moved herself and her children into the mansion. At fifteen and thirteen, Sheila and Neil had been kind in their own way but

21

the age difference had been too great for them to be her friends.

Zara had never been happy in that house again, especially after her father died of a heart attack in his office when she was fifteen.

She shivered and clutched the wool jacket tighter to her chest, sure she'd felt the wind reach through the fabric to touch her skin. She still believed that she'd made the right decision when she was eighteen. But it would have been interesting to see her aunt and cousins again.

Was Neil still the pompous weasel he'd been as a young man? And what about Sheila? Though she had been twenty-eight and a lawyer when Zara left home, her cousin had been more of a tomcat than any man Zara had ever met. And what about Aunt Lucy? Did she still hide from the world in the library, like a turtle in its shell?

Her smile died away when she remembered the accusation Rand had made and her anger rose again. How dare he criticize her motives? She'd never cared about Heinrich's money and nothing would get her back in that world again.

Then the memory of a decrepit, overcrowded building forced her to acknowledge her hypocrisy. If there were any chance a visit to the estate would benefit the Centre, she would go. Just as she had gone to the ForPac offices two months ago to ask, no, beg her grandfather to pay for structural work to make the building safer.

'Isn't this a little late to walk through alleys alone?'

When she heard the deep voice Zara stumbled back, staring wide-eyed at the looming shadow, then pressed her hand to where her heart was using her ribs as bongo drums. 'Are you insane? You nearly scared me to death.'

'I meant to,' Rand said as he took her arm and began to lead her toward the street. 'I couldn't stand the smoke any longer so I decided to wait for you outside. I thought you'd be out soon after the crowds left but when I knocked at the front door they told me you'd gone out the back. And let me tell you this neighbourhood makes me nervous. Particularly at two in the morning.'

'Who asked you to be here?' She yanked her arm free. As they walked she rummaged through her mind for the witty brush-off she'd been saving but now he was here she couldn't remember it. Typical! She'd probably remember it once she was at home in bed when he wasn't around to be zapped by her wit. 'I've been taking care of myself for a long time.'

'If this is an example, I'm surprised you haven't . . .'

'Oh!' At that moment they arrived at the street and under the lamps she got her first clear look at him. His stroll through the garbage cans had smeared something vilely green down the side of his camel overcoat.

'What?'

'Look.' He glanced down to where she pointed and she tried valiantly to hold back a giggle when she saw his pained expression.

'Great. First my suit is soiled in that bar, now the coat's probably ruined.'

'Too bad.'

'Try to restrain your sympathy. You're going to choke on it.'

'Nope. Don't think I will,' she said with a grin.

Rand pulled a handkerchief from his trouser pocket and bent to scrub at the offending stain. Blast the woman, he thought. If only her performance hadn't aroused such absurd reactions in his head and his libido, he'd have been able to wait for this talk in the relative comfort of The Kicking Horse.

Instead he'd had to stand outside in the cold, hovering in the street like some stage door Johnny. He looked up, just in time to see Zara disappearing into the back of a cab.

'Wait!' He tossed the crumpled square of white linen into a trash can and jumped forward to grab the door handle. After a short struggle, with her pulling against him from the inside, he managed to jerk it open again. 'I'll drive you home. We can talk on the way.'

'No, thanks.'

'I insist.'

'You are in no position to insist on anything.'

'Come on,' the cabbie interrupted. 'Enough, already. Either in the cab or out. I got a living to make, you know.'

'Let go of the door.' She stared at Rand for another minute until his hand dropped away.

'I was right, wasn't I?' He felt the frustrated anger building inside him. 'There's nothing in it for you, so to hell with an old man's last request.'

She didn't acknowledge him as she reached for the handle. The door's hollow thud punctuated his words. He stood there and watched the red tail lights pull away. Don't think I've given up, lady. I never give up, he promised silently.

But before they had gone half a block the brake lights flashed, and the cab began to back up, the rear wheel screeching to a stop only one foot from his toes. The door swung open again and Zara stepped halfway out.

'I'll be there.'

'Thank you.' Never doubted it for a moment, he thought.

His past had taught him the infinite value of a poker face but some of his triumph must have showed in his eyes because she leaned forward and flicked his tie with a disdainful fingertip.

'I'll go, but for reasons of my own. Don't forget I spent the first eighteen years of my life under the thumb of the greatest manipulator of them all and, ultimately, he failed with me. You'd be a fool to assume you were able to manipulate me into changing my mind.'

She flicked his tie once more, then climbed back into the cab.

'Do you really think so?' He stared after the tail lights until they were lost in traffic. 'I wonder which one of us is the fool, Zara Lindsey?'

CHAPTER 2

'I really appreciate the ride to the funeral, Billie.'

Zara lifted the ice cube wrapped in a paper towel away from her hand and turned so she could see her thumb better in the afternoon light slanting through the car window.

'No problem. It's on our way. I hope you won't be too late but if you are it's all your own fault. Does it hurt?'

'No.' Zara looked up when her best friend and landlady snorted in disbelief. 'Well, only a little.'

'Why don't you leave those jobs for someone who has more skill with tools?' Billie shook her fringe out of her eyes and signalled a left turn. 'Or at least someone who isn't quite so likely to kill themselves.'

'You're exaggerating.'

'First you knock yourself out walking into the scaffolding. Two days later you drop one of the cinder blocks on your hand. This morning you mistake your thumb for a nail. The other day someone asked me if you'd been mugged.'

'Billie . . .'

'I told them you're dangerous enough all on your own.'

'I want to help repair the Centre.'

'Man, we needed a singer for the benefit concert not an accident-prone construction worker. Although I wouldn't be surprised to hear you'd hit yourself in the face with the microphone once or twice.'

'Wilhelmina Jones, may I remind you that nobody "hired" me. I volunteered to put on the concert. I organized it and asked my friends to perform. If I want to help do the work, I will.' She tossed the ice out the window, put the damp paper towel in the trash bag, and experimentally wiggled her thumb. 'There, good as new.'

'Roggo came by yesterday and made us all promise to make sure you didn't get damaged again. He's fed up, Zara, and I agree with him. Why do you keep doing this?'

'Because the Centre and what the people there are trying to accomplish is very important to me. Because Kenny and children like him are important. Because you were there when I needed you.'

'But you keep getting hurt. Construction can be dangerous . . .'

'If I choose to hammer nails *or* thumbnails, I will. We all make our own choices. What about you? Why don't you,' she glanced at her friend's son in the back seat before finishing her sentence in a whisper, 'marry Abe? That man loves you.'

'Kenny's going to hear you.' Billie glanced in the rear-view mirror at the ten-year-old boy rapping his fingertips against the portable CD player and humming off key.

'The only thing he can hear is the music in those earphones.' Zara shook her finger at Billie. 'You're being an idiot. Abe loves you and Kenny as much as you both love him.'

'Just because I let you rent the other side of our duplex doesn't mean you know everything about my life.'

'Maybe not but I know I'm right about this. You need each other. You have to marry him, Billie.'

'The man hasn't asked me, Zara. He says he can't support a family until he's finished his last year of medical school.'

'He's being an idiot. But never mind, I've told you both that before.' Zara's heart beat a little faster as the car slowed for the turn onto Marine Drive, one of Vancouver's enclaves of stately mansions. 'We're almost there. Fourth set of gates on the left.'

'I remember.' Billie flicked on the turn signal and waited for the traffic to clear. 'Hasn't changed much since we were kids, has it?'

They drove through the open gates and Zara stared out the side window at the massive red brick building emerging through the bare branches of the oak trees lining the long drive. 'No, it hasn't.'

'Remember the time we caught Neil making out with his girlfriend in the tree fort?' She chortled, then lowered her voice. 'Too bad the first time we saw a naked man it had to be a little wiener like him, in more ways than one.'

'Billie!'

'So . . . is Rand Tremayne going to be here today?'

'Yes, I think so.'

'Oh.'

'Why?'

'Just interested. I get the feeling you are, too.'

Zara caught her friend's too-innocent expression but decided to deny her the satisfaction of knowing she'd guessed right. No way did she want to discuss Rand Tremayne with Billie. Deliberately she turned her head away and gazed out the window.

Billie was right, she mused. The estate hadn't changed in her ten year absence. Oh, the trees were bigger and the ivy thicker, but the impression of tranquil opulence remained. A minute or two from now the car would follow the drive's last sweeping curve through the trees and they'd arrive at the entrance.

'Please stop here. I think I'll walk up to the house.'

Kenny took off the earphones as his mother stopped the car. 'I think you should come to the

30

football game,' he said, his narrow face and dark eyes alive with mischief.

'I wish I could.' Zara grinned at the boy in the back seat. 'Now, no crazy driving around the stadium in that wheelchair. Remember what happened last time.'

'Yeah.' He giggled. 'But it sure was fun going full speed down those ramps.'

'Only until you freewheeled your chair around a corner and knocked over the security guard. You almost got us arrested.'

'You'd better get a move on, you're already late,' Billie said. 'Do you want me to pick you up on our way home?'

'I have no idea how long this is going to take so I'd better call a cab.'

'Come for dinner Sunday. You can tell me all about it.'

'Thanks. I will.' She stepped out and slammed the door. Billie turned the car and Kenny waved his hand out the window as they drove away.

For a moment she stood, silent, listening. And heard nothing. Not distant traffic. No neighbourhood kids at play. Not even a bird singing in the trees. In all her travels she had never been any place where the quiet was so intense. The urge to shout or sing or do something, anything, to shatter the hush was almost uncontrollable. Instead she hunched her shoulders inside her coat and left the drive for one of the paths that meandered through the estate.

Gravel crunched under her heels as she strolled, passing beneath the massive oak that had once upon a time held the perfect tree fort. She almost smiled as she skirted the velvety lawn where she and her childhood friends had played soccer and baseball and staged medieval jousts. Neil had been too lazy to join in such active sports and Sheila thought herself too mature.

Stone lions still guarded the bottom of the wide stairs at the main entrance. Tentatively she reached out and ran her fingers across the nearest lion's heavy mane. A long time ago she rode these lions into battle, pretending she was Boadicea defending the castle from the Romans. Or Annie Oakley, star of the Wild West Show. Or Jane taming Tarzan, Cheetah, and the jungle.

She pivoted slowly, conscious of her pounding heart.

Everything was the same. Everything was different. She would rather have gone to the football game with Billie and Kenny. So why was she here?

Curiosity about her old home? About her cousins?

Or was she determined to prove to a certain arrogant businessman that his accusations were wrong?

She couldn't come up with a rational answer.

'Hello, Margaret.'

Zara turned, looked up, then mounted the three steps to where her grandfather's housekeeper stood. 'Hello, Mrs Parker.'

'The service was scheduled for two o'clock.'

'So I was informed.' Zara stopped in front of the housekeeper, who hadn't moved. 'Can I come in?'

Eventually the other woman stepped back and allowed her into the hall.

Zara glanced at the ormolu clock that still graced the rosewood table in the foyer then shrugged off her yellow jacket. Quarter to three.

'They waited ten minutes, Margaret.'

She gritted her teeth at the censure in the middle-aged woman's voice. Just for a moment, while the housekeeper surveyed Zara's brown slacks and sweater with disapproval, she wished she'd bought a black suit or dress for today. But only for a moment. 'They shouldn't have. And I no longer use the name Margaret Forster, Mrs Parker. I prefer to be called Zara Lindsey.'

'Of course. The other mourners are in the gallery.' Helen Parker held Zara's jacket suspended between the forefinger and thumb of her left hand, nodded regally, and retired to the servant's quarters.

Zara gazed after the woman whose disapproval had been one of the miseries of her childhood. Though her hair was now steel grey instead of brown, Mrs Parker hadn't changed much over the years either. She still had the haughty look in her

33

eye, the straight spine and mincing walk, the slight flare of the nostrils as if the world exuded an unpleasant odour.

It wasn't until Zara was fourteen years old that she discovered how their grandfather knew about every misdemeanour committed by the three children; Helen Parker had reported to him every night.

So typical of Heinrich Forster, Zara thought as she stepped into the gallery. So practical to combine the duties of housekeeper, warden, and mistress in one salary. She wondered if the mayor, scheduled to deliver the eulogy, would mention this aspect of her grandfather's pragmatic nature.

As she reached the gallery's glass double doors a blonde woman slipped out, her slender legs emphasized by four-inch heels and a short skirt. Even after all these years, Zara would have recognized her anywhere.

'Hello, Sheila.'

'Well, if it isn't little Margaret.' Sheila flung her arms around Zara in an extravagant hug and the other woman's perfume stung Zara's nostrils.

Disconcerted by her familiarity, Zara recoiled. Sheila had always treated everyone she met as if they were her next best friend, talking about things other people would have kept confidential.

Sheila plopped down on a settee opposite the door. 'Oh, I forgot, it's Zara, now, isn't it? Being late to your grandfather's memorial service is bad form, my dear.'

'Car trouble.'

'Come over here and sit down.' Sheila lit up a cigarette and dragged a mouthful of smoke deep into her lungs. 'It's just too deadly boring in there and I had to escape.'

'Shouldn't you be inside?'

'No.'

Through the glass in the door they could see the mayor waving an expansive arm and Sheila shuddered delicately.

'I'll stay out here, thank you. I have to talk to most of those old jerks every day, either in court or at work, and that's more than any woman should have to bear.' They watched the mayor introduce Rand. 'All except him, of course. I'd never get enough of that man. What woman would?'

Zara couldn't ignore her cousin's suggestive tone. 'You're involved with Rand Tremayne?'

'Well . . .' Her gaze was pinned to the tall dark man. 'There's involved, and then there's involved, if you know what I mean?'

'No, I don't.' The interest she felt in his personal life dismayed Zara. 'We'd better go in, the minister is going to speak.'

'It's only old Henright. He won't even know we're not there. He'll ramble at the top of his lungs for ten minutes and then, finally, it will all be over. Except for reading the will, of course. Until then, let's talk about something more interesting.' She shifted around to face Zara.

'What?'

'Rand Tremayne, of course. I like a man who works hard and plays hard, don't you? He and I dated for a while a couple of years ago. Since then, well, let's say we've kept our options open.' She slipped off one shoe and wiggled her toes. 'My feet are killing me. I sure could use Rand's magic fingers right now. I swear that man gives a better foot rub than a professional. And his back rub! What that man can do with a little oil and the heat of his hands. Sheer magic.'

Zara couldn't prevent the blush that stained her neck at the intimate picture her cousin's words portrayed.

Sheila noticed and smirked. 'Still a prude after ten years in show business, coz? Who would have thought it?' She winced as she slipped her foot back into her shoe. 'I understand it was Rand who persuaded you to come here today. Tell me, what do you think of Heinrich's hand-picked protégé?'

'Not much. And I am not here because anyone persuaded me. I chose to come, no matter what interpretation Mr Tremayne gives the facts.' Abruptly she realized she was almost shouting and, shocked by the strong emotions roused by just talking about the man, Zara forcibly lowered her voice. 'Who is that with him?'

Sheila glanced into the other room. Rand was speaking, dwarfed by the very large man who stood behind his right shoulder.

36

'That's Rand's friend, Walt Kirkpatrick, one of the executives at ForPac. He's an amazingly ugly guy, isn't he? Body of a god and terminally faithful to his wife, more's the pity. He used to play professional ice hockey but now he and Rand play in a league with a bunch of middle-aged men who can't give up the fantasy they're athletes. Sure wish I could interest Walt in one of my fantasies.'

Zara shook her head. Obviously Sheila's habit of pursuing men hadn't changed. 'How's Aunt Lucy?'

'She died almost eight years ago.'

'I'm sorry. I didn't know.'

'You've been gone a long time.' She dragged hard on her cigarette, tilted her head back, and released smoke in rings that drifted lazily to the ceiling.

'Is Neil here?'

'Of course, darling. He wouldn't miss an opportunity to schmooze with wealthy potential clients.'

'Clients?'

'Neil and Fran run an auction house. Believe it or not, Neil's little wife is even more expensive than he is. Smarter, too, which is why she keeps him busy running after money. She's determined to keep a tighter leash on him than either of his first two wives. That's her over there.' She pointed at a brunette smiling vivaciously at no one in particular.

'She looks like . . .' Zara stopped herself from blurting out the unkind comparison.

'With those big boobs and little kiss curls around her forehead she looks like a cartoon character come to life. She even wiggles when she walks on those stilts she calls shoes. I, on the other hand, am a professional. A lawyer.'

Sheila stuck her nose in the air as she said it. Then she laughed and drew deeply on her cigarette again.

'How did Neil get into the auction business?'

'After Mother died Heinrich assured us that, for purely logical business reasons, he would not support Neil and me. After all, adopted by his daughter or not, none of his blood ran in our veins.

'Heinrich compelled old man Martin to give Neil a job at the auction house and he arranged for me to receive a grudging offer of a junior position with Cassidy and Kinley. They treated *me* like a gofer and of course I couldn't allow that to continue. Neil showed a surprising talent for estate sales but he didn't last long either. The old man did not raise us to be conciliatory, even for a salary.'

'What did you do?'

'We convinced him that, for the sake of appearances, he couldn't let us starve on the street. Neil thought he would finally get a top job at ForPac but Heinrich preferred Rand as heir apparent. The old man bought an almost defunct auction house and gave it to my brother, making it clear that he could sink or swim but not at ForPac.'

'Was Neil angry?'

'Furious. He owned a viable business but that wasn't much comfort as Rand gained a reputation as one of the wealthiest and most powerful men in the city.'

'What about you?'

'Heinrich finally agreed to set me up in my own practice on the condition that I act as his personal lawyer. He gave me an inexpensive lease for an office in the ForPac building. It's too small but I've managed to furnish it with style. My secretary is affordable and willing to do the work of two.'

'Is business good?'

'Things will certainly be different now that my one very demanding client is dead.'

'One?'

'Working for that old bastard left me very little time to develop any other clientele. He kept me at his beck and call to make sure he got his money's worth. You know, Neil and I thought you were so stupid to run away. Heinrich was enraged and, though he made sure we three paid dearly for your escape, it took us years to realize you were the lucky one.'

'I'm sorry.' Zara didn't know what else to say. Aunt Lucy, Neil and Sheila had evidently suffered because of her actions and nothing she could say now would change that.

Sheila's eyes flashed but, as if she regretted revealing bitterness, she shrugged and stubbed out her cigarette in the dirt of a nearby plant. 'We should go in.'

Zara agreed and followed her cousin as she slipped through the door and into the last row of folding chairs.

'Let's do this in the library. Helen has laid out a small buffet if anyone is hungry.'

Zara watched Sheila play gracious hostess, then glanced at Rand who was shaking hands with the departing minister in the entrance hall. Nobody was watching so she gave the others a chance to enter the library before she headed in the opposite direction. There was one thing she had to do before the reading of the will.

Sheila was answering a question from Mrs Parker and their voices faded away as Zara slipped up the curving staircase. She walked quickly along the hall. Would it still be there?

She twisted the crystal knob on one of the ornate doors and edged it open. Her hand slipped off the knob as the door swung wide and she halted on the threshold, almost afraid to enter what had been her mother's private sitting room. Had her grandfather followed through on his threat to get rid of the one item that meant more to her than all the valuable objects in this house put together?

She braced her hand against the door jamb as the mustiness of a room long shut up tickled her nose. There was no dust, no cobwebs. Mrs Parker's staff was very efficient, as always, even in a room unused since Eloise's death. Her gaze travelled slowly over the knick-knacks and Sheraton furniture so lovingly collected by her mother but Zara didn't move into the room until she saw the large picture, shrouded in a dust cover, hanging over the fireplace.

Her hand shook slightly as she tugged on the fabric. It finally slipped, whispering and sighing as it cascaded into a heap at her feet.

'Mama.' Her voice was a filament of sound, her heartbeat loud in her ears as she stared up at the people portrayed there, timeless in the swirls and textures of oils applied by a talented artist's brush.

The woman's curls were bright as sunshine, her eyes bluer than a summer sky. Her lips tilted in a winsome, loving smile as she combed out the tangles in the long black hair of the little girl perched on a stool in front of her chair. Zara thought she heard echoes of the child's giggle. The man crouched beside them was laughing, too.

He was laughing.

Zara rubbed away the tears in her eyes.

Regret. A wasted, wasteful emotion, she thought. Contrary to the dire warning her grandfather had uttered the day she'd told him she was leaving, she had never missed any of the possessions that had been hers while living in this house, living on his money. Except one.

This one. The only existing portrait of her mother, who had always refused to have her photograph taken. The only picture of them as a family because her father had so seldom allowed himself to be dragged away from business. The only proof that she had been loved.

Though the portrait had been given to her by her father on her fifteenth birthday, ten years after her mother's death and only weeks before his own, her grandfather would not let her take it when she left. She'd had no proof that it belonged to her and had been too young to fight him for it.

Somewhere in the distance a door slammed. Zara jumped, remembering the people waiting for her. She snatched up the dust cover and dragged a chair close underneath the portrait. She kicked off her shoes and stepped up onto the satin cushion and stretched out her hands to toss the cover back over the heavy frame but paused.

'I'll get you back, Mama. I promise.' Her fingers trembled as she reached out to touch her mother's face. But instead of living flesh they met only the texture of oil on canvas. She snatched her hand away and lifted the fabric, tossing it up to once more hide away the only tangible evidence of her happy childhood.

She stepped into her shoes, replaced the chair and strode across the room, pausing for a few minutes next to one of the soaring windows. She stopped and turned to face the shrouded portrait. A deep sigh shuddered through her body and she tilted her head back, blinking hard, forcing back tears. She gripped her purse tighter and opened the door.

At the other end of the hall Rand hesitated, then called her name but received no answer. Where was she?

He would also like to understand why, when her continued absence had been noticed, had he volunteered to look for her?

He heard a sound and glanced around, watching silently as Zara stepped out of a room, standing with bowed head and slumped shoulders before she dragged in a deep breath. Her sadness was so obvious he hesitated to intrude but if they were absent much longer Neil would be up here looking for both of them.

He strode up the hall but she didn't seem to hear him until he was very close. Her head jerked up and her shoulders snapped back. 'Oh, hello.'

'I was sent to collect you. Your cousins were worried you might be lost.'

'I wasn't, except maybe in memories. I wanted to take one last look.'

'Look?' His glance travelled to where her hand still rested on the crystal knob, then back to her face.

'At what used to be my mother's room.'

He studied her over-bright eyes and wondered if she'd been crying. 'Are you okay?'

'Yes, of course.' She pulled the door shut with a decisive snap. 'Shall we go?'

'Would you like a few more minutes? I could –'

'No, let's get this over with.'

'Zara.' He touched her forearm in a gesture of sympathy but he quickly withdrew when she flinched away. 'I'm sorry if this is difficult for you.'

'Oh. Does that mean you regret coming to Roggo's to find me?' she asked.

He felt a twinge of remorse which he brushed away. She'd feel better once she heard the will.

'I didn't think so, not when Heinrich had ordered you to do so,' she commented before he had a chance to answer.

'Does it have to be this way between us?' This time he did more than touch her arm; he grasped her hand and tugged gently until she faced him. 'We're not enemies, are we?'

'No, of course not.'

'Would you like me to stall them for half an hour?' He could feel the softness of her skin and the pulse beating erratically in her wrist. The urge to draw her closer, much closer, was so strong he immediately dropped her hand and backed away.

'No, thanks,' she answered as she began to walk back down the long hall. 'It's not necessary. I'm sure you have meetings scheduled this afternoon and I wouldn't want to make you miss them.'

He stiffened as he remembered her insults in the night-club. 'I have no business planned for the rest of today. You seemed upset and I wanted to help.'

'I'm sorry, that was uncalled for. You remind me of Heinrich and the resentment, the anger . . . comes out of nowhere.' She took a tissue from her purse and dabbed at the corners of her eyes. He could tell she hated him seeing her so vulnerable. 'Between the funeral and visiting my mother's room after all these years I guess I'm feeling emotional.'

'Don't worry about it.'

She shoved the tissue in her pocket and forced her lips to smile. 'Shall we go down?'

He nodded and fell into step. They descended the staircase together. Rand paused at the library door, waiting for Zara to precede him. They both heard the querulous tones of a spoiled child in Neil's voice.

'Why couldn't Fran stay, Sheila? She has as much right to hear the will as Margaret does.'

'Because that's the way Heinrich wanted it. And you should remember our cousin uses the name Zara now, Neil.'

'I don't know why Heinrich wanted her here. We all know he cut her out of his will years ago. He told us so every time he forced us to follow orders. He didn't change his mind, did he?'

'Sit down and be quiet. I'll read the will and then you'll know as much as I do.'

A reluctant grin tugged at Zara's lips as she entered the library. Sheila had abandoned her gracious hostess role and snapped out the command, much the same way she'd ordered Neil and Zara around years before. Her grin widened when he promptly obeyed the order but vanished when she noticed how Rand Tremayne was studying her.

'Ah, here they are at last,' Sheila said. 'Sit down. Please.'

Uncomfortable with the speculation in Rand's eyes, before she sat down Zara altered the angle of her chair so its high winged sides hid her from his scrutiny.

'Now that we're finally all here, I can begin.' Sheila began to read. 'This is the last will and testament of me, Heinrich Rainier Forster. I hereby revoke all former wills and codicils . . .'

Zara's eyes wandered to the portrait that dominated the room from its place of honour over her grandfather's empty chair. She stared at his long thin nose, curled down ever so slightly at its tip with nostrils flaring, the elevated eyebrow that seemed to question everyone else's mental acuity.

As she listened to Sheila recite the legal phraseology that disposed of her grandfather's possessions, she speculated that genetics had most generously provided the sneer his nature had required. Even dead his presence was so strong that no one, Sheila included, sat in his chair. Zara sighed as she focused her attention on Sheila's voice.

Rand received Heinrich's voting stock. The estate and its contents, as well as the apartments in London and New York, were to be sold and the proceeds invested in Forster Pacific Corporation. Heinrich's stock portfolio went to ForPac also. Neil and Sheila each received one hundred thousand dollars as a cash bequest and ten shares in ForPac.

She almost laughed out loud at the expression of shock on Neil's face; the bequest was closer to an insult than a windfall, considering the size of their grandfather's estate. Though Heinrich had compelled obedience from the others for years with promises of riches after his death, she wasn't surprised that he'd reneged on those promises. It was just like him.

'That's all I get?' Neil ran a hand across his scalp, sweeping long strands of mousy hair across his bald spot. 'I'll sell the shares.'

'No, you can't, except back to ForPac,' Sheila said. 'They will pay generous yearly dividends, however.'

'This is preposterous,' Neil spluttered. 'The old man was obviously insane. You should have told me what he intended while he was still alive, Sheila, so we could have taken action to stop

him. Had him declared incompetent or something.'

'I didn't tell because I knew you'd probably do
something stupid and cost us even this inheritance,'
Sheila said. 'He was a cruel old scoundrel, Neil, but
no way could you have had him declared incompetent. If you'd tried, he would have had *you* declared
unfit and saddled with a guardian.'

'Is there more?' asked Rand.

'Yes. If Margaret – no, excuse me,' she bent
graciously in her cousin's direction, 'if Zara is
present at this reading and will agree to work at
ForPac's executive offices for three months beginning immediately after this reading,' Sheila paused
when Zara gasped in disbelief, 'Grandfather's will
provides one million dollars to go to the charity of
her choice.'

One million dollars. If she'd do as she was told.
Zara pressed back into the chair and closed her
eyes. Oh, God, she wished she could stand up, tell
them what she thought of Grandfather's attempt to
control her from beyond the grave, and walk out.
Just walk out for the last time.

But she couldn't. She kept seeing the things the
money could change at the Children's Centre. The
paint peeling from the walls, toys so old they
weren't even fifth- or sixth-hand. The elevator
had settled to the basement level two weeks ago
and never rose again, forcing all children in wheelchairs to stay on the ground floor.

And what about the children? Children like Kenny who escaped to that haven every day. What could a million dollars do for them?

She pressed the fingers of one hand to her forehead, where she could feel a doozy of a headache starting up, then opened her eyes and tried to concentrate on what Sheila was saying.

'What about Crawford Forster?' Neil asked. 'I notice he isn't here today. Did the old bastard cut out his own cousin?'

That caught Zara's attention. Uncle Crawford was still alive?

As young men, Heinrich and Crawford had worked together to build Forster Pacific. A few years later Crawford asked Heinrich to buy him out so he could start a new venture. When that eventually failed he came back to work for Heinrich and had been an employee ever since.

'Crawford isn't here because he knows he isn't a beneficiary. Heinrich settled an annuity on him years ago.'

'That proves he's as cunning an old bastard as Heinrich. Crawford probably had some way to force Heinrich to pay up front. He didn't want to get screwed around like us. I can't believe we only get a measly hundred grand.'

'That's not exactly true. He also named me residual legatee in lieu of payment for my services as his personal lawyer.' Sheila flipped the page.

Her cousins began wrangling and Zara tuned them out. She could hardly comprehend what she'd heard. Her grandfather had put her back in his will. And under what terms!

The Children's Centre would get the money it needed if she would agree to work under the thumb of the Chief Executive Officer for three endless months. And of course, with his new voting shares, Rand Tremayne would remain the CEO. Zara felt him staring at her but she resisted the urge to look in his direction.

'We get a measly hundred grand and a handful of shares. Some charity gets a million and Tremayne gets everything else.' Neil began to pace. 'You get almost nothing after years of slaving as his lawyer. It's criminal.'

'Rand does not receive any of Grandfather's estate personally, other than stock,' Sheila reminded him. 'It's all going into ForPac.'

'Do you think I'm an idiot? He might not get any of the estate but he gets forty-nine per cent of the stock. Add that to his own ten per cent and he votes himself in as CEO. The family is no longer the major share holder, he is. He's running the whole show.'

Zara peeked at Rand without turning her head. He was leaning back in a brocade chair identical to hers, fingers laced and resting on his crossed knees, still staring at her impassively, completely at ease. Obviously the provisions of the will didn't surprise him. Why was he making no response to Neil's outburst?

When she met his gaze, he half-smiled and she whipped around to face forward again.

'I have half a mind to challenge this in court. No judge would –'

'You won't,' said Sheila.

'Why the heck not?'

'Because you would fail, Bendan,' Rand said. 'I guarantee it.'

'Feeling your oats already, Tremayne?' sneered Neil.

'Anyone who knew Heinrich would be willing to testify as to his mental competency right up until his death. Also, although Heinrich recommended I use your firm to handle the sale of the estate and its contents, I must remind you that such a contract has not yet been signed by me.'

'Oh . . .' Neil dropped into a chair as the meaning of Rand's words penetrated his anger.

'A hefty commission to risk on something so foolhardy, don't you agree?' Rand asked.

'I don't know about you guys, but I've had all of this place I can take for one day and I'm leaving.' Sheila stood up and began shoving all the documents into her briefcase.

'At least that old biddy Parker didn't get anything.'

'Yes, she did.' Sheila snapped the briefcase closed. 'Last year Grandfather gave her a house in West Vancouver and a generous annuity. She never has to work again, unless she chooses to.'

'That does it. I'm going to hire a lawyer tomorrow. I'm going to have him dig through the will –'

'You will not!' The concentrated venom in Sheila's voice silenced her brother. 'I'm out of here. Zara, let me know your decision by Thursday. If you still want me to give you a ride, Neil, we're leaving now.'

Zara knew she should ask Sheila for a ride. If she waited for a taxi, she'd be left alone with Rand. Which would be worse, listening to Neil whine or spending time with her grandfather's favourite person?

CHAPTER 3

Zara didn't move as Neil obediently trailed Sheila into the hall, practically treading on her heels, still complaining bitterly about the unfairness of Heinrich's will and his sister's secretiveness about its details.

'You seem annoyed.'

'Do I?' Zara glanced over at the man who would be ordering so many of her waking hours if she decided to accept her grandfather's deathbed challenge.

His suit didn't have one wrinkle, his shirt collar was crisply white, his tie knotted precisely. The muscles of his thighs flexed under the thin covering of navy wool as he stood and she caught a glimpse of his taut stomach and wide chest encased in what had to be a tailored shirt, before he buttoned his jacket. The man made her feel scruffy. Darned right she was annoyed.

'Probably because I'm hungry.'

But which had annoyed her more? she wondered. Her grandfather's will or the way her heart beat faster and her palms sweated every time she was near Rand Tremayne, businessman extraordinaire. A man formed in her grandfather's image.

'Perhaps we should eat lunch. Helen put out this wonderful buffet for the family and for some inexplicable reason,' he smiled down at her, 'no one ate anything. While we eat, we can discuss your plans to fulfil the terms of Heinrich's bequest.'

He would have a smile like that, she thought, and he would flash it in her direction right now when she needed brains, not mush, in her head. She bent forward to place her purse by the chair leg.

'This looks good.' At the long table against the windows he handed her a plate before taking one for himself. 'Helen does things like this so well.

'Yes, I know. She always did everything superbly. She managed to keep my grandfather satisfied and that was not an easy task. Certainly I never managed it. We three kids always used to wonder how she always knew if we'd planned something. She'd appear like a genie from a bottle, just before we were going to have some forbidden fun.'

Memories. Too many memories. She should have left with her cousins right after the will-reading. She could feel the old hostility building and struggled to repress it. The fork scraped along the platter as she stabbed at a piece of ham and forked it onto her own plate.

'Neil was upset.'

'He shouldn't have been. He knew better than to expect more than a token inheritance, no matter what the old man promised.' She chose tomatoes and broccoli from the array of cold vegetables and laid them beside the ham. She scooped a dab of honey-Dijon mustard onto the plate.

'Why shouldn't Neil have expected more?' Rand carefully layered ham and cheese into one of the buttered rolls.

Her head jerked up in surprise. 'How long did you say you'd known Grandfather?'

'Eight years, or so. Why?'

'Because I can't believe you'd need to ask.' She reached for a roll, then changed her mind and took a handful of carrot sticks instead. 'He'd disowned me and his only remaining heirs didn't have Forster blood in their veins. Of course he'd rather pass his life's work on to a "son" of his own choosing.'

'Me.'

'You.' She picked up the cutlery rolled in a linen napkin and was heading back to her own chair when she swerved abruptly, plopped the loaded plate onto the desk, and sat in her grandfather's chair.

'Wouldn't you rather sit over there?' He motioned toward the seating grouped around a low table at the other end of the room.

55

'No.' She leaned back and gripped the padded chair arms tightly before pressing her toes to the parquet floor and pushing off in a mad swing, around and around, on the swivel base. As the chair slowed she caught the edge of the desk with her hands and stopped. 'I always wanted to do that.'

He put his plate on his side of the desk, lay her purse on the opposite corner, and pulled up the high-backed chair she'd sat in during the reading of the will. 'You must have done it innumerable times as a child.'

'Oh, I came close once but Mrs Parker caught me. She was so angry! I had "defiled" the sacrosanct with my "childish impulses" and had to "pay the penalty for my behaviour".'

'What happened?' he asked.

She stopped eating and stared into the past for a moment before she shuddered. Resolutely she picked up, bit into, and chewed a pickle, relishing its sour tang.

'Zara?'

'Nothing much.' When she saw the way he was watching her she slammed down her fork, almost choking on the old bitterness and anger. The knife slithered across the plate, through the mustard, and bounced onto the desk top. She snatched up the knife and wiped away the yellow stain with her napkin.

'You want the truth? Grandfather lectured me on seemly behaviour, told me I should have greater

56

control over my conduct, and shut me in my room for a week. I was seven years old.' She stood, dropped the stained napkin onto her plate and picked up her purse. She was halfway across the room before he spoke.

'And you're still angry, aren't you?'

'Of course I am.' She whirled around and Rand rose from his chair. 'He's still doing it. Still trying to control me even though he's dead. That million in the will is my own fault. I went to see him and asked for money. I let him know how much I care about the Centre and he's using it to make me do what he wants.'

'What is this Centre?'

'A rehabilitation centre for underprivileged and special needs children. It's in an old building on the east side.'

'All you have to do is refuse. You don't have to comply with the condition.'

'Right. And then I get to go back there and watch them try to do too much with too little, knowing I could have helped.'

'It's only three months. What's three months for a million dollars?'

'You knew, didn't you?' Her hands tightened on her purse. 'You knew what he had planned for me.'

'I didn't know about the strings attached to the bequest, although I knew you were back in the will. He made me promise to get you here today without giving you even that information.'

'Uh, huh. Did he explain why I shouldn't know?'

'He said that you might not come if I was candid.'

'I don't think he needed to worry. I doubt you're capable of being open and honest, any more than he was.'

'Now that is a great exit line.' His lips thinned. 'Why don't you storm out and slam the door in my face? So melodramatic but so satisfying.'

She glowered at him as he paced closer, the percussion beat in her temples informing her she was in for another terrible headache. If she didn't leave immediately she'd be in no shape to perform tonight.

'Frankly, I'm getting tired of your insults,' he commented. 'I'm beginning to wonder if I wasn't right on target the other night. Maybe all this fury you're throwing around is because the money isn't yours to spend, free and clear.'

'I told you . . .' Horrified by the quiver audible in the words, she stopped speaking, gritting her teeth until she knew she had her voice under control, hating the sardonic amusement he didn't bother to hide.

He waited only a foot from where she stood. Too close for her to look anywhere but into his dark eyes, too close for her not to be uncomfortably aware of his imposing height and overwhelming masculine presence. She stood her ground, refusing to back away from the cold anger in those eyes and the rigid tension in his shoulders.

'I told you I didn't want anything from him and I meant it.'

'Then maybe this anger is something more. Maybe you don't like this thing, whatever it is, between you and me.' He reached out and brushed away a strand of hair that clung to her cheek, then slid his fingers beneath her hair to curve them around her nape.

'There is nothing between you and me.'

'No? I'm tempted to show you how wrong you are.' His thumb caressed her ear lobe. 'I'm going to tell you something I want you to remember. I am not, nor have I ever been, dishonest.'

His voice was quiet. Too quiet.

Arrested by the sensation of his fingertips moving smoothly on her sensitive skin, unable to answer, Zara felt the sparks of anger arcing between them splinter and reform into a dangerous attraction she had neither expected nor wanted. Her body swayed closer, so close she was enveloped by Rand's scent and heat.

'The taxi is waiting, Margaret.'

The housekeeper's voice was like a splash of freezing water as Zara realized how effortlessly Rand had woven a spell around her senses.

'Excellent timing, Mrs Parker, as always,' she said. 'Thank you for calling the taxi. Someday you might tell me how you always know your cue.' She stepped back to take the jacket the housekeeper was holding and Rand's hand dropped away.

'My office, Monday, eight a.m. sharp.' He shoved his fists in his pockets.

Zara shrugged into her jacket and wrapped it tightly around her chest as though she were already out in the autumn air. She looked up at him, not certain what she was going to say, knowing she had to do or say something, anything. He had to learn that she might comply for the sake of the Centre but she'd never be submissive.

'I'll be there. But if it weren't for those kids I'd tell you what you could do with that money. I might even help it along.'

She paused in the open doorway and let her glance travel down his body then back up to the face of the man, so sure of himself and his power over her.

'Is that the latest trim for men's jackets? Unusual but, you never know, it might catch on.'

'What? Oh, damn, not again.' Enjoying his exclamation of disgust as he found the mustard splashed across his hip, she swept through the door. Then, with considerable satisfaction and melodrama, she slammed it in both their faces.

'Ha! Take that.' Zara leaned closer to the television screen, her thumbs moving madly on the controller buttons. 'Here it comes. He's going, he's going. Touchdown!'

She dropped the controller and leaped to her feet. 'I am the champion, I am the champion.' She danced around Kenny's wheelchair, punching the air and singing, while he pouted. 'Can I play football, or what?'

'It's only a video game, Zara.'

'Right. And you've been lording it over me for months that you always win when we play this game.' She planted a smacking kiss on his cheek. 'That's okay, I understand you can't help it. It's built into your Y chromosome. Men can't stand to lose. You'll just have to get over it 'cause I'm the best.' On the last word she flung both arms into the air.

'I bet you can't do it again.'

'Oh, yeah?' She put both hands on her hips and bent down to look him in the eye.

'It's getting late, you two.' Billie stood in the door between the living room and the kitchen, wiping her hands on a dishtowel. 'Time for Kenny to get ready for bed.'

'Aahh, Moomm, it's not even nine o'clock,' Kenny whined.

Zara's arms dropped. 'You were supposed to call me so I could help with the dishes.'

'There weren't many and you guys were having so much fun I didn't have the heart to interrupt.'

'We'll just play one more game, okay, Mom? There's nothing important going on at school tomorrow.'

'Bed, young man.' Billie pointed a stern finger in the direction of his room which, along with the bathroom, opened onto the kitchen. 'Brush your teeth. Now.'

'We'll do the rematch next Sunday, Kenny. Be grateful the coach, here, is getting you some practice time before you have to play me again.'

While Billie talked and Kenny splashed in the other room, Zara occupied herself putting away the game cartridges and winding the remote wire around the controllers. Their house was a duplex. One building but two homes, each half a mirror image of the other side, with a shared wall between the two living rooms and kitchens.

She'd rented the right half from Billie since she'd moved back to town eight months before. At the front of the house you entered one small bedroom from the living room. At the back an even smaller bedroom and a minuscule bathroom adjoined the kitchen. Behind the kitchen another small room held the furnace and hot water tank.

She'd finished tidying the mess they'd made and put the kettle on to boil when Billie came back and collapsed into one of the shabby but comfortable arm chairs.

'I swear the older he gets, the more exhausted I get. I don't know what I'm going to do when he's a teenager. After spending time with the kids at the Centre, I've decided the old nursery rhyme about the girl with the curl applies to teenagers.

They're either loving or hating their parents. What's worse is us poor parents never know which to expect.'

'I suspect that when he's a teenager you're going to love every *other* minute of it,' Zara said. 'The rest of the time you're going to feel as if you're living in a torture chamber.'

'Oh, yeah, you're the voice of experience.'

'Hey, I was a kid once. And I met lots of young people when I was on the road.'

'Want another piece of pie?'

'Too full after your great dinner.' She dropped into the other chair and patted her stomach. 'Thanks, anyway.'

'You haven't told me how your grandfather's service went Friday. Was you-know-who there?'

'Who?'

'The guy you're attracted to, of course. Tremayne.'

'Drop it, Billie. He's not my type.'

'Oh, really?'

Zara glared.

Billie grinned but let it go. 'What else happened?'

'Let's see. First, I was late and had to listen to a lecture from both Mrs Parker and Sheila. Then I sneaked upstairs to see if the painting was still in my mother's old sitting room and Rand caught me. All in all, it should have been quite humiliating.'

'You don't sound like you were embarrassed.'

63

'I stopped caring what people like them thought a long time ago, especially Helen Parker.'

'Why did your grandfather want you there? Did he leave you something after all?'

'That was interesting, too. When Sheila read the will Neil had a temper tantrum because Grandfather didn't leave them the fortune he'd promised.'

'So, I guess Neil hasn't changed much since we were kids, has he? Remember that time he went nutso because the cook didn't give him the biggest piece of his birthday cake?'

'No, he's still the same weasel as ever. Grandfather left most of his money to the company, of course, and put Tremayne firmly in the driver's seat. If I slave at his office as a clerk for three months, the Centre gets a million bucks.' She jumped to her feet. 'Kettle's boiling, I'll make the tea.'

'Whoa, girl.' Billie leaned forward and grabbed Zara's wrist. 'Wait just a darned minute. Did you say a million dollars? For the Centre?'

'Yeah.'

'A million dollars! I can hardly believe it.' Billie pressed one hand to her chest. 'Just imagine what we can do with that much money. Fix the elevator, get better equipment for the physical therapists, hire more staff. Oh, my heavens, the list is endless. We could repair the whole darned building and have money left over for other years.'

'Did you also hear me say I'd have to work at ForPac, nine to five, for three months?' Zara shook her wrist free. 'With Tremayne in charge I'll probably be stuck in some menial clerical job the whole time.'

Billie followed her into the kitchen. 'So? You're not qualified for anything else, are you?'

'I can type.'

'Hunt and peck. I've seen you writing letters on your old electric typewriter. Have you ever used a computer?'

'Yes, I have.' She snatched the teapot out of Billie's hands. 'Sit down. You made dinner, I'll make tea.'

'Tell me when you've used a computer.' Billie sat at the table and propped her chin on her hands.

'The drummer on my last tour had a laptop and during all those endless hours on the bus he showed me how to play some computer games.'

'Most office jobs need particular knowledge or experience. Where I work the receptionist needed training just to run the phone system. The warehouse staff operate specialized machinery and work with a computerized inventory system. In my job as secretary I use desktop publishing plus a spreadsheet and two different word processing programs.'

'I could learn.' Zara dropped two tea bags into the pot, poured in boiling water, and covered the pot with the quilted warmer.

'Do you want to? For a job that's only going to last three months?'

'You're assuming I'm going to do it.' She got two mugs from the cupboard and put them on the table with the teapot.

'But . . . But you have to. It's a million dollars.'

The expression on her friend's face was priceless. Zara almost choked trying not to laugh out loud. She opened the fridge to get the milk and leaned in behind the door to hide her face from Billie. This little game was too much fun to give it up right away. 'It would be three months of hell for me and you know it.'

'I can't believe what I'm hearing. I refuse to believe it.'

'What's in it for me? Nothing. It won't even be fun.' Zara poured a little milk in each mug, then put away the carton. 'Of course if someone added a little extra incentive . . .'

'What do you mean, incentive?'

She sat down beside Billie and poured the tea, then picked up the mug and contemplated the steaming liquid.

'Weeelll . . . I might do it if you phoned Abe and finally accepted his invitation to spend a weekend with him at his family's cabin. It's time for you to stop waffling about taking the next step in your relationship.'

'That's blackmail.'

'Yup.' She sipped the tea, savouring the fragrant jasmine blend.

'What about Kenny?'

'I'll take care of Kenny. Roggo owes me some time off.'

'You're a pain in the you-know-what.'

'Yup.'

'Fine. I'll call Abe tomorrow.'

'You'll call him now.'

Billie muttered but obediently made the call to a surprised but jubilant Abe.

'He said to thank you,' she told Zara afterward. 'And I'm calling the Centre's other board members tonight to tell them about the money, so don't even think about reneging on our deal.'

'I won't.'

'I can't believe you made me do this.' Billie picked up her mug and drank. 'Now it's your turn. Call Rand Tremayne to ask him when you should start.'

'Eight o'clock tomorrow morning.'

She choked on her tea and Zara leaned over to thump her back. When Billie could finally draw breath, she glared at her friend.

'You were stringing me along, weren't you? You'd already committed to working at your grandfather's office.

'You'll never know.' Zara rinsed out the mug, put it in the sink and picked up her keys.

'Thanks a lot. Now what am I going to tell Abe?'

'Nothing. You'll go to the cabin, have a good time, and finally find out what it's like to be alone together for more than a couple of hours.'

'Geez, Zara.'

'I've got to go home to bed. I'm not used to getting out of bed so early in the morning and I wouldn't want to be late my first day.'

'You know what?'

She swung her jacket around her shoulders for the dash next door. 'What?'

'You might have tricked me into this weekend with Abe but I'll enjoy knowing you'll be spending the next three months working for Rand Tremayne. I don't care what you say about his type. Something tells me there's heat between you two.'

'Don't be daft, woman. He's a businessman. He doesn't understand heat, much less feel it.'

Zara thought she still heard Billie laughing as they locked their respective doors and turned out the lights.

On Monday morning Zara set her teeth and shoved harder at the heavy revolving glass door. Finally a gap opened, air whooshed into the tiny space, and she stumbled free into the steel and glass tower owned by the Forster Pacific conglomerate. In the lobby she leaned against the circular reception desk to catch her breath and glanced at her watch. Almost eight-thirty.

It wasn't supposed to be like this.

Before she went to bed last night she'd planned the scene carefully. At seven fifty-five she would stroll through the main entrance. The elevator would whisk her to Rand's office on the top floor at exactly one minute after eight, just late enough to make him understand he couldn't order her around.

She'd booked a cab so she wouldn't have to worry about finding a parking space. Her black dress and turquoise jacket were classy enough to dazzle and intimidate even Rand Tremayne. The shoulder pads she'd added to the jacket made her feel strong and powerful.

She'd even put her hair up in a hellishly uncomfortable chignon in an attempt to look cool and sophisticated, with dozens of hairpins anchoring it to her scalp.

Then the taxi had been ten minutes late and they'd been caught in two traffic jams. Two blocks short of her destination they'd hit another traffic snarl that even the cops couldn't seem to clear so she'd decided to jog the rest of the way. Just outside the building a gust of wind had come out of nowhere and knocked the chignon loose. She could feel hanks of hair hanging down her neck.

'Can I help you, Ma'am?'

Two male security guards, one very tall, the other shorter than herself, were staring at the top of her head. Their fascinated scrutiny made her glance at her image in the mirrored wall behind them and she barely suppressed the shriek that rose to her lips. She looked like Medusa. No.

She looked worse than Medusa. She gathered a fistful of wayward hair and held it at her nape.

'Ma'am?'

'My name is Zara Lindsey. I'm here to see Mr Tremayne.'

They both appeared surprised. 'But it's Monday morning.'

'Yes. Is there a problem?'

They looked at each other, then one shrugged and consulted the computer screen in their security console. 'The appointment's listed here, Sam. Eight a.m. She's to go right up.'

After a moment's hesitation, the shorter guard came out from behind the desk.

'Mr Tremayne's office is on fourteen. This way, please.'

'Fourteen? I thought . . . Aren't the executive offices on the top floor any more?'

'Mr Tremayne and his staff are on fourteen,' he said firmly as he escorted her to an elevator.

Grateful it was empty except for herself, she dug frantically in her purse for a brush and glanced up at the flashing numbers indicating each floor as the car rose. Second floor. Fifth floor. Her groping fingers snagged the bristles. Ninth floor. She dragged the brush ruthlessly through her hair, ignoring the hairpins scattering around her feet. Twelfth floor.

She used the elevator doors' burnished steel surface as a mirror to check her appearance. Her hair was presentable if slightly lopsided because of the hairspray she'd used on the chignon. She jammed the brush back into her purse, stabbing her index finger on her fingernail file.

'Ouch!' She put the bleeding fingertip in her mouth just as the doors opened. She took one step forward then stopped, uneasy about what she was about to do and who she was about to see.

A woman strode past, looked curiously at Zara frozen inside the open elevator, but said nothing as she went about her own business.

This was real, she thought. She was actually here. The doors began to close but at the last moment she put out her hand and the shiny steel gates to her own personal Purgatory slid open again.

'Come along, Margaret, come along. You're holding up production.' The querulous voice came from down the hall that led to a set of double oak doors. 'Don't stand there like a ninny.'

'Uncle Crawford?' She looked at the man who'd seemed so old when she was still a little girl and now was even more bent than she remembered. What had been wrinkles on his face ten years ago were now deeply carved grooves. His face looked

71

like a topographical model of a mountain range. 'Is that you?'

'Heh, heh, heh,' he cackled. 'Thought I'd be dead by now, did you? So did Heinrich, the old fool. Warned him I'd out-live him if he didn't stop carrying on with that woman.' He bustled toward her as she stepped out of the elevator.

'Sheila didn't tell me you still worked here.'

'I don't have nothing to do with that woman or her brother, and neither should you. Those two were hellions as kids and they ain't changed none.'

Her grandfather's cousin had never liked children so finding new ways to irritate him had been one of Neil and Sheila's favourite pastimes.

'I've always said they'll have to carry me out on my desk, m'dear.' He beckoned her closer. 'Come on, then, come on. Enough chit chat. I've got work to do.'

'I can't visit with you Uncle Crawford. I'm already late for my appointment with Rand Tremayne.'

'On Monday morning? Pshaw.'

'Why does everyone seem so surprised it's Monday morning?'

'Don't dawdle, girl.' He seemed to be struggling as he tried to push open the massive doors so she jumped forward to help him. He muttered and glared but allowed her to assist. Once inside he grabbed her elbow with clawed fingers and moved

72

her toward the receptionist who sat behind a black reflective desk that served as a barrier.

'Betty, this is Margaret, Heinrich's granddaughter. Margaret, Betty.'

'Good morning . . . Margaret?' The woman peeked at the paper in front of her, then looked up, bewildered.

'Hello. Mr Tremayne probably has me listed as Zara Lindsey. Uncle Crawford doesn't know I use my other names now.' She was about to shake the older woman's hand when Crawford yanked on her elbow.

'I don't take notice of such foolishness. Margaret is your name and that's that. Enough chit chat. Let's move along.'

He yanked on her elbow again and she obediently followed him along a hall. They passed two doors set with glass panes before he stopped in front of the third. She leaned around him to pull it open, then followed him in.

'Timothy? Where are you, boy?'

A young man popped up from where he'd been kneeling behind another black desk. He couldn't have been older than twenty-one. 'Mr Forster. Hello.'

'What were you doing down there?' The young man opened his mouth to explain. 'Never mind that. Time's a'wasting. Margaret, this is Timothy Hayes, Randall's secretary.'

'I'm his executive assistant, Mr Forster.' The young man smiled at her while he corrected

Crawford, who snorted in disdain at the job title. 'Hello. I'm Tim.'

'My name is Zara Lindsey.' She held out her hand. 'Nice to meet you.'

Timothy blushed, wiped his hand on his pant leg, then shook hers.

She looked at the double oak doors beyond his desk. Was that Rand's office?

'Have you got the paperwork ready, Timothy? Where have they put the girl?'

'Ms Lindsey will be working upstairs in marketing, for Steve Moore. Mr Kirkpatrick's clerk is on her way down right now with the documentation.'

'I don't have time for this. You know I have important work to do.'

'That's okay Mr Forster. I'll take care of Ms Lindsey.'

'He asked me to deal with this, get her settled. You should have had things ready half an hour ago, when she was supposed to arrive.'

Zara looked at the two men who appeared to have forgotten she was standing there. 'Excuse me. I was supposed to see Rand Tremayne this morning.'

'It's Monday,' Tim said, surprised, as if the day was an explanation.

'Why do you all keep telling me that today's Monday as if you're surprised?'

Crawford snorted and shook his head. 'Don't be ridiculous, girl. Of course we know it's Monday.'

'The guards downstairs mentioned it, and so did you and Tim, when I said I was here to see Rand Tremayne.'

'Well, of course. It's Monday.'

'Uncle Crawford!' Her mouth snapped shut as she counted to ten. 'Please tell Mr Tremayne I've arrived,' she said to Tim, hoping he'd make more sense than the old man.

'Mr Tremayne's not here.'

'He's not?' She tightened her grip on her purse. 'Where is he? We had an eight o'clock appointment.'

'Not on a Monday, you didn't. He doesn't work on Mondays, never has. Heh, heh, heh.' Crawford's wrinkles deepened into crevasses when he grinned for the first time since he'd met her at the elevator. 'That boy's up to no good, I bet. Probably fooling around with some woman. It's going to put him in an early grave, just like Heinrich.'

'Mr Forster!' Tim frowned and shook his head. 'You shouldn't say things like that.'

'Why not, boy? Everyone in the whole damned building talks about it.'

Zara glanced from one to the other, wondering what they were talking about.

'If you want to leave, Mr Forster, I'll show Ms Lindsey around.' Tim turned to her. 'Please sit down, Ms Lindsey. The paperwork should be here from Mr Kirkpatrick's office in a few minutes.'

'Thank you.' She hesitated, then quickly kissed the old man's cheek. 'Thanks for meeting me, Uncle Crawford, but I know you're busy. You don't have to stay.'

'Then I won't. My own work's suffering while we dilly dally up here. Can't keep everyone waiting, you know.' Crawford patted her hand. 'Stayed away too long, girl. Heinrich missed you.'

Her scepticism must have shown in her expression.

'No, no, girl. He did. After Lucy passed on you were his only kin, other than me.'

'What about Neil and Sheila?'

'Those Bendan hellions aren't blood, you know that. Bye now.' He scurried out before she could respond. She sat down in one of the chairs beside Tim's desk.

'I was wondering, Ms Lindsey . . .'

'Please call me Zara, Tim.'

'Zara.' He blushed again. 'I was wondering . . .'

'Yes?' Heavens, he's young, she thought.

'Would you have lunch with me today?'

'Thanks for the invitation, Tim. Maybe another day, after I've learned my way around and settled in?'

'Sure. That'd be great.'

He sat down behind his desk again but said nothing, just looked at her. Eventually the silence began to bother her.

'So . . . I'm going to be working in the marketing department?'

He nodded.

'That might be interesting. Did you know I'm a singer and song writer?'

He nodded.

'Marketing is very important in the music business. I've had some ideas I've always wanted to try but the producers wouldn't listen to me. Maybe some of my ideas would be effective here.' She tapped a finger on her chin and smiled. 'I didn't want to work here, you know, but maybe it's going to fun after all.'

Maybe it was just as well Rand was away. With any luck she wouldn't have to see him at all.

'Aw, come on, Tim.' The pretty young woman batted her eyelashes at the equally young man on the other side of the wide desk and sidled one step nearer the oak doors that barricaded Rand's office. 'Let me see him. I'm sure if I can have just five minutes alone with him, I can change his mind.'

Zara shifted restlessly. Even after spending three weeks working at ForPac she didn't like being anywhere near Rand's office. Today she hadn't had a choice. She was waiting her turn to talk to Tim, trying not to stare at the amount of breast and leg revealed by the other woman's skimpy outfit. The woman had obviously dressed, or undressed, to persuade Rand about something.

'No, Debra. He won't see you. You'll never work for him again and you know it.'

'Shit.' Her persuasive smile and fawning posture disappeared as she cursed. 'All this over some paper and stuff. Everybody does it.'

'It was more than just "stuff" and you know it. You've been stealing ever since they hired you.'

They argued back and forth until finally the young man lost his patience. 'Look, either you leave right now or I'll call security.'

'What makes him think he's better than me? Since he's so secretive about what he does on Mondays, I bet it's something awful or disgusting. I bet if everyone knew . . .'

Ignoring the other woman as she grumbled her way out the door, Tim blushed as he smiled at Zara. 'Hi. Changed your mind about lunch?'

'No, but thanks for the invitation.'

'How ya doing in the research department?'

'It's interesting. Much better than marketing and accounting. Peggy asked me to drop off . . .' The door crashed closed behind Debra and they both stared as the glass panel vibrated, wondering if it was going to shatter. 'That girl was really angry.'

'Yeah, I guess so. I don't know why she even bothered coming here today. Mr Tremayne would never give her another chance and everybody knows it.'

'Never?' Zara felt uncomfortable gossiping about Rand with his staff but the conviction in Tim's voice made her curious.

'He's got this little quirk. Won't tolerate dishonesty. Kind'a nuts about it.'

'I can imagine.' Her grandfather hadn't tolerated dishonesty either. Anyone who lied to Heinrich Forster had paid stiff penalties. Of course he'd considered his own remarkable ability with lies to be a good business tool.

'Mr Tremayne's a great boss.'

'He is?'

'Yeah, just look at me. I was stocking shelves in that chain of pharmacies ForPac owns. One day he comes through on some kind'a inspection and we get to talking. He finds out I really want to make it into management but can't afford to go to college. So he says, "can you use a computer?" I say sure and, bingo, I've got a job downstairs. Now, two years later, I'm executive assistant to the boss of Forster Pacific Corporation.'

'And that's good?'

'You bet. What better short cut into management is there? I make a good salary, too, enough to go to night school and still pay all my bills. The boss even makes sure not to keep me late on school nights.'

'I didn't know.' She really didn't know, she thought as she shook her head. It seemed that almost every day some small thing happened that forced her to realize there was a lot about Rand she didn't know.

Like his mysterious absences every Monday. Absences nobody seemed to think were odd despite the fact that most senior executives worked more than four days a week, even if Rand's days sometimes lasted ten hours. None of his employees knew where he went but speculation was plentiful and ran the gamut from a mistress to laziness, though they figured the former was more likely.

'Did you want to see him? You'll have to wait. He's got company and the lady said she didn't want to be disturbed,' he leaned forward and winked, wiggling an imaginary cigar, 'if ya know what I mean.'

She studied Tim's idea of a suggestive leer, then glanced at the closed doors to Rand's office. 'Oh . . .'

'Neil's going to make trouble.' On the other side of the oak double doors, Sheila trailed a finger along the edge of Rand's desk as she wandered closer to him.

'How?'

'I've kept him quiet in the weeks since the reading but today I found out he's calling in a lawyer to contest the will. If he gets it into court, ForPac's stock will drop.'

'You said you could handle him.' Rand glanced at the long red fingernails that were creeping closer to his hand and leaned back, arms crossed.

'His wife is encouraging him to play the big man so I'm having a little difficulty managing him. Things'll be back to normal soon, but in the meantime . . .'

'You want me to take care of the situation.'

'Well,' she smiled playfully and walked her fingers up his arm, 'it will be your problem if he drags ForPac into the lawsuit.'

'Why don't you want him to contest the will?' Abruptly Rand stood up and walked over to the wall of windows. 'If he wins, you'll get a bigger share of Heinrich's millions.'

'I wrote the will. If he breaks it, how will that make me look as a lawyer? Besides,' she followed him and slid both hands up to his shoulders, 'there's no guarantee that everyone on the Board would vote you in as CEO. Other than myself, of course. You'll always get my vote.'

She leaned into his body and pressed a kiss to his throat when he turned his face aside. 'Neil's my brother and I love him but if he got control of ForPac my shares would be worth little or nothing in a very short time.'

'Do you honestly think anyone on the Board will vote for Neil to run the company?' His hands came up to rest on her hips but he restrained the impulse to shove her away. He was so surprised at his own lack of response, he wasn't really listening to her answer.

What was the matter with him? They had been lovers once and they'd been together occasionally since then, usually at her instigation. But never before had he felt repulsed by her advances, whether or not he'd chosen to accept them.

'We both know that the timing is incredibly bad for ForPac board members to be involved in a legal squabble. The negotiations with that Swiss firm are at a particularly sensitive point.'

'I'll take care of Neil.' He caught at the hand that was edging below his waist and levered her away. 'I've, uh, got a lot of work to do, so perhaps you should leave now.'

She allowed him to walk her to the door, where she turned and leaned back against it, using his tie to tug him closer. 'I've got the use of a cabin up at Whistler for this weekend. How about it? A little wine, a big fire, you and me?'

He had to smile when she batted her lashes at him. 'I don't think so, Sheila. But I'm flattered by the offer.'

'Is there someone else?'

He gritted his teeth as her words immediately summoned an image of Zara.

'No!' He was as startled as Sheila by the explosive denial, and he offered a wry smile. 'No, thanks.'

'*C'est la vie*.' She shrugged.

He opened the door for her and they came face to face with Zara.

'Hi, coz. How's it going for you in the real world?' Sheila asked.

'Tolerable.'

'Yeah, I guess anything's tolerable if it nets a million dollars.' She brushed a kiss across Rand's cheek. 'Ta, ta, darling.' She was gone in a swirl of perfume.

When he turned around Tim had his head down, industriously shuffling papers on his desk, but Zara met Rand's gaze.

'Were you looking for me?' he asked.

'Peggy asked me to drop off the blueprints on my way to lunch. She asked me to tell you she'll be hearing from the city engineers by three o'clock.'

'Thank you.' He wondered what caused the odd expression on her face.

'You're welcome. I'd better get going or I'm not going to have time to eat.' Still she stood there, staring at him.

'Was there something else?'

Zara was trying to ignore the odd sensation of distress she felt. Daily contact with the man had forced her to recognize Rand's few good points but she still didn't like him.

Why should it bother her to see Sheila and Rand so obviously intimate? Sheila had hinted at a relationship, so why was she surprised to see them together this way? Just drop it, she told herself, you don't care who he kisses.

Yeah. And his dishevelled hair, crooked tie, and the streak of red on his cheek and collar that matched Sheila's lipstick didn't matter either. Instinct, denial or self-preservation? She didn't know which caused her flippant reaction.

Tim choked on a laugh when she waggled her finger and sang a few lines from an old Connie Francis song about a woman finding unfamiliar lipstick on her boyfriend's shirt.

Rand's frown deepened. 'What's that supposed to mean?'

She pointed at his collar. He glanced in the mirror behind Tim's desk, his jaw tightening when he saw the pinkish stains.

'Nothing happened . . .' Rand broke off and glared at his assistant's carefully blank face. 'Zara, would you please come into my office?' He indicated she should precede him then followed her inside. The door didn't slam when he shut it behind them. Not quite.

'What was that little song routine for?' he asked.

'I'm doing a rock'n'roll revival every night this week, fifties and sixties stuff. When I saw the lipstick stain . . . I'm sorry.'

'There is nothing between Sheila and myself. Just a good bye kiss from a friend.' He opened a corner cupboard and studied his reflection in the mirror over the enclosed bar. He jerked the shirt-tails out of his slacks and began unbuttoning it.

'Damn. Now I have to change my shirt and I've got a lunch meeting in five minutes. Why do I end up a mess almost every time I see you?'

'I have to go, I'm starving.' She averted her eyes and bolted for the door, trying to convince herself she wasn't running away just because she was about to see his naked chest. 'At least you can't blame this one on me.'

A minute later he was alone.

She's wrong, Rand thought with a sense of shock as he reached into a drawer for one of the shirts he kept on hand. He *could* blame this craziness on her. Before he'd met Zara, Sheila's lipstick would not have ended up on his collar because he wouldn't have felt compelled to avoid her kiss.

Yes, it was definitely Zara's fault.

CHAPTER 4

'It's either her or me.'

Rand looked up in amazement at the big man who'd charged into his office and slammed the door. 'Walt?'

'She's driving me crazy. She should'a stayed in research. Then she'd still be Peggy's problem. You know what she did today? Carl Winterstein from Receiving at Smithson Brothers called up to ask for a week's advance on his paycheque 'cause his father's dying in Florida and he needs plane fare to get out there. She's been nagging at me to give him *two* weeks worth.'

'But –'

'I know. I told her he isn't getting a paycheque next week because he's going to be laid off and you know what she said?'

'Calm down, Walt.' Rand stood up and urged his vice-president of human resources into a chair. 'This can't be good for your ulcer.'

'What ulcer? Since you dumped her on me I

don't have a stomach any more so I can't have an ulcer in it, can I?'

'You're getting hysterical.'

'She said "all the more reason. What's two weeks' pay to a big company like ForPac?"' The man covered his face with one meaty hand. 'Why did I let you convince me to get out of professional hockey? I might have ended up a cripple or an unemployed slob but at least I wouldn't have had to deal with her.'

'I'll talk to her.'

'No, that's not good enough.' Walt stood up and grabbed Rand by the shoulders. 'We've been friends a long time but even friendship will only get you so far when it comes to that woman.'

Rand winced when the agitated and much bigger man's fingers tightened, lifting Rand up onto his toes.

'Uh, Walt? Could you –'

'I'll admit she's intelligent and a hard worker who eventually gets the job done but she's got this little quirk in her personality. She thinks corporations like ours should support the world. Either you get her out of my department or I quit.'

'Of course.' Rand tugged at Walt's wrists, dropping back onto his heels when Walt finally released him. Carefully he rotated his shoulders, making sure nothing was dislocated before he leaned over his desk and buzzed his assistant.

87

'Yes, Mr Tremayne?' Tim's voice echoed out of the speaker phone on the corner of his desk.

'Please call payroll and ask Ms Lindsey to come to my office.'

'Right away, Mr Tremayne.'

Rand punched a button, cutting off the open line.

'Thanks.' Walt kneaded his stomach and popped an antacid. 'I'm sorry. I know you were counting on me.'

'Counting on you?'

'To keep her occupied and out of the way.'

'Oh.' Rand rubbed his forehead. He'd thought his motives were well-hidden. Hopefully only their friendship had allowed Walt to see through Rand's actions. 'You haven't mentioned this to anyone else, have you? It's just that —'

'Hell, no, buddy. And you don't owe me any explanations. Remember, I've worked with her.'

Rand propped himself on the corner of his desk, rolled down his sleeves, and refastened his cuffs. 'Thanks. At lunch Don mentioned that he needs two more clerks. I'll send her up there.'

'He won't take her.'

'Why not?'

'The word's spread, Rand. Steve in marketing, Wendy in accounting, Peggy in research; none of them kept quiet about her stay in their departments.'

'But you —'

'The only reason I gave her a chance was because you asked and I owed you big time. Now we're even.' He groaned, still massaging the pain in his stomach. 'You know what else? She hums while she works.'

'That's so bad? She's a singer.' Rand grinned. 'At least she'd hum in tune.'

'You don't know what it's like. First she starts to hum something, pretty soon she's swaying and . . . and sort'a wiggling around with the song. The women are listening 'cause she sings so beautiful, and not a man in the room can keep his mind on work, myself included, because she's so damned gorgeous. Some of the guys are making bets on which one of them gets her into bed first.'

He scrubbed his fist across his closely-shaven scalp. 'It's ridiculous. Things are at the point where Zara's the only one concentrating on the job.'

Rand's eyebrows drew together and his lips tightened into a stern line as he struggled to control a rush of fury. 'Are they harassing her?'

'The dumb part is she doesn't even know she's driving the guys crazy. It's like they're not even there, you know? No, it's worse than that. She doesn't seem to comprehend they're male, just sees them as people.'

Rand turned away so his friend couldn't read the expression in his eyes. 'Yeah, I know. Last night –'

He was interrupted when a brisk rat-a-tat heralded Zara's arrival. 'Come in.'

She halted immediately inside the door when she saw Walt standing beside Rand. 'Oh.'

'Please sit down. Walt was just leaving.' Rand lifted his jacket from the back of his chair and shrugged it on, concentrating on slipping each button through the correct buttonhole and brushing a tiny speck of lint off his black wool sleeve.

Which was it, he wondered. Which idea had caused that flash of anger during Walt's recital? Was it the thought of how she was disrupting the office or that she might be subjected to sexual harassment? Or was he afraid one of those other men might win that bet?

He tugged at each cuff until it settled into place. Where did that last thought come from? Nothing could be further from the truth. Even though he hadn't been able to resist dropping by the bar to watch her performance last night, it didn't mean he wanted her for himself. It had only been curiosity. Of course he felt a natural concern.

Then he really looked at Zara.

A long white wool sweater dress clung to her body from neck to wrist, from shoulder to knee. A jangly length of gold chain snuggled the fabric to her hips. Her hair was braided into a single fat plait and hung over her left shoulder, dark as night and tied with a white ribbon, ending in a curl above her breast.

No! He dragged his eyes away. He would not allow something as inappropriate as lust, to use its real name, to confuse their association. She would only be here a few weeks and then they would never see each other again. The barbed twinge caused by that last thought made his expression even bleaker than it had been a minute before.

Guess this proves he does take off his jacket occasionally, Zara thought as she watched him don his well-tailored armour, then stand behind his desk at parade rest, hands linked behind his back. Black suited him, as did his black vintage Mustang. All he needed was a helmet and sword and he could be the Black Knight complete with steed, constant scowl and all.

'Why do you do it?'

'Do what?' She sauntered across the room and sank into the big chair opposite his desk. To heck with him, she thought as she crossed her legs. She wasn't going to stand in his presence like some school child brought before the principal to be reprimanded for a misdemeanour.

'Don't play games with me, Zara. You knew Winterstein's advance wouldn't get approval from Walt, no matter how much you badgered him.'

'The poor man had a family emergency. I promised him I'd try.'

'The man's employment is being terminated, for chris —'

He snapped his teeth shut on the curse and swung around to stare out at the sailboats in the marina far below.

'Walt told me. So? The poor man is losing his job and his father and you're worried about money. Why are you laying him and the other employees off? Smithson is a prosperous concern. Never mind, I already know the answer. You probably wanted to increase your profit margin.'

'Oh?' He spun around, planted his fists on the desk, and leaned toward her. 'Does your great financial expertise tell you that?'

'There are Smithson Brothers Appliance stores all over the country. They're huge.'

'Yes, too big. They'd been in the red for over two years when we acquired them. Cutbacks have to be made and one-quarter of those outlets are being closed out, the rest down-sized.'

'Oh.' She felt some of her righteous anger evaporate. 'Carl is a very nice man. You should make the cuts somewhere else.'

'Where would you suggest? Perhaps we should fire his boss, who is also a very nice man? A man with three kids and a wife to support, unlike Carl who is single.'

He snapped erect and walked around the desk to tower over her. She wished she'd stayed on her feet. Maybe she wouldn't have felt quite so small.

'Or would you suggest we fire the staff in the outlets, all of whom are very nice people I might add, and move the head office staff into their positions? How about I give you the list and you can choose who stays and who is out?'

'It's only two weeks' pay.'

'We have to lay off one hundred and forty-two people, Zara. Do you think Smithson can afford to give them each an extra two weeks' pay?'

'Maybe not but Forster Pacific can.'

'And do you think ForPac's shareholders will be pleased to know they are supporting a charitable organization? Perhaps you'd care to come to the next general meeting and explain to them why they won't be getting dividends this year.' He grasped the arm rests on either side of her and leaned close. Way too close.

Her cheeks flushed as his scent filled her nostrils, his breath warmed her skin.

'And guess what? Some of those shareholders are very nice people, too. Nice people who count on their dividends to get them through these tough times.'

'Fine.' She shoved him away and stood up, rubbing her hands together, determined to erase the tingling caused by contact with his chest. 'You've made your point. I guess I was too naive. But it's a good thing someone like you has this job.'

'What do you mean by that? Oh, I get it. You think I like firing people.'

She didn't answer, only shrugged as she turned away.

'Wait a minute.'

She ignored his low-voiced order and opened the door.

'I said wait.' He reached around her and slammed it shut. She spun around to face him. 'It's hell to tell someone they're out of a job. Most of them look sick, some cry, some beg.' Disgust vibrated in his voice. 'I hate it.'

'Then why do you do it?'

'Because it's my job. And I don't delegate difficult responsibilities.'

They stared into each other's eyes, ignoring the buzz of his telephone.

Zara studied his face, the whiteness around his lips, the icy storm swirling in his eyes. And she remembered how her grandfather had celebrated every increase in profits whether or not his decisions had created misery for his employees. Could this man be different?

He was hard. Driven. She'd seen many examples of the ruthlessness of his decisions in the weeks she'd spent at ForPac but his staff admired him as much as they feared him.

Now she wondered if he was as lacking in compassion as she'd thought.

'Winterstein will be told there is no advance.'

'But I told him . . .'

'You had no authority.'

'Fine.' The softening she'd felt towards Rand evaporated.

'Go home now. Collect your belongings from payroll before you leave.'

'Collect –? Does this mean you're firing me? You can't. I have to stay here almost nine more weeks to . . .'

'Forty-three working days.' He laughed cynically at her expression of surprise. 'I counted.'

'Why?'

'Because you'll spend the rest of your time in my office.'

'In *your* office?' Her stomach flip-flopped at the thought of spending even one day in the same room with Rand. The reaction was dislike, she assured herself. Of course she didn't want to work so close to Rand.

'You can help my staff. If I put you anywhere else I'd have a mutiny on my hands. No one feels capable of controlling your philanthropic impulses.'

'And you are?' Zara flicked the braid over her shoulder with a toss of her head.

'I think so.' He smiled. 'Don't you?'

'Damn, damn, damn!' For the fifth time Rand had run the column of figures through his calculator. For the fifth time he'd arrived at an entirely different total. He glared at the opposite corner of what had once seemed a spacious office.

Zara was oblivious.

She was also driving him insane.

First he'd had her sharing an office with, and helping, Tim. That arrangement had only lasted three days. Three days of misplaced files, forgotten messages, botched appointments, all the actions of his formerly efficient, now besotted, assistant.

Then his receptionist, Betty, had a week's holiday and, to get Zara away from Tim, he'd thankfully asked her to fill in. She'd been excellent at the job, as at every other assignment he'd given her.

But he'd fallen over one or more of his male employees every time he'd stepped out of his office door. Finally he'd moved a desk for Zara into his own office the day Betty returned. At least with Zara out of sight, the rest of the staff would get back to normal.

For ten days she'd been sharing his office.

Ten days ago he'd have bet any amount of cash against her ability to distract him from his work. Since then even during his weekly trips to Treville he hadn't been able to forget her.

Reluctantly he raised his eyes. A desk, a computer terminal and scanner, and a chair didn't seem to take up as much space as the presence of one small woman. She had turned the desk to face the window, claiming the work was so boring she needed the view to make it bearable.

His view was becoming every day more unbearable: trim, jean-clad hips, sneakers hooked around the base of the chair and a swinging mass of dark silky hair. Yesterday it had been a cotton print dress trimmed with lace both below the flounced hem and in the deep vee neckline. One day last week she'd worn bicycle shorts, a baggy tee shirt printed with environmental slogans, and a pony-tail. Why couldn't the woman wear appropriate office clothing?

But the eccentric way she dressed wasn't the worst.

If only she would quit that blasted *humming*. As he watched she stopped feeding documents, sang two bars about lovin' kisses, then leaned sideways to scribble notes on blank sheet music she kept near at hand. Afternoon sunlight glimmered on her hair, her skin, her mouth as she murmured lyrics. She pursed her lips and his slacks grew uncomfortably tight as she studied what she'd written, nodded, then resumed feeding documents and humming.

'Will you *please* stop that.' He wound his fingers around the chair's arm rests and squeezed in an effort to keep himself from rising and walking close enough to bury his hands in her hair and explore those lips with his own.

The rhythmic beat she'd contrived out of her chair's squeak, the documents feeding into the scanner, and the occasional tapping of her toes, halted abruptly.

'Stop? I'd be glad to.' She sneezed when she slapped down the stack of yellowing papers on the files beside her, raising a cloud of dust. 'This has to be the most boring job in the world. Why do you want this done anyway?'

'We need to clear out old files but I want to keep copies of all documentation on computer disc. Federal law requires . . .' His jaw snapped shut and he drew in a deep breath before continuing. 'You don't have to understand. It has to be done and it is the only task I could think of where you would be unable to disrupt business. Or should have been.' The correction was muttered under his breath.

She stretched and covered a yawn with one hand. 'Sorry. Late night. I'm beat. What do you want me to do now?'

What a question! The supple movements of her torso, the elegant arch of her neck combined to evoke a series of erotic images in his brain which shot heat to his groin. He swallowed a groan.

'Nothing,' he snapped back harshly.

She looked surprised at his tone and he moderated his voice. 'I mean, I do want you to continue.'

'But you said . . .'

'I know what I said,' he interrupted. 'I just . . . I meant would you please stop singing.' He winced and hoped she wouldn't recognize the desperation in his voice.

Her mouth dropped open. 'Singing?'

'Singing. Humming. Whatever.'

'I can't believe this. Between sitting in this building eight hours a day, keeping up my tasks at the Centre, performing, and rehearsals I haven't got a minute to myself. I need some time to write the darn songs.' She jumped to her feet and marched over to his desk. 'I get the work done, don't I?'

'Yes, of course.'

'There are no mistakes?'

'No.'

'How can you sit there and order me to stop? You have no right . . .'

'I have every right.' He stood and leaned forward until they were almost nose to nose, glaring at each other across his desk. 'I'm the boss, remember?'

'You have no legitimate reason for this.'

'I can't concentrate, dammit!'

She shook her head. 'Are you trying to tell me you need absolute quiet to work? 'Cause if so, let me move my desk back out into the general office. You'll get quiet and I'll get some songs done so my time here isn't a total waste.'

'I can't believe you're really as naive as that statement indicates. If I put you back out there for another five weeks my entire operation will be a shambles.'

'Just because one or two of your staff have been friendly and helpful?'

'Come off it, lady. Don't you have any idea of your effect on men? Compared to the women they know you're . . . you're exotic. They're even making bets on which of them is going to get you into bed first.'

For a second her eyes widened in shock, then they narrowed to slits of disbelief. 'That's ridiculous.'

'Is it?' He flattened his palms on the surface of his desk and leaned closer, close enough to see the flecks of gold in her dark brown irises.

'Yeah. It is.' She planted her fists on her hips and stuck out her chin.

Rand wasn't sure if she heard the crack as his self-restraint snapped. A cry of outrage tore from her lips as he grasped her upper arms and lifted her up on his desk, sliding her across the slick surface on her hip, scattering the last few days' worth of mostly useless paperwork to the floor.

His pulse pounded in his temples as he hauled her into his arms, tangling one hand in her hair as he'd been tempted to do since he'd first seen her in that disreputable bar.

'Let me go! Are you crazy?'

'I think I must be,' he murmured. Slowly, staring into her eyes, he lowered his lips to cover hers. Softness. Heat. Both exploded on his tongue as he traced the edge of her mouth before plunging deeper.

His arm tightened around her waist, drawing her closer until her breasts pushed against his chest. Inch by reluctant inch her arms crept around him and clung with a strength and urgency that fired passion even as the last thinking fragments of his brain questioned his sanity. He hesitated until she moaned faintly and snuggled closer.

'Zara,' he whispered as he stepped back, tugging her with him until they fell into his chair.

This explains the love songs she'd been compulsively writing, Zara thought fuzzily. Spend time with Rand and poof – a woman's got romance. Just like the flu. She trailed kisses around to the sensitive flesh behind his ear and smiled against his skin when he shuddered. Wonder if it's catching?

He lifted the mass of her hair and brought it to his face, inhaling deeply. And then they were kissing again, with a depth and passion that shook her world.

'Rand, I've got those papers for you –' After one look at the couple entwined in the arm chair, Walt backed out.

Zara shoved at Rand's shoulders. *What had they done?* His arms tightened for a second, then fell away, and she clambered out of his lap. *Away. She had to get away from him. Later. She'd think about this later, much later.*

She took one step back, staggered and grabbed his desk for balance, shaking her head firmly when he reached out to catch her.

'Are you okay?'

'Yeah,' she brushed her hair back out of her face, 'just dizzy for a second.' She tugged at her shirt until it was straight, tucked the hem back into the waist of her jeans, and walked over to her own desk where she shut down the computer.

'We have to talk.'

'About what just happened?' She glanced over her shoulder as she shoved sheet music into her purse. He sat in the big chair, motionless, his face as blank as his voice. A flicker of emotion threatened to disturb the numbness she'd wrapped around her thoughts and she jerked her gaze away. 'No, I don't think so.'

'I'm sorry.'

'So am I.' She zipped her purse shut and slung its long strap over her shoulder.

'I don't understand why things always go a little crazy when I'm around you. One minute I was furious at you, the next I was –' He sucked in a deep breath and exhaled noisily. 'It's my responsibility.'

'*Your* responsibility?' She felt the numbness begin to crack and anger seeped in. 'We kissed each other, Rand. It's called equal participation, something you can't accept in business or sex, right? Always have to be in charge, always calling the shots. You know what's really crazy? I wanted that kiss as much as you did.'

'I didn't say I wanted . . . I mean you're not exactly –' He mouth snapped shut.

'Not exactly what, Rand? Your type?' His disparagement hurt, but she wasn't going to let him see it. 'Isn't it weird what sexual attraction can do to a person's standards?'

She yanked her jacket out of his closet and shoved her left arm into its sleeve. 'Never in a million years would I have guessed I'd kiss a money-grubbing bloodsucker like you. Grandfather must be giggling in his grave.'

'A bloodsucker?' Indignation splintered his cool facade. 'What about you? If you had your way ForPac would be trapped in a financial quagmire, sinking fast into bankruptcy, and dragging along all our employees. But who cares, as long as there are sleazy bars for you to perform in?'

'Sleazy bars? If that's the way you feel, I'm surprised you've shown your face there four times since Grandfather's funeral.' She enjoyed the fact he wasn't able to hide his chagrin. 'Didn't think I'd know you were there, did you? Someone like you sticks out in The Kicking Horse like an oak tree in a dandelion patch.' She swore and tried again to jab her right arm though the jacket's sleeve.

'It might help if you removed your purse first.'

She looked down. Her purse's long strap was tangled around both her shoulder and the buttons decorating the jacket's cuff, creating a vice through which her arm couldn't penetrate. How had she become entangled in her clothing? she wondered. Or entangled with Rand Tremayne? And why on earth should she care what he thought of her?

'I'm sorry, Zara. I didn't mean to offend you. A difference of opinion doesn't need to sink into a childish exchange of insults.'

When she looked up and saw his reluctant grin, she had to smile at the absurdity of their argument, especially when she didn't know if she was more angry at him or at herself. 'Me, too. How 'bout we just forget today ever happened?'

'Right.'

'There are only a few more weeks and, after all, neither of us wants to get involved. What happened was just . . . just hormones.' She struggled to free her arm from the trap of purse and jacket sleeve. It was worse now because her hair was snarled in the buttons.

'Of course.'

'Truce?' she asked, ignoring the flash of dismay she felt when he agreed so quickly.

'Truce,' he said.

She bent her head to study how the leather was knotted around the buttons, concentrating so hard she jumped when she heard his voice beside her ear.

'Here, let me help.'

'No.' She jerked away as if, once burned, she was afraid to come too close to the flames a second time, and pain shot through her scalp. 'Owww.'

'You're only hurting yourself. I promise, I won't touch you any more than I have to.' He held his hands shoulder high, palms facing her.

104

The man just wants to help, Zara chided herself. Why was she so jittery? She had no intention of allowing him to kiss her again. And he certainly didn't want to kiss her.

'Okay. Thanks.' She stood still while his long fingers carefully separated the long strands of hair from the jumbled mess, stroking each silken thread behind her ear before going on to the next.

He was too close. As he bent over her arm her eyes were helplessly drawn to the tendons in his nape, the curve of his ear, the shadow of beard on his jaw. Abruptly she swung her gaze away and tried desperately not to breathe, not to absorb the mingled scents of cologne and man. Even if he wasn't just like Heinrich, he was still a business-man with rigid priorities. Priorities she couldn't understand, wouldn't live with.

If only . . .

'All done.' He reached around her and pulled the sleeve up her arm, then tugged the lapels until the jacket settled around her shoulders. His hands met under her chin and he gazed down at her for a second, then let go.

'Great.' She blinked up at him, trying to drag her mind back from never-never land. 'Thanks.'

'See you tomorrow.' He shoved his hands in his pockets and stepped back.

'Yes.'

'Good bye.'

'Bye.'

Rand nodded when she smiled uncertainly and clenched his hands harder until she was gone. Then he yanked his hands out of his pockets and groped behind him for a chair. Once he'd found it his knees buckled and he dropped hard into the seat.

What the hell was he going to do? he wondered. No way could he spend even one more day closeted in here with her.

He bent forward, propped his elbows on spread knees, and contemplated his hands. His fingers were still shaking from the effects of touching her, from being just so close and no closer. From wanting to explore, to discover the texture and fragrance of Zara when she was aroused – a woman who wanted him as much as he wanted her.

And no matter how hard he tried to convince himself he felt merely lust, it didn't work. The clues and confusion were mounting every day.

Her smile was a shot of adrenaline he was afraid he would miss long after she was gone. Since she'd plunged into his life he kept finding himself in that damn bar, watching her perform. He ached to kiss her even when they were at loggerheads over a decision he'd made. Then there was the heart-pounding excitement of arguing with her.

But he saw life and business as a chess game. He always planned five moves ahead so no person or event could take him by surprise. Zara didn't and good intentions were no excuse for imprudence in business. He couldn't deny the rush of hostility and resentment every time he saw evidence of her reckless nature.

Imprudence would ruin ForPac if she were given free rein with the company. Recklessness could drive all his employees into unemployment and poverty. Almost exactly the same way his family had destroyed Tremayne's and, over the fourteen grinding years since, the town and people of Treville.

Several long filaments of black hair clung to his sleeve. His mind wandered as he plucked them off the fabric, dragging them between his fingers, testing their strength, remembering the weight and texture and scent of her hair when he'd held it in his hands.

He ignored the knock on the half-open door and didn't look up at Walt when he entered.

'You have to sign these.' Walt tossed two letters on the desk. 'That was a pretty hot clinch. Sorry if I broke things up.'

Rand shrugged.

'You guys an item?'

'No.'

'Looked intense from where I was standing.'

'There's nothing between us. We just got a little . . . carried away.'

'I'll say so. Have a look at what you've made.'

Rand slowly focused on his hands. He'd woven the strands of Zara's hair around the third finger of his left hand. He swore and yanked off the improvised ring.

'Don't you have work to do, Walt?' He scanned the letters, scrawled his signature twice and thrust the papers at his friend.

'Just going.' The big man grabbed the door handle. 'See you at hockey practice tonight?'

'Yeah, I'll be there. Wait. Is there still an empty desk in Crawford's office down on the third floor?'

'Yeah.'

'I'm going out of town for two days. Have this stuff,' he nodded in the direction of Zara's desk, 'moved in there before I get back.'

'So she got to you, too, huh?'

'No one gets to me.'

Walt looked doubtful but didn't say anything. Rand was grateful his friend didn't try to drag him into a debate on the truth of that denial. Right now he didn't want to talk about Zara or his reaction to her.

'Crawford will be livid,' Walt reminded him. 'He hates it when someone rearranges his space.'

'I'll deal with Crawford before I go.'

Walt rubbed his chin and looked thoughtful. 'That might work. At least we can be sure there's no way her presence will keep him from concentrating on his work. Even more important, there's no way he'll give her any authority or encouragement to make decisions.'

'Just do it, Walt.' Rand surged to his feet and turned to stare out the window.

'Don't worry.' Walt started to chuckle. 'I'll make sure she's out of sight before you get back.'

Once he was alone, Rand sat down at his desk again and dragged together the file he'd been trying to work on before Zara and he had started to argue. After ten minutes he gave up and stuffed it into a drawer.

Would out of sight put her out of mind? he wondered. Could he be so lucky? He leaned back, dragging his knuckles back and forth along his jaw as he thought back over the way his life had changed since he'd complied with Heinrich's last request and persuaded a certain sexy singer to come to the reading of her grandfather's will.

His subconscious chose that moment to replay the kiss they'd shared and Rand decided his luck had probably run out.

CHAPTER 5

That night Zara struggled in her sleep but didn't wake. Nothing would stop her subconscious from playing out old memories as nightmares.

Margaret tried not to giggle. She covered her mouth with both hands but out burst the excited titters and chortles. Father was going to be so surprised when he came home.

She crawled beneath his desk, wrapped her arms around her bent legs and planted her chin in the flannel night-gown covering her knees. Father's office always smelled just like him, even when he wasn't here. She stared up at the painting of her and Mama and Father that hung on the wall behind his desk. If she held her head just right she could see Mama's eyes sparkling and smiling, just like they always used to.

The only light in the room came from the full moon outside the arched windows but she wasn't scared. She shuddered, delighted with her own daring – awake at midnight! Any minute now

Father would come home. He'd turn on the light and she'd jump up to surprise him.

Mama always teased Father 'cause he had such ticklish ears. She wrapped her arms around him to tickle him and tickle him and tickle him. When Mama did this Father laughed until he nearly cried.

Tears threatened through the giggles but Margaret blinked hard and the wetness went away. Tonight Father would laugh and swing her around in his arms. He'd swing her so hard and high that they'd both feel dizzy and sick, just like he did last year at her birthday party when she turned five.

Maybe he'd kiss her and brush her hair with long, long strokes, just like Mama always did before . . .

Margaret pressed her face hard into her knees until the sharp bones dug into her eyes and the stars flashing behind her eyelids forced away thoughts of 'before'. This time Father would hug her. Then everything would be right again. Father loved her. He did. He did. He did.

She covered her mouth with her night-gown when the light clicked on and she heard his voice. He was here! Any minute now he'd see her and . . .

'No, no, no, no!' The mounting scream tore at the adult Zara's throat and rang in her ears, loud enough to shake off sleep. When she jerked up on her elbows, the pillow thumped to the floor.

111

She pushed the sweat-soaked strands of hair off her forehead and stared at the moon beams angling through the venetian blinds, casting a broken grid of light and dark stripes on the quilt bunched at her feet.

She dragged her legs from the snarled sheets, wrapped the quilt around her shoulders and left the bedroom. She knew from experience that she couldn't stay in bed. If she did fall asleep again, she'd have to play out the dream.

She swayed groggily as she dragged herself into the living room of the small duplex. When she rounded the table beside the couch, the bulky quilt knocked over the half-empty mug of tea she'd left there the night before and splashed icy liquid on her toes. She wiped it up with a handful of tissues from the box on the table.

She plopped onto the couch, swung her legs up and buried her bare feet behind the cushions heaped at its other end, shrugging deeper in the quilt's warm folds. Her eyes burned with exhaustion but she couldn't allow them to close.

She didn't want to see the end of the dream, like a terrible old movie that played out its tragedy again and again. She didn't want to re-live how the child buried in her mind had learned that she'd lost everything that mattered on the day her mother died.

Zara's head fell back and she stared up at the blank expanse over the fireplace. A space almost exactly like those she'd deliberately left empty in every apartment or house or room she'd rented since she'd left her grandfather's house.

The space she'd promised herself would some day hold the painting. A promise she had to keep.

Neil would be at Sheila's party Friday night. Zara could talk to him there and arrange to get the painting back. Because when she did, finally, maybe, the nightmares would leave her alone.

She loathed cocktail parties. Zara shifted her weight onto one foot and eased the opposite heel free of the maiming grip of her high heels. It wasn't just the smoke, or the annoying buzz of gossip, or the way strange men pushed intimacy in kisses they would never have tried for in private.

She smiled automatically when the cluster of people she was standing with laughed at a joke she hadn't bothered listening to. It was all so fake.

Tonight was an excellent example. If Sheila hadn't wanted to show off a relative who possessed a nodding acquaintance with some of music's megastars, Zara wouldn't have received an invitation to this party. In exchange for a little genteel name-dropping, Zara could corner Neil in a social situation where he might be more persuadable.

At least here he wouldn't find ignoring the situation to be as simple as refusing to take her phone calls or having his secretary pretend he wasn't in the office. Now if he would only arrive so she could go home before her feet swelled up to the size of pumpkins.

Her stomach growled.

Why didn't Sheila serve real food or own real furniture? The hors d'oeuvres were displayed on a sheet of bevelled glass balanced on the wingtips and head of a burnished iron Pegasus. She'd thought the display was art until she saw other guests plucking items from the arrangement and eating them. Amid chattering, flattering guests, the azure room held only three other pieces of furniture, none of them designed for comfort.

Where did Sheila sit in the evenings, on the marble floor?

When Zara knew her ten years ago, Sheila had been as dedicated to her own physical comfort as she'd been to exploring the sexual skills of every man she met.

'Isn't that right, Ms Lindsey?'

'Hmm?' Zara glanced around the small circle of women she'd been mostly ignoring.

'Does Rico really insist on cream cheese being licked off his whole nude body by two naked women before he'll sing?'

Startled by the question and the breathless silence of the women waiting for an answer, Zara blinked at the sweet-faced young woman whose eyes gleamed with curiosity. 'What did you say?'

'You made that up, Darla.' The second speaker so closely resembled the first they might have been sisters. Only the unnatural tautness of the mother's skin gave away her age.

'Did not. It was in one of those magazines at the check-out stand. They say one night he ordered fifteen containers of it.' The younger woman leaned forward, her air of trustworthy confidante meant to encourage Zara to spill any secrets she might know about music's latest superstar.

'Sheila told us you were a back-up singer on his Silvercity tour last year. Does he really do that with the cream cheese?' She shuddered delicately and licked her lips.

'No, he doesn't. His wife, whom he adores, was pregnant and craved cream cheese. If you'll excuse me,' Zara gritted her teeth as she slid her foot back into the shoe, 'I need another drink.' Make that two, she thought as she threaded her way toward the bar. Especially if even one more person asked her to confirm another stupid tabloid rumour.

Thank God she'd walked away from that life. Perhaps she'd never be a big star but at least she'd escaped having her life picked apart by a tabloid microscope. The paparazzi never cared about the song writers, only those poor souls up on the stage.

Turning away from the bar, Zara spotted a staircase on the opposite side of the crowded room and knew she'd found a place to hide. She could sit at the top in the darkened hallway, finish her drink in relative peace, and still be able to watch for Neil. She could even take her shoes off.

Fifteen painful minutes passed before she sank down onto the thick carpet, settled her back against the railing with her legs stretched across the hall, and moaned with relief as she kicked off the shoes.

Heavens, her feet burned. Why had she let Billie talk her into borrowing the red shoes? Just because they matched the one decent party dress left from Zara's previous life on stage was no reason to put herself through this misery. In this crowd, no one would have noticed or cared if she wore moccasins.

She closed her eyes and slowly dragged the arch of her left foot up and down the shin of her right leg, trying to rub away the ache. A sudden yearning for a foot massage reminded her of Sheila. What had she said about Rand?

Zara thought for a minute and then changed feet. Ah, yes. Magic. The man had magic fingers.

And magic eyes and a magic smile. Magic lips, too. Zara sighed. Sheer magic.

Her eyes blinked open. It was happening again. Buried alive in Uncle Crawford's office for days, she'd only seen Rand at a distance, if at all, when he'd appeared in the building. Yet whenever she relaxed, even for a moment, the man invaded her mind.

Why couldn't she forget that day? That kiss? Why did her body retain the heat and longing her logical mind wanted to deny?

She should be grateful there were only a few more weeks until she could sleep in every morning. Instead she had to fight a crazy urge to panic when she thought about how little time she had left at ForPac. Why would she want to be anywhere near Rand?

Suddenly the door beyond her toes opened about four inches and she was trapped in a bar of light. She scrambled for her belongings, mortified that one of Sheila's guests might catch her sprawled across the floor.

She'd gathered her purse and glass in one hand and was reaching for her shoes when she recognized the voices of the room's occupants.

'I mean it, Bendan, don't contest the will. Cross me on this and you'll regret it,' said Rand. 'Do as you're told, and we've got a deal.'

'To hell with commission on the estate sale. Why should I give up a chance to get millions of dollars? I deserve more than a few measly shares.' Neil's voice was muffled, as if he were across the room. Obviously it was Rand who had opened the door.

'Remember the old saying, a bird in the hand. . .? Do you know what happened to the clever cat who released the small sparrow he held to go after two much plumper birds?'

The icy mildness in Rand's voice made Zara's skin crawl.

'I'm sure you're dying to tell me,' Neil replied bitterly.

'The branch to which he'd entrusted his weight snapped and he came crashing down, scaring away all the birds. He was left with nothing. You should be careful or you might be left with nothing.'

'I won't sit still to be threatened by you and I won't keep quiet. You're going to be sorry.'

'As you please, Bendan. Just remember to check the strength of that branch you're on.'

'Go to hell, Tremayne.' Neil's voice shook with anger.

'I'm sure you'll be there to show me around when I arrive.' Rand had stepped out and swung the door closed before he noticed her kneeling at his feet. 'What have we here?'

Zara had frozen in a crouch, so stunned by the conversation of the two men that she'd forgotten the possibility of discovery. Now she looked up the length of his body to meet the green glitter of his eyes and felt desire clench in her belly.

'Allow me,' he said as he extended a hand.

Hesitantly she laid her free hand in his. He cupped the other under her elbow and drew her to her feet. He didn't release her immediately, but held her close to his body. So close that the ruffle on her bodice brushed the lapels of his jacket. So close that if she leaned forward at all, they would be pressed together, from thigh to breast.

So close that her senses swam and she was tempted to forget how incompatible they were.

118

'These must be yours.'

Rand dropped to one knee and scooped up the red high heels. His gaze travelled up from her stocking-clad toes curled into the thick carpet, to the tight skirt that stopped short mid-thigh, to the raspberry-red ruffles framing the upper swells of her breasts, to the silky hair that for the first time since he'd met her was severely drawn back and pinned up off her neck in a smooth twist.

'Yes, they're mine.'

He placed the shoes on the floor beside him and smiled. 'Lean on me.'

'Why would I want to . . .'

Her voice died as he slid one hand under her arch and lifted her foot to his raised thigh. As she wobbled and almost lost her balance, she grabbed for his shoulder and clung.

Rand's smile vanished. One hand encircled her ankle while his fingers gently massaged her toes where they were pink from being squeezed into too-tight shoes. With her eyes closed, she sighed deeply. He was conscious of only warmth. The warmth of the foot he cradled and the warm tingling deep in his body.

Her breathing grew so ragged the ruffles on her dress fluttered as he slid on her shoe. Her weight shifted as he placed the shod foot on the floor and lifted her other foot to his thigh, proceeding to bestow on it the same therapy. Gradually his movements slowed and he slid one palm up to cup her calf, his thumb stroking back and forth across her shin.

His gaze travelled back up her body, studying every curve on the lingering journey until at last his gaze met hers. Rand's heart skipped a beat when he read both hunger and wariness in the brilliance of her eyes.

'Rand . . .' His gaze held hers as her voice died away on a groan. The thigh muscles under her foot flexed as she leaned forward, turning her hand to cup his neck, her thumb grazing the pulse that beat hard and fast in his throat.

'You have gorgeous legs.' One hand still held her foot to his thigh while the other slid higher, caressing the sensitive skin behind her knee. 'Long, supple, elegant.'

His fingertip dipped beneath the hem of her skirt as he tugged her foot higher on his thigh, edging her toes closer to his groin. 'A man might be willing to risk anything to feel them wrapped around him.'

She had to feel it, too. The growing desire, the craving that had taken on a life of its own in the dark hall.

Something shattered on the other side of the door, reminding him of where they were and who they were. His jaw tightened and his hand dropped from her thigh to clench in a fist.

'Rand?'

He closed his eyes. What in God's name was happening to him? When had his life careened out of control?

When he looked at her again, the flush of arousal was fading from Zara's face. First pleading, then doubt and anger took its place as her cheeks whitened.

As the overwhelming passion ebbed he remembered that she was the wrong woman, just as he was the wrong man for her. But even though he cursed himself for wanting her, when she tried to move her foot his hand tightened instinctively on the fragile bones of her ankle.

'Let me go.' Her words were no less fierce for being uttered in a whisper.

He knew she was right. But ordering himself to resist the urge to touch her didn't make it any easier to obey. Not when everything that made him a man demanded a quiet place where he could wrap her in his arms and make love to her.

He looked down at her foot, at her toes curled in the effort to hold them away from his thigh, to pull away from his grasp.

'Let me go!'

He studied her face and knew he had to walk away. He willed his fingers to loosen their grip and eventually they obeyed him. He placed her foot on the floor. After a moment he stood up and turned toward the stairs.

'Rand,' she said, her voice tense but quiet, 'why did I come in on Monday morning to find you'd ordered my desk moved to Uncle Crawford's office?'

When he looked at her again, her gaze burned unafraid, bright with anger and pride.

He, on the other hand, was afraid. 'You know what I said a few minutes ago, that a man might be willing to risk anything to be with you?'

'Yes.'

'You're a very dangerous woman and when I kiss you, when I touch you . . . Hell, even when I'm alone in the office with you, I forget that fact.'

'Dangerous? Me?'

'Good bye, Zara.' He walked down the stairs.

Zara stared after Rand, not quite believing he'd left without saying another word. She hobbled over to lean on the railing and look down while she slipped on her other shoe. He nodded politely at anyone who greeted him but he didn't deviate from a straight course across the wide room. A handshake for one man, a peck on the cheek from Sheila, and he was gone.

Gone.

She sucked in a deep breath and pressed her fist hard against her breastbone, trying to ease the unexpected ache where her heart thudded heavily, painfully. What had happened? There'd been so much gentle passion in his touch, yet it was gone so quickly. For some reason it hurt to watch the man, the lover, change into Tremayne, the ultimate businessman. Afterward she'd felt like a vulnerable fool with her foot resting on his thigh, his fingers encircling her ankle.

What had he meant – dangerous? That he was determined not to want her? To feel affection for her?

She shook her shoulders and lifted her head. So what? Life went on. There was still Neil to confront and convince.

Her hand was on the knob when she hesitated. His argument with Rand had been explosive and hostile. Perhaps she should wait for a more opportune moment?

No. The contents of Heinrich's estate would be valued any day now and she had to talk to Neil before the picture was listed. She pushed the door open and blinked at the decor, so different from downstairs.

So Sheila really hadn't changed so much. She'd only hidden this side of her life from her society acquaintances.

The room's indirect lighting showcased an entertainment centre the length of one wall. Each of the three upholstered arm chairs with matching ottomans invited one to recline in their depths. Against the far wall between the windows a highly polished antique table was flanked by two matching chairs, their fragility emphasizing the sturdy comfort of the other furniture.

Sheila was going to be furious when she saw the shattered glass and the liquor dripping down the wall to soak into the deep carpet.

Neil stood across the room, his head bowed in thought. Obviously he hadn't heard her come in.

'Neil?'

He swung around. 'What the hell are you doing here?'

'I want the painting of my family, Neil.'

'No.'

'It's mine and you know it.' She perched on the edge of a chair and clasped her hands together in her lap as Neil slouched in the delicate chair by the window. 'My father gave it to me before he died and you were there when grandfather made me leave without it.'

'Your father might have mentioned he would give it to you some day.' He stirred restlessly and the antique chair creaked ominously. 'I don't know that he actually did it.'

'I told you I'd pay for it.'

'You don't get it, do you, Margaret?'

She was tempted to correct him on her name but decided not to push him on something that, compared to the picture, was so unimportant. 'Get what?'

'Singleton was a two-bit artist starving in a garret somewhere when your mother hired him but the guy's famous now. One of his paintings sold for over twenty grand last month.' He heaved himself to his feet. 'The picture you're talking about is not the quality of his work today, but it is still worth a small fortune.'

She felt her jaw drop as her heart thudded to her shoes. 'Twenty thousand dollars . . .' She would never be able to raise that much money. 'But it's mine. Father gave it to me.'

'I only have your word on that, don't I?' He smirked at her, then opened the door and started down the stairs. 'My firm is handling the sale and it's my responsibility to get the best price possible for the entire estate.'

'Is this about the commission you'd earn?' She followed him so closely she almost fell over him when he stopped. 'I'll match any percentage you would've made. You won't come out the loser, Neil.'

'Are you trying to bribe me?'

'Of course not.' What a joke, she thought. Where was all this righteous indignation coming from? He'd perfected the art of running dubious deals in his cradle and she doubted he'd changed.

'I grew up watching the old man shower you with everything while he made it clear that Sheila and I had second-class blood. After you left, for a few years I thought . . . But no, Heinrich brought in Mr Wonderful Tremayne to be the crown prince.'

'Neil —'

'Get legal proof of ownership and the painting's yours. Until then, forget it. Of course you could always get the cash from loverboy. He got more of the old man's money than he deserved.'

Her mouth fell open. He must have heard the conversation between Rand and herself through the door.

He smirked, enjoying her discomfiture.

'Yoo hoo, Ne-il! Over here, sweetie.' Fran called from across the room. 'There's someone I want you to meet.'

'Neil, wait. We're not finished talking.'

'Yes, we are.' He obeyed his wife's summons.

She was getting tired of men who thought walking away was the best way to end a conversation, she thought as she stared daggers at Neil's disappearing back. And she was more than tired of Billie's high heels.

She stepped out of the shoes, picked them up in one hand, and grabbed her jacket before stalking boldly out of Sheila's place in her stocking feet. Hiking two blocks to her car over cold asphalt and the occasional sharp piece of gravel was better than limping one more step in self-inflicted torture.

On her way home she spent over an hour stuck in a traffic jam on Lion's Gate Bridge with nothing to do but brood. It was after midnight and she was peering blearily at a police car speeding by in the opposite direction, lights flashing, siren shrieking, when a plan, born of equal parts desperation, resentment, and determination, sprang full-blown into her mind.

Tonight, she promised herself.

CHAPTER 6

Rand dropped another stack of files onto the desk and sank into the big chair with a sigh. This wasn't going to work. He had hoped that spending the rest of the night going through Heinrich's study at the estate, sorting documents either for return to the office or disposal, would occupy his mind.

It seemed nothing could. He couldn't stop thinking of that woman whether he was working or at home in bed, which is where he'd been until he gave up on trying to sleep. It had been a big mistake to touch Zara at Sheila's earlier tonight. Very big. Immense.

He refused to believe it might be life-altering.

A faint rattle echoed in the distance and Rand looked up from the papers spread across the wide surface of the desk. The utter silence of the night hung thick and heavy and unbroken. He tossed a folder back onto the desk and pressed the heels of his hands against his closed eyes. Now he was hearing things. What the hell was the matter with him?

He couldn't concentrate, even here in the room where the old man's presence was stronger than Zara's. God, he wanted her!

Not just naked in his bed – though every time he thought of making love to her, his body's reaction was potent enough to drive him crazy. He wanted more than their bodies to be naked, pressed together, clinging and sweaty and satiated.

With Zara he wanted it all. Bodies, souls, and hearts, naked and vulnerable. That was what had his head spinning and his stomach in knots. That was what terrified him.

She was full of crazy ideas for robbing a corporation of its money and giving it away like some modern day Robin Hood. And a singer, for chrissakes. In one town for a few weeks, the next town for a few days, then the next and the next. Doing whatever was necessary to achieve success as a singer, a job notorious for chewing up and spitting out almost everybody who had a yen for fame.

He'd probably just get used to having her around and she'd be gone.

And what about him? He had commitments that took all his time, damn near all his money and, until lately, all his thoughts. He was in no position to take on any kind of permanent relationship, even if she would have him. And she wouldn't – if she knew.

Zara would not love the man responsible for ruining so many people's lives. If he told her the truth she would despise him –

There it was again.

Rand lifted his head and listened carefully but the indistinct noise was not repeated a third time. He'd reset the alarm system after he'd arrived. Still . . . with a big house so full of valuable items and the notices of Heinrich's death in the newspapers telling anyone that the place might be empty, he probably should check around.

He pushed back from the desk and strode silently into the hall, pausing at the base of the staircase that curved up into the night, one hand on the heavily carved newel post.

Where had the sound come from? Upstairs? Or at the back of the house? He held his breath and listened. A moment later, grateful he had worn dark clothing, he melted back into a heavily shadowed corner to wait. And as he waited, he bared his teeth in an expression that wasn't quite a smile.

He'd had a killer of a day. Dealing with a sneak thief would fit his mood exactly.

Maybe this wasn't such a brilliant plan, Zara thought.

She wiggled a little, trying to dislodge her jacket from the jagged window frame without letting a splinter stab through the fabric into her skin. She hadn't noticed it before she'd tried to slide through the opening.

She'd decided it was an omen when she'd discovered the estate staff no longer slept in and that the basement window had never been fixed. Though she'd hoped the bushes shielding it from the estate's garden and the fact that it opened into a remote storage room would have kept it unnoticed, it had been a long time since she'd been a teenager using it to escape when she'd found life painful and lonely.

She'd never dared to attempt anything riskier than sipping ice cream sodas at the local hangout with school friends like Billie. But the risks she'd taken had added excitement to the adventures. Though Mrs Parker had always reported her absence and assigned punishment, no one had been able to discover how she'd left the house unseen.

Tonight she was using her old escape route to get back into the house but there were a few problems. She was no longer as rail-thin or agile as she'd been at seventeen. The splinters on the ancient window frame were like iron-hard thorns; she felt like she was crawling through a barbed wire fence. And now, when she was hanging upside down, half inside the house, she felt uneasy about what would happen if she were caught.

Was she being foolish? Neil would know right away who was responsible when the picture went missing. He'd call the police and what would she say? They wouldn't believe it was hers, especially if Neil could prove it had been in the house before tonight. There were no guarantees that removing it before the evaluation and listing would be enough.

As she wavered about forgetting the whole thing, her weight tore her jacket free and she pitched head-first onto old magazines stacked inside the room. Just in time she tucked her head into her shoulders and turned the tumble into a somersault.

Dust choked the air and she swallowed a scream as the piles collapsed and she toppled to the ground. Sneezing, coughing, and rubbing a bruised hip, Zara hauled herself to her feet and picked up the small flashlight she'd dropped in the fall.

She slapped her clothes free of the worst dirt ground into the fabric during her crawl through the bushes and winced when the twig she pulled from her braid snagged a few strands of hair.

For about two seconds she contemplated leaving without the painting, then she stiffened her spine and gulped a mouthful of air. Neil wouldn't call the police; he'd avoided cops like the plague ever since he was a kid.

Onward and upward, she told herself as she picked up her backpack.

Ten minutes later, in the upper hallway, for what felt like the hundredth time, Zara's nape itched and she felt as if watching eyes were spearing her between the shoulder blades, following her every move. She stopped and peered back up the shadowed hall. Nothing.

She reached for the crystal knob that glittered in the narrow beam of light. A minute later she stood the flashlight on its end so the light it cast hit the white ceiling and was reflected downward, creating a soft glow that lit that part of the room. She tugged down the cloth covering her family portrait.

'Hi, Mama. I'm here, just like I promised.'

In the dim light her mother's blue eyes seemed to sparkle approvingly. She reached into her backpack and pulled out a screwdriver, a miniature hammer, masking tape, and a package of brown wrapping paper.

'I bet you thought I'd forgotten.'

She grasped the bottom of the frame and lifted, grunting as her arms took the full weight of the painting. She staggered back a step as she crouched to balance it against a chair. Picking up the screwdriver, she peered at the painting's backing, trying to decide how to remove the canvas from the heavy frame.

'Just a few minutes and we'll be out of here.'

'Do you really think so?'

She tensed, then carefully laid the tool on the table before she swivelled around on her heels. 'Hello, Rand.'

'What's happening here, Zara?'

133

'I didn't expect to see you.' Slowly she stood up and shoved her hands deep into her jacket pockets.

'That's very clear. I didn't expect to see you either.' He rubbed the back of his neck and sighed. 'Will you please explain? Can you?'

'The painting is mine. I came to get it.'

'And . . .'

'And that's all.'

'How did you get in?'

'A window.' She bit her lip then picked up the screwdriver and crouched in front of the painting again. She placed its tip beneath a staple, preparing to lever the sharp teeth out of the wood.

'That's impossible. Heinrich had an excellent alarm system installed years ago.'

She shrugged. 'Not that excellent.'

His hand snaked out and grasped hers, squeezing until the ridges on the screwdriver's handle dug into her fingers. 'Which window?'

'Downstairs. In the basement.' Her efforts to pull away from him were futile. 'Do you mind? You're hurting me.'

'Sorry.' He tugged her to her feet, then pried loose the screwdriver without releasing her hand. 'Show me. Now.'

She twisted around to face him, but any argument she might have made died unspoken when she saw the fury on his face. She'd lost her bid to recover the painting secretly. She scooped the

134

tools into her backpack and silently led him downstairs.

Down in the cellars he stopped her as they passed the handyman's workshop. 'Did you break the window?'

'No, I didn't break the window. Sheesh, what do you think I am? It's been broken since I was a kid.'

He looked at her silently for a minute, then picked up a piece of plywood and a hammer and nails.

'Let's go.' He pointed with the hammer and she grimaced but led on. She ducked a tangle of dusty spider webs but he didn't notice and walked straight through. She felt a small amount of guilty satisfaction as he swore roundly and wiped his face. So what? Why should she point out every little hazard?

'There it is. Are you satisfied now?' She opened the obscure door to the storage room and pointed at the small window she'd used to enter the building. He stepped past her and stumbled over the fallen piles of magazines. She heard the grate of a chain and blinked in the sudden light. The shadows rocked crazily as the single light bulb dangling from the ceiling swung on its cord.

'Not entirely, but I'll have it repaired and wired into the alarm system in the morning. In the meantime,' he held the board up to the window and wielded the hammer with loud, angry blows, 'I'll make sure this is secure from any would-be thieves.'

'I told you I'm not a thief,' she snapped. 'The painting is mine.'

'And you felt it would be more fun to retrieve it in the middle of the night through a basement window?'

'How many times do I have to tell you? It was a present from my father but my grandfather wouldn't let me take it when I left.'

'And no one else knew about this?'

'Neil does, but he won't admit anything.' She couldn't help staring at the muscles that bulged in his arms and rippled across his back as he fished one nail after another out of the pocket of his jeans and hammered them into the wood so hard there were pockmarks around the nail heads.

Comparing the man she saw at the office to this one clad in snug jeans, black leather boots, and a thin black tee shirt stretched taut over sleek musculature, was like comparing a Siamese cat to a panther. One was secure in its superiority, the other was beautiful but perilous.

'And you have no documents at all to support your claim?'

'I told you . . .'

'Yes, you told me.' Rand drove in the last nail and shook the board to make sure it would hold. 'But without something to substantiate your claim if you take the painting you are stealing, especially when you sneak in through a broken window at,' he checked his watch, 'three in the morning.'

'It's mine,' she said. He yanked on the dangling chain, plunging the room into darkness, and she scrambled after him as he left. 'It's not fair.'

He laughed cynically. 'Life isn't fair, never has been. Haven't you learned that yet?'

Zara followed him through the labyrinth-like cellar, up the narrow stairs, and into the kitchen, an immaculate expanse with glaring fluorescent lighting that glinted off the copper pots neatly aligned over the cooking island. When she entered he was already halfway across the room and his long legs were steadily increasing the distance between them.

'Wait.' When he ignored her request, she felt her temper begin to heat. 'I asked you to stop.'

Rand stopped but not because of her words. It was the desperate plea he heard in her voice. Despite his anger it bothered him. A woman like Zara should never have to beg a man for anything.

'I am tired of men walking away from an argument with me, as if once they've had their say that's the end of it.' She widened her stance and planted her fists on her hips. 'Well, Mister Tremayne, this discussion isn't over. I insist you listen to me.'

'Okay.' His lips twisted in something close to a smile when his casual agreement left her with nothing to argue about. Her teeth shut with a distinct click and he ignored the little voice warning him it was a mistake to be alone with her in the empty house. All alone with a dozen empty beds in the rooms upstairs.

'Sit down. I'll get us something to drink and we'll talk.' He opened the fridge and scanned its contents, deliberately leaning into the frosty air. He needed something to cool himself off. 'Orange juice?'

'Okay.' She hesitated, as if unsure he meant what he said, then unzipped her bulky jacket and hung it on the back of one of eight chairs that circled the long glass-topped table.

Her curves outlined by the clinging burgundy turtleneck made him aware that those beds were either too far away or much too close. Distracted by the potent urge to drag her into his arms right then and there, his hand squeezed the open box he'd just pulled from the fridge, shooting a geyser of juice into his face and chest.

The string of curses that exploded from his mouth didn't come close to relieving his frustration as he groped his way to the sink. He dropped the box, slapped up the silver lever that controlled the tap and started splashing cold water into his stinging eyes.

Damn. Even when suffering acute pain he could sense her hovering close behind him – even before she spoke.

'Rand! Let me help you.'

'Get me a towel, would you?'

'Yes, of course.'

Drawers opened and shut while he continued to rinse his eyes and by the time she'd found the towels the pain was easing.

'Here.'

The water stopped gushing into the sink when he whacked down the handle. 'Just a sec.' He turned aside and tugged his sopping tee shirt from the waistband of his jeans, off over his head, and tossed it in the sink.

Zara froze, hoping he hadn't heard her gulp for air when he stripped off his shirt. Rand was a beautiful man and at this moment she had a close-up, personal view of smoothly sculpted muscles which she knew she would probably never forget.

What would happen if she let her fingers follow the dusting of curly hair in the middle of his broad chest, hair that drifted downward to swirl around his navel then disappeared beneath his jeans. Was all of him as stunning, as masculine, as powerful as what she could already see?

'Zara?'

'Huh?' Her gaze snapped up from its fascinated fixation on the brass button fastening those jeans, jarring loose her heated imaginings of what lay beneath the clinging denim.

'The towel?'

'Oh. Here.' She held out the thick towel she'd found, her arm stretched to its full length in an attempt to avoid getting any closer.

'Thanks. Why don't you sit down?' He scrubbed it across his face, around the back of his neck, then dragged it up and down his chest a couple of times. 'Still want something to drink? There's no more juice. I wore it all.'

She turned quickly and walked back to the table, feeling stiff and awkward as she pulled out a chair at one end of the table and sat down. 'No, thank you.'

'I need some coffee.'

She watched as he moved smoothly around a kitchen he obviously knew well as he ground coffee beans, then filled the high-tech white and silver machine with water.

'There,' he said as he pushed a button. 'Hot coffee in a few minutes.' He wrung out his shirt and draped it and the towel across the middle of the divided sink.

'Isn't amazing how I always end up a mess when I'm with you?'

He slouched down in the chair next to hers and propped his feet up on the one opposite, effectively fencing in her legs. She stared through the glass top of the table. Her knees were only a quarter of an inch from his damp thigh, maybe less. If she moved just a little their legs would touch.

'So?'

She jerked her eyes away from his thigh. 'Huh?'

When her gaze skimmed the muscular arms he'd crossed on his naked chest her heart began to pound. She bit her lip and resolutely trained her gaze on his face.

It's ridiculous, she told herself, to practically swoon like some heroine out of a Victorian novel at the sight of a man's chest. During her years in show business she'd probably seen hundreds of half-naked male bodies even more beautiful than Rand's and none had disturbed her equilibrium to this extent.

'You wanted to talk?' he asked.

'Why are you at the estate?'

'I'm working.'

'Here? At this time of night?'

'I often work at night. As for why I'm here, for the last few years Heinrich did most of his work from the estate. All his papers have to be sorted before the auction.'

'Shouldn't Sheila be doing that?'

'She was solely his personal lawyer. I'll set aside anything personal as I organize the business files. Why are *you* here?'

'To get the painting, of course.'

'Why don't you just buy it?'

'Because I don't have twenty thousand dollars, that's why.' She winced at the shrill accusation in her tone and dragged in a deep breath, counting as she inhaled and exhaled in slow rhythm, forcing herself to a calm that wouldn't come naturally.

'What's so important about that particular painting?'

'Because it's the only picture of my mother that still exists.' Zara studied his expression. Maybe if she explained she could leave, painting in hand, and he'd be willing to forget she'd been here tonight. 'I was five when she died. Everybody loved her. She was fun and beautiful and exciting. Around her – things happened. My father adored her. We all did.'

She looked back at the table but this time she didn't look at his body through the glass, focusing instead on the fingers she'd twisted together on its surface.

'After she died he changed, everything changed. I was just a little girl who believed that if I could somehow talk to my father things would be the same as they'd been before. But he'd been working long hours, never coming home before midnight. So I waited in the office he used at home and . . .'

'And . . .?' he prompted when she stopped speaking.

'I know now he was probably drinking to make it easier to return to a house that felt so empty but I was terrified. I heard him cursing and yelling in the hall from where I was hiding under his desk.'

Rand swallowed hard. Though he was still angry, he didn't like to see the bleakness in her eyes.

'He must have been out of his mind with grief and anger and alcohol. When he came into the office he heaved his briefcase through the window and began tearing the room apart, sobbing as he shattered ornaments on the floor and tossed chairs against the walls.

'When he went for the painting, somehow I knew he was going to destroy it so I tried to stop him. He shoved me away so violently I fell out the broken window after the briefcase.' She touched the scar so near her throat. 'Luckily my grandfather had heard all the noise and came before I bled to death in the azaleas.'

'Zara . . .'

'I don't remember what happened next. When I came home from the hospital the few photographs of my mother had disappeared, the painting had been moved into what used to be my mother's sitting room, and my father's sister was living on the estate with her two children.'

'Neil and Sheila.' Rand reached out and tugged away the hand she'd pressed to the scar, winding his fingers through hers.

'The smell of scotch still makes me nauseous. And I can't bear to go near a hospital.'

'What happened when the police arrested him?'

'Charles Forster, Heinrich's only son? In police custody?' She opened her eyes wide and looked shocked.

'He wasn't charged?'

'Of course not. Grandfather hushed it all up. Society was very sympathetic about little Margaret's terrible accident so soon after dear Eloise's tragic death. Father was suitably devastated, of course, but buried himself in his work and recovered quickly enough. I've always believed he gave me the picture out of guilt.'

Zara flinched when Rand's feet hit the floor. It wasn't until he lifted her to her feet and wrapped his arms around her, rocking her gently, that she realized her cheeks were wet with tears. Why? She hadn't cried since . . .

She couldn't remember the last time she'd cried.

Her arms slid around his waist and leaned into his strength. Gradually her body absorbed his warmth, driving out the old painful memories, and she became aware of the damp, wiry curls on his chest tickling her nose, his heart thumping solidly beneath her jaw, his hands rubbing slow circles on her back.

It felt good. Too good.

'I'd better leave.'

'Why?'

'Before we do something foolish.'

'Zara.' When he whispered her name, she tilted her head to meet his gaze. She saw compassion and desire mixed with fading anger in his eyes. He lowered his lips to hers, so slowly, giving her every chance to pull away.

But she didn't. Instead she lifted her hand to his cheek, gently scraping her fingernails through the bristles that darkened his jaw.

The kiss, when it came, wasn't the explosion on her senses she expected. Rather it was an invitation. A promise.

'We're all wrong for each other, you know that,' she said.

'Do I?' He bent to press his mouth to the pulse throbbing in her neck, then tasted her with his tongue. 'So sweet.'

He swept aside the thick braid and moved his lips on the exposed flesh. She shivered as his breath caressed her skin.

'On the other hand,' she couldn't ignore the magical persuasion of his touch and she leaned into him, sliding her hands up his arms, grasping his shoulders and hanging on as the floor seemed to sway beneath her feet, 'maybe I'm wrong. Maybe we can be friends. Good friends.'

Rand cupped her face in his hand and traced her bottom lip with a thumb that trembled as he stared down at the woman who had haunted him, waking and sleeping, ever since he'd walked into The Kicking Horse.

Reality was much better than fantasy. His fantasies had never been as intense as the reality of holding Zara in his arms. 'Is that what we are? Friends?'

'You know, it's a stunner to me, too,' she turned her head to press a kiss and a smile to his palm, 'but for a person I'd decided not to like, you can be pretty darned nice. Pig-headed, but nice.'

The desire in his eyes blazed brighter as he tightened his arm around her, his hand sliding down to the upper curve of her buttocks to press her firmly to his hard length. 'What if we want more than friendship?'

Zara's heart lurched, then began to thud painfully as he drew her hand to his mouth and pressed a kiss to her fingers. She forgot to breathe when his tongue traced her life line, pressing wet and hot between two of her fingers, then withdrawing as he nipped gently at the fleshy base of her thumb.

'You said I was dangerous to be around.'

'I live for danger. Maybe we should stop trying to convince ourselves how wrong we are for each other,' he kissed the inside of her wrist, then placed her hand at the back of his neck, 'and discover how right this could be.' His arms tightened until her breasts were crushed against his chest.

'And this.' He pressed kisses to the outer corners of her eyes. 'And this, and this, and this . . .' He explored her face with his lips, kisses punctuating the words.

Cool air seeped up her back as he slid a hand beneath the hem of her sweater. She gasped and arched closer. The heated imprint of his fingers and palm scalded her tingling skin. She quivered as his thumb caressed each vertebra of her spine, from the waist of her jeans to the clasp of her bra and back down again.

His body was taut against hers, nothing hidden. She heard his arousal in his quickened breathing, saw it in his glittering eyes, felt it as his hips moved restlessly against her own.

Zara fought back the swirling passion evoked by his touch, by his words, struggling to deny her own body's demands as she attempted to focus on what had brought them together, here, tonight.

It was too soon. Passion was not enough. Need was not enough.

She wanted more. She wanted it all.

Her eyes squeezed shut and her forehead rested against his shoulder as she admitted to herself that what she felt was stronger than like, deeper than lust. She wouldn't settle for less and they would never have more until several problems were dealt with.

'What about the painting?'

'What?' He became absolutely still.

'The painting. I need . . .'

His hands tightened into fists, then dropped away as he stepped back. 'Are you trying to make a deal? In exchange for sex I look the other way as you walk out of here with that damned painting under your arm?'

'No.' She pressed the heels of her hands to her eyes as the passion drained away, leaving emptiness. Her arms dropped to hang limp at her sides. 'See, we are wrong together. I ask a question and you . . . you . . .'

Rand's gut twisted as his angry accusation echoed in his ears. What had he done? Instinctively he reached out for her, reacting to the sadness in her eyes, but she stepped back and shook her head.

'I didn't mean it,' he said.

'Yes, you did.' She picked up her jacket, refusing to look at him as she shrugged it on and turned toward the door.

'Please, Zara.' Rand reached out again, only releasing her arm when she stopped. 'I'm sorry. It just . . . came out.' He shoved his hands in his pockets to keep from touching her. 'It's no excuse but, dammit, we were so close to making love and you come out with something from left field.'

'You're right, that's no excuse. My question wasn't from "left field", something you'd understand if you knew me better. I can't make love with a man I don't know.'

'Then get to know me. Let me learn about you.' He felt a whisper of panic when she still wouldn't look at him. 'I care, Zara. Give me a chance to show you.'

'If you cared about me you wouldn't stop me from taking my mother's picture.'

'Do you know how that sounds? I've heard it before. "If you loved me you would . . ." Hah!' He began to pace, long, angry strides across the kitchen floor, stopping when the table blocked his way, then turning on his heel to reverse direction.

When he was brought up short against the counter he slapped his hands down and leaned on them, staring at its surface before he swivelled to resume pacing. 'One has nothing to do with the other. Caring is emotional, taking that out of here would be illegal.'

'It's mine . . .'

'I've heard that, too,' he rushed on. 'From my mother, as she bought yet another expensive toy, whether it was jewellery, or clothes, or men. From my father . . .' his voice faltered, then continued, 'every time he needed another drink on the job, or another dip into petty cash for a stake because he had a "sure tip" from his buddies at the race course.'

'I'm not like that, Rand.'

'Neither were my parents, or so they said. Well, they got their way. They lied and they cheated until they'd sucked all the blood from what was "theirs". When I got it there was nothing left.'

The silence was thunderous when he came to a halt, their toes almost touching as they stared into each other's eyes.

He was aware of his lungs heaving as he struggled to bring his breathing under control, aware his throat ached from forcing himself to speak calmly.

'You meant money, didn't you, when you said "blood"?' she said. 'To you money is life's blood.'

After interminable seconds of his silence her gaze dropped, and they both watched her fingers fumble the jacket's zipper together and listened as each tooth clicked into place.

'I need my mother's picture, Rand. Not like a useless woman needs another symbol to prove her importance; not like an alcoholic needs a drink or a gambler needs a stake. To me, that picture is proof that love and caring and honesty existed for me – once upon a time.'

She flipped her braid outside her collar, then hunched her shoulders as she buried her hands in her jacket pockets.

'You should try to recognize the difference and until you do we can't resolve this situation or our future.'

'It's only a painting . . .' He stood there, fists clenched at his own idiocy, and watched her walk away. He waited as her footsteps receded, waited until he heard the heavy thump of the front door, waited for the last trace of her perfume to fade. Waited as he acknowledged the futility of chasing after her.

He shivered. Only because he was shirtless and the old house's furnace wasn't running, he told himself. Not because she was gone.

Rand filled a cup before turning off the coffee machine. He sipped the hot liquid while he looked for a plastic bag in which he could carry his wet shirt home. When another shiver racked his spine he hunched his shoulders. This chill could have nothing to do with the way they'd parted, he thought.

He glanced back, flicked off the light switch, then exhaled, rubbing the back of his neck. She was unreasonable to expect him to let her walk away with the portrait.

They were wrong together. That had been apparent from the beginning. They were wrong for each other and she had obviously accepted that fact.

Now he just had to convince himself. He'd go to Treville for a few days and when he returned he'd have himself and his life back under control.

CHAPTER 7

'It's about time you came back.' Walt slapped Rand on the back in greeting. 'Not that we noticed you were gone, mind you.'

The elevator doors opened and they both stepped inside. Rand nodded a greeting to the two men already occupying the car, Forster Pacific's senior accountant and the vice-president of marketing.

'Although why you'd bother showing up in the office at six on a Friday night is beyond me.' As the doors closed, Walt moved to stand next to Rand. 'The team's pissed off that you missed the game on Thursday. Where've you been?'

'I'm sorry about the game but I was . . . busy.'

'Never mind. I should know better by now than to ask about your mysterious "business" jaunts. Of course, if you'd care to mention why you were away mid-week rather than your usual Sunday and Monday, I'd be happy to listen.' He lowered his voice to a hoarse whisper that was as loud as most people's normal tone. 'The staff think you keep a mistress hidden away. Is it true? Do you spend every Sunday and Monday in an orgy of sexual satisfaction?'

'What do you think?' Rand almost smiled when he noticed the thinly disguised curiosity of the elevator's other occupants.

'I have several different theories. Probably all of them are wrong, same as everyone else's. The only thing I know for sure is, wherever you go, you never drive the Mustang.'

Rand said nothing more and eventually the other two men reluctantly got off at their own parking level.

Walt shook his head as he and Rand exited into the lowest level beneath the company's building. 'I hate parkades, they always stink. It's especially disgusting after sitting in that office all day. Why did I let you talk me into leaving hockey? I miss the thrills and the travel.'

'Do you miss the broken bones or concussions?'

'You really get a kick out of being a smart ass jerk, don't you?'

'See you next week.' Rand fished inside his overcoat pocket for his keys.

'This is some car.' Walt stood back to admire the gleaming lines of Rand's vintage Mustang. 'I don't know how you can stand to drive that box leased by ForPac when you have this baby.'

'It's practical.'

Walt used the sheepskin lining of his jacket to polish away a smudge on the car's shiny black fender. 'When are you going to give in and sell her to me?'

'Never.'

'Why?' Walt ticked off the car's faults on his fingers. 'She guzzles gas. Parts, when you can find 'em, should be cast in platinum for the price you pay. You can't leave it anywhere except secure parking 'cause it's number one on the chop shops' hit parade.'

'Give it up, Walt.'

Walt patted the car's roof. 'Some day, old girl, it'll be you, me, and the highway.' He had unlocked his own car door two stalls down when he suddenly laughed and slapped the heel of his hand against his forehead.

'Ha! I can't believe it took me so long to see it.'

'See what?' Rand unlocked the trunk and placed his bulging briefcase inside beside the suitcase he'd used on his recent stay in Treville.

He'd hoped that concentrating on securing another new employer for his home town might distract him from wanting Zara. He'd succeeded with the parts manufacturer but he might have accomplished just as much by staying in Vancouver. Certainly Zara had never been out of his thoughts.

Why had he been so stupid that night? A woman like her would never use sex as a tool to get what she wanted. And if he'd been thinking with his brains, he would have realized the stupidity of the idea before he opened his mouth. Of course, that didn't excuse her attempt to steal the painting.

'I can see your weakness. I always knew you had one. So much for Mr Need-nothing-and-no-one.'

'What are you talking about?'

'The Mustang. You pretend to be so cool but let anyone suggest you sell your grandfather's car and – bingo – brick wall.'

Walt's comment arrested Rand mid-motion. A second later he pressed shut the trunk, leaning heavily on the metal as he stared at his friend. Oh my God, he thought.

Suddenly he felt as if he was going to gag on the stink of gas fumes and musty walls. Walt was right, he did have an emotional investment in the Mustang he'd inherited from his grandfather. Perhaps much like Zara and that painting of her family?

He'd been a prime, A-one jerk. He had to call her. Rand rounded the car, opened the door and reached for the car phone, then drew back. Why on earth would she listen to him? Unless . . . He rubbed his chin, deep in thought. Maybe there was one way . . .

'Randall Tremayne, sentimental about a car.' Walt leaned on the roof of his Jeep and chuckled. 'That's rich.'

'You have no idea how rich, Walt.' Grateful his

155

friend didn't know about his confrontation with Zara, Rand turned around. 'Could you give me a hand for an hour or so?'

Walt glanced at his watch. 'Why?'

'I need some help with about a dozen boxes.' He glanced at his own watch, then reached around Walt to remove the keys of the Jeep. 'You can use my car phone to call Marcy and tell her you'll be late.'

Walt spluttered protests as Rand gently urged him toward the Mustang.

'I can't be late for dinner again, not after what happened last time.' Walt crossed his arms across his chest and stopped moving his feet, becoming as solid as one of the columns holding up the building.

Rand grinned. 'You can drive my car. I'll take yours.'

'Well, heck, why didn't you say so in the first place?' Walt held out his hand for Rand's keys. 'Marcy will understand. Where are we going?'

'The estate, then my apartment. I have some extra paperwork that might take all weekend.'

'What about your usual Sunday and Monday mystery jaunt?'

'I'll have to skip this weekend.'

Walt dropped the keys. 'You're going to *what*?'

Rand didn't need Walt's shocked stare to know he'd just said something totally out of character For the last six years he'd never allowed anything to interfere with his commitments in Treville. Amazing how a woman could change a man's priorities.

'Oh, wow! What a beaut of a Sunday.' Walt upended his beer can and gulped noisily. 'They squeezed the goalie out of his net just like the zit he is. Couldn't happen to a nicer guy.' He righted the can so he could read the brand name and frowned. 'Why do you buy this light stuff? It ain't got no real flavour. Rand? Rand?'

'What?' Rand looked up from the papers stacked on his dining room table.

'Man, what's with you? The coach who made my life a grief is losing big and you're buried under a stack of paperwork.' Walt heaved himself to his feet and headed for the kitchen. 'Why the heck did ya invite me over here if you weren't even goin' to watch the game?'

'You invited yourself.' Rand stretched and yawned. 'Something about the size of my television compared to your own, and some mention of escaping your wife's friends.'

'There are fourteen women at my house right now. Can you believe it? Lucky for me you decided to stay in Vancouver this weekend.' He hoisted his empty beer can at Rand and cocked an enquiring eyebrow. 'Want another?'

When Rand nodded, Walt retrieved two more cans from the fridge. 'Marcy invited her charity committee over even though she knew there was a big game today.'

'I'd forgotten she was in charge of charitable donations for her sorority.' Rand nodded his thanks for the can and leaned back as he popped the lid. 'Does she know anything about the children's rehab centre over on the east side?'

'I dunno. Maybe. Want me to ask her?'

'Yes. No. Yes.'

'So make up your mind, already. What do you want to know?'

Rand shrugged. 'Just general stuff, I guess.'

'Isn't that the place Zara goes? The place that's getting the million?'

'So what if it is? She made it sound like a worthwhile cause. I thought I'd look into it.'

'Jeez, no need to get huffy. I was just asking.'

'Fine.' Rand put down the beer can and bent over the papers again.

Walt stood there and watched silently for a moment as Rand picked a piece of paper off the slowly diminishing stacks, scanned it, then dropped it in one of the six bulging boxes on the floor. 'Those are the ones I helped you with on Friday, aren't they? What's in them?'

'Heinrich's papers.'

'Your first weekend off in almost two months and you bring home someone else's musty paperwork? Isn't that stuff Sheila's responsibility?'

'I'm looking for something, all right?' A muted roar rose from the television. 'Better get over there. You're missing the action.'

'Need some help?'

'What about the hockey game?'

Walt glanced over his shoulder at the television just as the score flashed on the screen. 'It's a blowout. The Rangers have them by eight points in the third period. His butt is toast.' He snagged the chair opposite Rand and spun it around before he straddled it. 'What are we looking for?'

'Any mention of a painting that once belonged to Charles or Eloise Forster. The artist's name is Singleton.'

'That's all? Can't you give me a little more info?'

'I don't know much more than that myself.' Rand sighed and slumped back. 'At the estate there's a portrait . . .'

'. . . of my family and nobody cares enough to listen when I try to explain.' Zara dipped the brush into the can of paint. 'They just quote dollars and legalese at me.'

'This cruel and mysterious "they" . . . are we talking about Neil or the gorgeous hunk who just happens to run Forster Pacific?' Billie picked up a small tool and began scraping dried paint splatters off the windows.

In what she knew was probably a futile attempt to ward off discussion, Zara concentrated on aligning the long, steady strokes of her brush so no hint of sickly pea green showed through the creamy yellow paint they were using to refurbish the classroom furniture of the Children's Centre.

'That isn't Hepplewhite, Zara. Talk to me.'

'I already told you what happened.'

'If you ask me, you were lucky he didn't call the police. I can't believe you were so crazy.'

'I didn't ask you.' Zara dipped her brush in the paint can again.

'Right.' They were silent for a few minutes, the only sounds the swish of the brush, the scrape of the blade along the glass, and the faint din from the games room down the hall.

'That had to have been some kiss to get you this rattled. I know you ended up yelling at him instead of getting on to better things but . . .'

'Billie, just drop it, okay? Or I might come here to help you next Sunday, too.' She took one last swipe at the desk leg, then set the brush onto the plastic drop sheet and centred the lid on the paint can. Three sharp blows with the hammer and it was airtight, pinching the flesh on her finger in the process.

She bit back a yelp, then turned her back so she could examine her hand without Billie realizing she'd hurt herself again. No way did she want another safety lecture.

'I mean, I only got a glimpse of him a few weeks ago at The Kicking Horse but, whew,' Billie whistled and fanned her hand in a gesture of appreciation. 'Why did you need to talk to him about the darn painting just when things were heating up? Couldn't it wait half an hour or so? Maybe even,' she scrunched up one side of her face in an exaggerated wink, 'until the next morning? As it is, I don't think I blame him for getting the wrong idea.'

'How could he even think that I wanted to trade it for sex?' Zara lowered her voice and hissed the last word. 'Shows what he thinks of me. The man's totally out of line, totally ridiculous.'

'Totally ridiculous, huh?' Billie wiped the paper towel over one window and moved on to the next. 'Didn't you tell me about some woman trying to come on to him to get her job back? I imagine a man in his position has things like that happen quite often.'

'That's different.'

'Uh, huh. If you say so.' Billie started on the next window as Zara gathered up brushes for cleaning. 'You're out of luck, girl, if you're looking to me for excuses.'

'What about you? You and Abe had something special. You could have tried to understand his point of view. You wouldn't even listen . . .'

'I don't want to talk about Abe.' Both women cringed when the scraper in Billie's hand screeched up the glass.

'And I don't want to talk about Randall Tremayne.'

'Too bad we didn't find what you were looking for.'

'Thanks for your help.' Rand glanced up from the document he was examining, smiled briefly at Walt, then began flipping the pages, his frown deepening as he scanned them.

'Are those the papers you found in the last box? What are they?'

'I'm not sure. Looks like the rough draft of the will Heinrich wrote just before he died. But something about this doesn't jibe with the copy of the will Sheila gave me.'

Rand frowned and flipped back to the figures listed on the top sheet. 'Keep this information to yourself until I can do some checking, okay?'

'No problem. I'd better get going. The hockey game was over two hours ago.' Walt shrugged into his jacket. 'I'll pick you up at five o'clock Tuesday.'

'For what?'

'The old-timers hockey game. The party starts at five-thirty sharp, remember?'

'We have to stop at the Forster estate on our way.' Rand picked up the can at his elbow, grimacing when he got a mouthful of flat, warm beer.

'I thought the estate was sold to that crazy movie director. Isn't she using it to make a series of television movies?'

'Yes. But Neil Bendan's company received

permission to hold the auction in the estate ball-room before her crew takes possession.'

'Why would I want to go to an auction?'

'To see how the other half live? It won't take long. I think I should be there but we don't have to stay for the whole thing. The art's scheduled to be sold early in the afternoon.'

'You're doing this because of Zara, right? You've already spent an entire weekend looking for a piece of paper which, if it exists, might prove she owns the painting. Isn't that enough?'

Rand tilted the can, idly sloshing the liquid back and forth as he contemplated the boxes stacked against the wall.

Would Zara go to the auction? Heaven knew most people would stay away, avoiding the bitter memories, reluctant to watch the painting be sold to a stranger who only cared about the value of the artist's signature.

Something told him she would be there. He was amused by his decision to attend, as if he felt his presence might make the sale of the painting easier for her to bear. How laughable.

'Was it enough?' Rand's smile was wry when he answered. 'Apparently not.'

Walt plopped into the last empty seat at the back of the estate's ballroom, leaving Rand to stand near the door, the auction programme in one hand as he scanned the room. Where was she? Had he

163

misjudged . . . Ah, there, a dozen rows from the back.

Today her hair was coiled into a mass low on her neck, although a few rebellious strands of silken ebony had slipped free of confinement and gleamed starkly against her yellow jacket.

He eyed the empty chair on her left, trying to decide if it would be smart or masochistic to sit so close to her but before he could make up his mind an elderly woman took the seat.

He stepped back until his heels bumped into the wall near the rear door, then trained his eyes on the programme. It was just as well.

His shoulders moved restlessly beneath the silky grey fabric of his jacket, feeling an unusual constriction in the business clothing he'd worn with ease every day of his adult life. The uncomfortable sensation became more noticeable as Neil's staff placed the Singleton painting on an easel.

He watched Zara's profile as the bidding opened high and soared higher, as the pain she was experiencing showed in her posture, in the expression on her face.

'Sixteen, I have sixteen. Ladies and gentlemen I must remind you . . .' The urbane man at the podium flashed a white smile as he expounded on the investment value of Singleton's early work.

Neil stood to the side of the improvised stage, arms crossed on his chest, his face showing distinct pleasure in the rising prices. Rand knew he was also relishing his swelling commission.

'Thank you, Mrs Roth-Williams. I now have seventeen. Is there another bid? Ah, yes, the gentleman by the rubber tree, eighteen . . .'

The auctioneer's practised patter continued for several minutes until he raised his hand. 'I have a bid of eighteen thousand dollars. If there are no more bids, I shall close . . .'

Zara leaped to her feet, apologizing as she stumbled over the legs of the elderly woman in her haste to leave. Rand opened the door at his side, stepping back to allow her room to escape.

'Going . . .'

'Zara . . .'

She glanced up, her eyes widening as she recognized who held the door for her. Time seemed to stretch and sound deadened as he stared into her eyes, her misery striking a chord in his heart, her tears soaking into his soul. Then she was gone and he was back in real time, the door vibrating with the force she'd used to close it behind her.

'Going . . .'

'Nineteen.'

Rand looked up in amazement at the hand in the air, listened as the auctioneer repeated the words that had just been uttered by suddenly numb lips.

'Nineteen thousand. Going, going, gone.' Rand

forced his mouth shut as his hand fell heavily to his side.

The auctioneer bowed and smiled. 'Sold to Mr Tremayne.'

Walt laughed. 'I'd like to be a fly on the wall when you explain to Zara how this happened.'

'Let's get out of here.' They were almost out of the room when Sheila stepped in front of Rand.

'I didn't know you liked Singleton's work, Rand.'

He looked down at the blood-red fingernails resting lightly on his sleeve. 'You didn't?'

'Unless you had a reason. What could it be?' Sheila tapped one long fingernail against her lips as she pretended to ponder the question. 'Perhaps you are trying to win the fair maiden? Little Zara has become quite a pretty woman. Or perhaps her naiveté is the attraction for a man of your experience. Who knows how she would show her gratitude to the man who gave her what she wants most in the world.'

'You can be so common, my dear.' He lifted her hand off his arm and curved his lips in a smile that held no warmth.

'You used to like my common touch, Rand.'

'I did?' His gaze travelled from her carefully arranged blonde curls to her elegantly clad feet. 'I wonder why? If you'll excuse me, I have a cheque to write.'

'Mrs Parker tells me you took several boxes from the estate this weekend.'

Rand had turned to follow Walt out but something in her tone made him pause. 'Yes, I did. Why do you ask?'

'As Heinrich's lawyer, I should have been present to verify the nature of the documents. A formality of course, in your case, but these legal procedures have to be observed.'

'What legal procedures? Everything necessary was completed at the time of the estate inventory. The boxes were due to be shipped to ForPac at the end of the week in any case. I needed some documentation and saw no reason to wait.'

Sheila pulled a cigarette from her purse and lit it with time-consuming ceremony. She leaned a little closer, so only he could hear her voice.

'Actually, someone misplaced one of my files and I had intended to have a look inside before the boxes were sent away. I was doing a lot of work at the estate these past few months, finishing up Heinrich's stuff and setting up my own practice. I wouldn't want any clients to think I was careless. Bad for business.' She winked.

Rand contemplated her 'just-between-us' manner. 'I'll have my assistant check the boxes before they are stored. Tim is very dependable.'

'You didn't look inside?'

'Excuse me, young lady. You shouldn't light that thing in here.' An elderly man shook his finger at Sheila and coughed into the cloth handkerchief he held across his face. 'You smokers just don't show enough consideration . . .'

Rand and Walt saw their opportunity and made their escape.

After returning home from the hockey game that evening, Rand had the delivery men prop the painting on the chest of drawers against his bedroom wall, then smiled mechanically as he ushered them from the apartment. Ignoring the urge to unwrap the painting, Rand threw together a sandwich and had a quick shower.

It wasn't until he walked back into the bedroom, naked except for the towel slung around his neck, that something drew him back to sit on the edge of the bed facing the wrapped parcel. He sighed, leaned forward to tear off the brown paper, and gazed at the smiling, black-haired child depicted with oil and brush and canvas.

'All right, now I've got you. What do I do with you?'

He tossed the towel on the floor, stretched out on his back and buried his head in the thick, fluffy pillows, covering his eyes with his forearm. 'Nineteen thousand dollars.' He shook his head in disbelief and groaned. 'What in hell is happening to me?'

Rand slowly clenched and unclenched his fist against his forehead, timing his breathing until it had steadied into the usual, controlled rhythm. Then he rolled to his side and tucked his bent arm under his head, propping himself up just enough so he could see the canvas.

The longer he stared, the more he felt that at any moment a child's giggle would break the silence of his bedroom. The sensation of her presence was so strong he gripped a handful of the bedspread and dragged it across his lap. That Singleton was a very talented artist, he acknowledged with a wry grin. Rand knew she was only a figure on canvas but he kept himself covered as he slumped back onto the pillow.

What was Zara going to say when she found out he had purchased her precious painting? He had to tell her before she heard it from someone else. Neil, being who and what he was, would likely phone her tomorrow to gloat, so that meant going to see her at Roggo's damn bar. Tonight.

He glanced at the clock on the bedside table, then rolled to his feet. He'd forgotten both his nudity and the picture until he was standing in front of it. With warm cheeks and a roll of his eyes at his own absurdity he snatched up the damp towel and wrapped it around his hips. Then he grabbed clean briefs and slacks and disappeared into his bathroom to dress.

This was another embarrassing incident Walt would never hear about.

Forty-five minutes later he pulled into a parking

space directly across from the alley access used by Roggo's employees after hours, the same alley where he and Zara had argued the first time they'd met.

He turned off the car but his hand slid from the handle without opening the door. He couldn't go inside the bar.

He'd couldn't think straight while Zara sang.

He sank back against the car door and stared at Roggo's back door. He desperately needed time to think and now was as good as any.

What was he going to do about Heinrich's will? What was Sheila's involvement? If his suspicions were correct, the situation at ForPac was about to blow up in his face.

More urgently, how was he going to tell Zara *he* now owned the painting?

And with all his resources already committed to rebuilding Treville, how was he going to juggle his finances to pay for the damn thing?

Which question would be easier to answer, only heaven knew. Or hell.

It wasn't long before the last customers had departed. When the staff began appearing beneath the single lamp angled out over the short flight of stairs in the alley, Rand got out of the car and waited to call her over. He watched the huge bartender walk down the street to the bus stop with a waitress but no one else came out of the building.

His fingers began drumming on the car roof

when another ten minutes passed and there was still no sign of Zara.

Where was she? He couldn't have missed the bright yellow jacket she wore every day. His gaze sharpened as something stirred in the shadows beyond the stairs. His heart jerked into a faster rhythm when, just as Zara stepped out, the shadows solidified into three menacing hulks. Between one breath and the next, the brightness of her jacket had been enveloped by darkness.

'Zara!' His shout and her scream ricocheted off crumbling brick walls. rand leaped across the front end of the car, barely aware of the traffic he dodged as he dashed across the street. 'Zara!'

By the time he reached the spot where they'd grabbed her under the light, nothing remained but the absurd suitcase she called a purse, its contents spewed carelessly on the ground beside the yellow jacket. Bile rose in his throat as he snatched up something he saw lying there and raced on into a scene lit eerily by the full moon, passing first one of her shoes, then the other, drunkenly askew, abandoned where they had fallen.

As he passed a dumpster Rand ran up against a wall of rancid flesh.

'Whatcha looking for, man? This pretty little piece? Finders keepers.'

Rand jerked away from the hand that had grabbed his shoulder. Beyond the leering face he caught sight of Zara struggling, held off the

171

ground by two other attackers. Her arms flailed, drawing grunts or curses when her fists connected with part of their anatomy.

One mugger had a hand across her mouth, the other arm crossed her chest with a hand squeezed around her breast. The second man held her legs chest high, his fingers digging deep into the tender inner flesh of her stocking-clad thighs, bared by the struggle that had forced her skirt to her hips. Both grinned at their buddy's witticism.

'Put her down.' Rand dragged his gaze away from Zara's terrified eyes and the bloody scrapes on her knees, back to the man facing him. 'Now.'

'Why would we do that? At three to one, your odds ain't so great.'

'Three to one?' Slowly Rand brought up the hand he'd hidden in the folds of his overcoat, revealing the gun he'd picked up from Zara's belongings. 'More like six to three, I'd say. Two bullets each.'

'I make it a little higher than that, boyyo.'

In his peripheral vision Rand saw Roggo's skinny arms come in to view, wielding a shotgun, its butt nestled against his shoulder, its business end pointed at the man opposite Rand. 'I've got this one, boyyo.'

Rand brought the gun he held a few inches to the left, levelling it at the head of the mugger whose grip shifted from Zara's mouth to her shoulders. Rand went still when he saw the blood smeared

across her lips and chin. He stepped around
Roggo, careful not to get between the little man
and his target, moving closer until he could see the
sweat beaded on the faces of the men who held her.

'Let her go,' he sayd. 'Now!'

'Shit man, I don't need this crap.' The guy
holding her legs dropped them and took to his
heels. A second later the other guy swore, flung
Zara directly at Rand, and ran.

Rand staggered back and dropped the gun as he
absorbed her weight against his chest. After a
moment he wrapped his arms around her, pressing his face to her hair. The hand he rubbed up and
down her back trembled.

Zara squeezed her eyes closed and breathed
deeply of his scent: clean sweat and cologne,
needing to absorb some part of him into herself,
to believe in the reality of this moment, that she
was safe.

'If you two are finished there, boyyo, I think
we'd better tie up this scum for the cops. I've got
twine inside.'

She felt Rand's arms tighten slightly before his
lips touched her forehead.

'Can you stand?'

'Yes,' she said, then used all her strength of will
to make it true as he removed his arms. She swayed
and almost fell but when he reached for her again
she shook her head. 'I'm fine, just light-headed.'

'You sure?'

'Yes. Help Roggo.' She shivered.

'You're freezing. Here.' He removed his coat and helped her slide her arms into the sleeves before he buttoned it. Then he picked up the gun.

Zara crossed her arms around her chest, sliding her hands deep into the opposite sleeves until each grasped and elbow, then leaned against the filthy steel wall of the dumpster and concentrated on staying on her feet. She watched through a deep fog of exhaustion and residual fear as they used Rand's belt to bind their stuggling captive's wrists.

'We'd better get inside in case this bastard's friends come back,' Rand said.

'You got that right.' Roggo shoved the barrel of the shotgun into the back of the mugger's neck and nudged until he began to climb the steps. Rand wrapped his arm around her shoulders and slowly guided her back to her scattered belongings.

He dropped to one knee and gathered everything back into her purse. When he was done he slung its long strap across his shoulder and scooped up her jacket. At first his hand brushed briskly at the filth that clung to the yellow wool, then moved slower and slower until his fingers stopped and dug into the folds of fabric.

'Rand.' Her voice was hoarse, barely above a whisper, but he heard her. His shoulders hunched, then he stood and turned. Zara wanted to cry when she saw the expression on his face. 'I'm okay. They didn't hurt me.'

'They didn't hurt you? My God, look at you.' He strode the few steps between them and dragged her back into his arms as if he would never let her go. She nuzzled her cheek into the soft white cotton that covered his muscled chest.

'You're covered in blood. Your legs, your mouth . . .' With one finger he lifted her chin until he could study her face in the moonlight. 'He cut you.' His finger left her chin to track the curve of her bottom lip.

Zara blinked at the savagery she heard in his voice, more than ever reminded of the panther she'd once compared him to. Then the world rocked dizzily as he swung her into his arms and carried her into the bar.

CHAPTER 8

'Put her there. Everything's ready.' Roggo locked the door behind them and pointed to one of the curved benches lining the back wall. He'd placed a first aid kit on the nearby table.

'Where'd you put the slimeball?' Rand asked as he lay Zara on the bench.

'Tied him to the bar's footrail.' Roggo pointed over his shoulder with his thumb. 'Had to stuff a towel in his mouth to shut him up. He'll hold 'til the cops get here.'

While Zara listened to them talk she lay back on the cushioned vinyl, grateful when Rand folded her jacket inside out and placed it beneath her throbbing head.

'Get me some water, Roggo. I've got to clean these cuts.' He swept her hair off her forehead.

'Sure thing.'

As soon as the older man went behind the bar Rand dropped to his knees beside the bench and slid his hands beneath her skirt to grasp the

176

waistband of her shredded pantyhose. He tugged them down and off, moving very carefully near the scrapes on her knees and shins.

Zara bit her lip, struggling to contain rising hysteria. Whether she would laugh because he was so matter of fact while he partially undressed her or cry for the same reason, she had no idea. How could he be so calm?

It wasn't until he smoothed the fabric of her short skirt back down around her hips, and pressed his cheek to her thigh, that she noticed the tremor in his hands and the fury in his eyes.

'Rand –'

'Be quiet.' He dumped the kit out on the table and began sorting through its contents until he found the packet of sterile gauze. He ripped it open with his teeth and pressed it to the blood still seeping from her cut lip.

'Call an ambulance, Roggo.' He placed one of her hands over the pad to hold it in place, then turned to work on her legs, repeatedly dipping the cloth into the bucket of warm water Roggo had placed on the table.

'No.' Zara cleared her throat and tried again. 'No ambulance.'

'Call the ambulance, Roggo. Now.'

'Rand.' She grabbed his hand and waited until he met her gaze. He knew why she hated hospitals. 'Don't. I won't go.'

Understanding showed in his face, then disappeared. 'That was a long time ago. You were a child.'

Tense, Zara watched him and waited. If he was ever going to understand her, he had to take this first step.

His expression revealed indecision, frustration, and finally resignation. 'No ambulance.'

Roggo shrugged and grabbed a bottle of scotch before he dropped into a chair and hooked his heels over the bar rail by the mugger's head.

'Thanks.' She blinked back sudden tears.

'But I'm taking you home. And I'm staying the night.' Rand's cheeks reddened slightly as he glanced at her face from the corner of his eye. 'Just to make sure you're okay. Nothing else.'

'That's –'

'That's the deal, or I call the ambulance myself.'

Her instinctive protest died when she noticed his averted gaze and deliberately blank expression. He was worried about her, she realized. His pushy attitude caused no more than a hiccup of anger amid the pleasure she felt. She nodded, then relaxed under his gentle ministrations, content to enjoy his touch while the two men talked.

'How did you know what was happening to Zara in the alley?' Rand asked Roggo as he dipped a clean towel in the water and wiped away the worst of the dirt that streaked her face, gliding softly over the bruise that was forming around her cut lip.

·'Heard her scream. Grabbed the gun. Didn't know you were there until I got outside, though.' Roggo took a swig from the bottle as he eyed Rand speculatively. 'Seems to me most businessmen don't walk around with a gun in their pocket.'

'Most don't.'

'Seems to me the cops are going to ask questions about that there gun. Maybe we should come up with some answers before they get here.'

'Why?'

'Gotta licence?'

'No. I don't need one.'

'Now that's plain stupid.'

'It's not my gun.' Rand walked over to the bar, piled a handful of ice cubes onto a towel, then knelt again to hold it against the growing bruise on her jaw. 'I took it from Zara's purse.'

Up until that moment she had enjoyed watching Roggo grill Rand but his comment brought her upright in shock.

'From *my* purse? I don't own a –' Her mouth open in shock, she pushed away the ice-filled cloth and stared at him. When he tried to urge her down again she shoved away his hand. 'Oh, my Lord. That's Kenny's gun. You faced down those thugs with a toy gun!'

'I know.'

Zara swung around until her feet were on the floor between his knees and they faced each other.

'You knew? You idiot!' Her voice rose, squeaking on the last word.

'It was a very realistic toy. Until I picked it up, I thought it was genuine. In the moonlight, they would see what they expected to see if I was credible.'

'Don't that beat all. Your talk about those six bullets was just that, talk.' Roggo's wheezing laugh almost drowned out the growls emerging from behind the gag in the mugger's mouth as he twisted furiously in his bonds. 'Seems she's not the only one who's upset.'

'Let me –'

Zara swatted away Rand's hand as he tried to hold the ice against the side of her face again. 'Forget the darn ice. What were you thinking of? You could have been killed. They might've –'

'Zara.'

It was only one word but she closed her mouth and looked at him. His eyebrows were pinched together in a heavy frown and his lips were tight and grim.

'You took a hard blow to the jaw. If you don't use this ice to keep the swelling down, tomorrow you won't be able to talk or eat without a great deal of pain.'

'You do as he says, girlie.' Roggo cocked his head and listened before he got to his feet and headed for the front door. 'Besides, it sounds like the cops are here, so you'll have enough talking to do without scolding the poor man.'

She snatched the ice away from Rand and held it to her face. 'What you did was stupid.'

'Yes.' He rested his hands on the bench beside her hips and looked steadily into her eyes.

'Not carefully thought out.'

'No.'

'Totally out of character.'

He shrugged.

Her heart skipped a beat. She barely heard the clatter as Roggo unlocked the door for the police. 'Why?' she whispered.

'I'm not sure.' He glanced at the two officers who had entered the room, brushed a kiss against her unhurt cheek, then stood up and slid his hands into his trouser pockets. 'But I'd do it again.'

She couldn't interpret what he'd meant by the last muttered sentence. The gentle words were at odds with his bleak, almost resigned expression.

She tried to concentrate on the look she'd seen in his eyes, to decipher the significance of what he'd said, but beneath the throbbing of assorted aches and pains, her thoughts were becoming fuzzier by the second.

Giving up her attempt to sort out a reason for his actions, she lay down on the improvised cushion and closed her eyes, letting the ice provide some respite for her painful jaw. When something warm settled over her, she opened her eyes and smiled, or tried to smile, at Rand as he tucked the folds of his overcoat around her body.

Time. She needed time to understand the look she'd seen in his eyes. If he was really going to take her home and stay with her, she'd have that time. But would it be smart to be alone with Rand?

She yawned, wincing as the movement made her jaw throb. Determined to relax while she could, she dropped the damp towel, snuggled her face into the collar of his coat, inhaling his scent, smiling as his hand drifted across her forehead, the gentle caress smoothing her hair away.

Later. She'd worry about this . . .

The low rumble of male voices dwindled to background noise as Zara slipped into a light doze.

Rand stared down at Zara, studying the fan of her eyelashes against her skin, the way she'd curled on her side and tucked her hands beneath her cheek for sleep. He reached out to tuck the collar higher around her throat and noticed the streaks of blood on his hands and coat. Zara's blood.

He could feel the urge to kill rising again and flung back his head, squeezing his eyes shut as a shudder worked its way down his spine. What would have happened tonight if he hadn't arrived when he did, if Roggo hadn't heard her scream?

He sucked in a deep breath, then exhaled through his mouth, counting to ten as he slowly brought himself under control. Then he leaned forward, tucked his coat higher around her shoulder.

No matter what, he would never allow her to be in danger again.

Just for a second he remembered what Zara had said about Heinrich's attempts to control her, then shrugged it off. This wasn't the same. Her life was at risk every time she came to work down here and safety was more important than independence. She'd understand why he couldn't allow her to make foolish choices.

Rand nodded in response to a policeman's request, then touched her hair once more before he moved away.

'I'm exhausted.' Zara kicked off her shoes the minute she stepped inside her front door. 'The half-hour snooze on a hard bench in The Kicking Horse didn't help much.'

Rand held his overcoat and searched the overcrowded closet for an empty hanger, then gave up and used one that already held a windbreaker and scarf. He put his shoes neatly together beside the door.

'Can you believe it?' she asked. 'Two hours of interrogation and the police still want to talk to us again tomorrow. Who would'a thought the jerk we caught would turn out to be the mayor's nephew?'

She tossed her purse and jacket across the hall table before she padded into her living room and dropped onto the couch with a sigh of relief. 'Your shirt is probably ruined.'

He glanced around her living room and she wondered what he thought of her home. Billie rented it out furnished and Zara liked the comfortable, if faded, furniture. The first time she saw the little house, when Billie offered her a place to live, she'd sensed that it had been here forever and would still be here for many years to come. It made her feel settled, as if she too had lived in the little house for years.

He sat beside her on the couch, one arm along its back, his hand only inches from her shoulder, and looked down at the rusty brown streaks marring his formerly pristine white shirt.

'Our relationship is probably going to cost me a fortune in clothes,' he said with a rueful smile. 'Zara, I realized something tonight.'

Relationship? Startled, she leaped into speech. 'Garbage on your coat, mustard on your suit.'

'Don't forget the lipstick on my collar.' His fingers played with a lock of her hair.

'That one wasn't my fault.'

'You don't think so? But if I hadn't met you, Sheila's lipstick wouldn't have been on my *collar*.'

'It wouldn't?'

His hand moved from her shoulder to her hair where he tugged lightly until she looked up.

'It wouldn't.' The smile on his lips didn't quite reach his eyes.

She shivered. 'You'll be glad when I'm out of your life.'

'Will I?' He swept her hair aside and slid his fingers around her neck, his thumb gliding over the pulse beating rapidly in her throat.

'Your shirt . . .' Zara looked down at her fingers and carefully wove them together in her lap. 'If you soak it in cold water right away the blood might come out.'

Finally his hand withdrew and she gulped air, able to breathe again. Then the rustling of fabric jerked her gaze his way.

He was unbuttoning his shirt. The couch springs rocked as he stood up.

'I didn't mean . . . Shouldn't you . . .' She gawked, unable to look away as he yanked the shirt-tails from his slacks, unbuttoned the cuffs, and removed the shirt.

'Where's the bathroom?'

'Huh?' She blinked and dragged her gaze away from his chest. 'Through the kitchen, on the left.'

'Thanks.'

She watched him stride away. The bathroom light blinked on, bathing him in a yellow glow before he disappeared from sight. But not from view as her eyes played tricks on her, letting her see his chiselled features, muscled chest, and taut abdomen as if he still stood there.

She blinked rapidly, dispelling the image. She groaned when, though his likeness had faded from her mind, the unfamiliar jolt of desire did not.

On the contrary.

She closed her eyes and arranged a cushion to ease the fading ache in her head. Worse, all her body parts were kicking up a ruckus, as if determined to get her attention. Her throat was tight, her heart pounded, her knees shook, and her palms sweated. No doubt about it, she felt horny. The word was appropriate, if crude.

Any scrapes and bruises received during the scuffle outside the bar were nothing when measured against the fire of arousal in her belly, a fire she feared would never be doused by common sense.

What chance did common sense have when she was in the same room with a man who made her want to step into the fire? A man whose touch, scent, and naked chest gave her disordered equilibrium a wild ride.

'Zara.'

His voice rumbled, like the low, deeply felt thunder that followed nearby lightning. She squeezed her eyelids together tighter, as if by refusing to look at him, she would be safe from the storm.

Safe?

Her face relaxed and one corner of her mouth turned up. Since when had she ever avoided life's storms just to be safe? Why shouldn't she experience the tempest, bathe in the tingle energizing her skin as the storm's power spent itself all around her?

She could feel his nearness though he wasn't touching her. Yet.

Her eyelids fluttered open.

He stood in front of her, his toes only inches from her own. His long legs, draped in fine linen, were slightly apart in the aggressive stance so many men assumed when they had a point to make or an argument to win. His arms hung loosely at his sides. His expression was carefully bland.

'Zara?'

Too bland. He was wasting time trying to mask his passion. The heat in his eyes and his clenched jaw screamed tension. Not to mention the impressive and very masculine bulge under his fine linen slacks.

'Yes?' His thigh muscle jumped when she brushed his ankle with her toes. She allowed her mouth to curve in a genuine grin and held out her hand. He wrapped his fingers around hers, tugging sharply. The action brought her to her feet, her breast brushing his knuckles briefly before he averted his eyes and released her.

'You'd better get some sleep.' He eyed the short couch and shuddered. 'I don't think I'll fit on that thing. Is there a bed for me?'

'Yes.' She rested one hand on his chest, fingers threading through the dark curls that shielded the unsteady beat of his heart. 'Mine.'

'No.' He touched her cheek. 'Not now. Not just because of what happened at The Kicking Horse.'

'Why did you face those thugs down with a toy gun?'

He swore and his hand dropped away in a fist.

'Is it so difficult, Rand? How about if I go first?' She moved closer until her breasts pressed against his chest. She stood on tiptoe, her hips cradling his arousal, and cupped his jaw with her hands, urging him to meet her gaze.

'You're an impossible, incredible man. Your logic often baffles me, your orders infuriate me, and your touch drives me crazy.' Her lips brushed his chin, inching upward toward his mouth. 'I've decided I like crazy.'

'Stop it.' He grabbed her hands in both of his, bringing them down to his chest. He sucked in a deep breath, then continued, his tone eminently reasonable.

'You're overwrought. You need sleep. You're feeling vulnerable. You are experiencing an understandable reaction and want to be physically close because of what happened.'

'Damn you!' She snatched her hands away. 'Nobody tells me what I'm thinking or feeling. The only person who decides what's best for me, is me.'

'Yeah?' The expression in his eyes lightened to something perilously close to a smile.

'Yeah.'

'And what's best for you?'

'You.'

'Have you decided what's best for me?'

'Me. Since you're feeling skittish we'll have to start slow.'

She slid her hands up his chest, enjoying the way he groaned as her nails dragged across his nipples before she laced her fingers together behind his neck. She pressed her open mouth to his neck just below his jaw and licked the pulse beating there.

'You call that slow?' His hands slid up her bare arms and across her shoulder blades until his arms were wrapped around her body. His fingers played idly with the zipper tab on her dress.

'Think you can do better?'

He didn't answer but she wasn't sure she liked the glint in his eyes as he tugged the zipper down, releasing one tooth at a time. He slid one hand inside the dress and pressed his palm against her waist. She waited but, other than the fingertips gliding back and forth across her hip, he didn't move.

'Well?'

He chuckled. 'Too slow?'

She leaned back in his arms so she could see his face. 'I think you're teasing me.'

'And if I am?'

'It's nice to know you can loosen up now and then.' She wrapped one leg high around his thigh, pressing her heat to his hardness. 'Although perhaps "loose" isn't exactly the most correct word at this moment.'

He reached down for the hem of her dress which was now twisted around her hips, drawing it up inch by inch. She raised her arms and he lifted the garment over her head. He dropped it on a nearby table without taking his gaze from her face.

He slid both hands down from her shoulders and over her hips, stroking his palms over the satin camisole and panties. 'You feel good.'

'So do . . .' She gasped when he lifted her up, his hands supporting her thighs as her bare legs instinctively wrapped around his waist. He shuddered heavily as she settled against him. When he spoke his voice was deep and rough.

'Still want to go slow?'

'No. I don't think slow is an option. Not now.' She held on to his shoulders with both hands and brushed a kiss across his lips. He growled and deepened the kiss, exploring her mouth until they were both trembling. 'My bedroom is through the door behind you.'

He staggered slightly but managed to carry her into the other room where he collapsed backward onto the bed. The springs groaned in protest when they bounced once, twice. Laughing breathlessly, they slowly, carefully untangled themselves until they were stretched out side by side.

Still smiling, Rand tugged the camisole up and over her head. Though the only light came from the lamps in the other room, Zara could see the desire in his eyes as he cupped her breasts, gliding his thumbs across the hardening tips.

'So soft. So responsive.' He bent his head, dragged his tongue across a nipple, then blew gently. She shivered.

'I want you, Zara. I didn't know how much, until today.'

'We're going to be good together, aren't we?' She pushed at his shoulder, rolling him onto his back. She fumbled open his buckle, then unfastened his zipper, sliding it down one tooth at a time, as he had done to hers.

He groaned and moved restlessly. 'Are you trying to make me crazy?'

She laughed. 'Sorry.' He lifted his hips so she could slide the slacks and white briefs down and off his legs. Feeling oddly shy, she averted her gaze from his nakedness.

'Wait, I need something from the pocket.'

She tossed his clothes onto the floor and lay down on her side, facing him. 'Check the table beside you.'

For a moment Rand thought about the next morning, when he'd have to wear wrinkled clothes if he left them where she'd thrown them, then shrugged. Right now he didn't give a damn about any morning, much less what he'd wear. He picked up the small box from beside the glowing digital clock and read the label. 'Extra large?'

'I wasn't sure what size . . . Your hands are so big and I'd heard . . .' She looked flustered, then grinned. 'I had no idea companies manufactured such a selection of condoms.'

'You bought this box for me, for us?' He dumped the packages out on the table top and tore one open.

'A few weeks ago, before . . .' She lapsed into silence.

He finished her sentence. 'Before our midnight meeting at the estate.'

She nodded.

'I'm sorry for what I said about . . .'

She covered his lips with her hand. 'I think it would be better if we didn't talk about that night, not right now.'

She was right. A smarter man wouldn't have brought up that fiasco in the first place. Soon enough to talk about the painting tomorrow.

'I'm glad you'd been thinking about the possibility of us, too. We should have known how good this was going to be. We've wasted so much time denying the attraction.'

He pulled her on top of him and strung kisses around her neck to nibble on her ear. He bent one knee, lifting his thigh between her legs, separating, opening her. He could feel her, hot, damp, ready.

She put her hands on his shoulders for balance and looked down at him, passion in her eyes. Her gaze held his as she slowly moved her hips, shifting against him. His head spun and he sucked air deep into his lungs. Slow down, he reminded himself. She wanted to take things slow.

He slipped his other leg between hers, opening her wider. Her fingernails sank into his shoulders when his hand touched her inner thigh.

'Rand!' she cried out softly.

'Yes, sweetheart. Yes.' His fingers cupped her heat, went deeper. Her hips moved, reaching, reaching. 'I'm here. Come to me, honey, come to me.'

'Now, now. I can't wait.' She sobbed out his name again, her entire body trembling.

Her need, her honesty made his head spin. He knew he was losing control and he didn't care. All he could see, all he could feel was hunger, hunger for her. He needed to be inside her. Now. He cupped her buttocks and pulled her down onto him, thrusting deep and hard.

'Rand. Rand! Oh, God, it's so right.' She moved, again and again. 'Faster, darn you, faster.'

He heard himself chuckle and felt distant amazement. Never before in his life had he found anything remotely amusing during sex. Now, listening to Zara urging, no, commanding him to greater speed, struck him as exquisitely funny.

She moaned and wrapped one hand around the back of his neck, holding him still for her kiss, plunging her tongue into his mouth, matching the passion and action as his body moved in hers. All thoughts about laughing were wiped from his mind.

Rand knew he couldn't last much longer. He reached between them and touched her again. Her body went taut above him, her spine arched as he felt the inner ripples of her release. Her muscles clenched around him and he called out her name as the tension exploded.

Rand groaned when Zara pressed her knee higher on his thigh, dragging her toes along his calf as she nuzzled her cheek into his chest. 'Are you trying to kill me?'

'I don't know. Could I?'

She drew circles on his inner thigh with her fingernails and he shifted restlessly, then grinned. Totally exhausted and, he'd thought, totally satiated, still his body swelled slightly in response.

They'd made love twice but the second time they'd both been able to keep things slow. Now the early morning sun was lightening the sky outside the window. The air was cool, the quilt and sheets lay somewhere on the floor, but she felt deliciously warm draped across his body.

'I guess I'd die happy.' He idly combed his fingers through her hair, tangled and damp from passion. She winced when his hand grazed the back of her head.

'Ouch.'

'What's wrong?'

'Nothing much, just a bit sore where my head connected with the wall in the alley.' She smiled. 'Before you say anything, I'm warning you. People who say "I told you so" are odious.' She kissed his chin, then rested her head on his chest. 'Did I thank you for being there?'

What in hell would have happened if he hadn't been there? He struggled to control his rage as he re-lived the gut-wrenching fear he'd felt when those thugs had dragged her deeper into the alley.

'Every night I knew you were working at The Kicking Horse I couldn't stop thinking about how dangerous that part of town can be. Then there were the hours we spent together at the office. Those were worse, if you can believe that's possible. I almost went out of my mind.'

'That's why you moved my desk down to Crawford's office?'

'You'd hum or sing under your breath, just loud enough so I could hear you and sometimes you'd wiggle your hips.' He caressed the offending piece of her anatomy. 'I didn't get any work done, at least none that was worth anything. All I could think about was making love to you.'

'Things weren't any better for me. No matter how the writing started out, I'd end up with a love song.'

Her words startled him for a moment. She couldn't possibly mean . . .? No way. Just a figure of speech.

'Tomorrow you can tell Roggo you won't be back. I'll use my connections in the city to find you a job in a more reputable place.'

'Reputable?' He winced when her fingers dug into his chest as she pushed herself up. 'Are you saying my job and my friends aren't respectable?'

He recognized her outrage and closed his eyes in resignation. He'd committed a tactical error, something unheard of before he'd met Zara. On a normal day and with anyone else he would have achieved his purpose without confrontation.

'Look at me, damn you.' Her tone was as cold as the dawn air striking his body. He opened his eyes as she pulled away from his touch.

'You are a very talented singer and I'm sure they are all very, ah, nice people. I merely meant that Roggo's place isn't safe. You won't want to work there any longer.'

'I won't?' She swung her legs over the edge of the bed. She picked up a pair of jeans and yanked them on. She jerked open a drawer and pulled out a sweatshirt. When her head reappeared from the neckline, so did her scowl.

He propped himself on his elbows to watch her stomp around the room, resisting the cowardly urge to grab the sheets off the floor to cover himself. He'd never felt so exposed, completely naked and half-aroused in a rumpled bed still redolent with their passion.

'Zara, be reasonable. Tonight's incident . . . it could happen again. You could be seriously hurt, even killed.'

'I write songs. To do my job I need to stay close to my audience. It's what I am, what I do. Women are attacked every day and believe me, as sad as that fact is, not all of them are entertainers.'

'Please, sit down. We can talk about this.'

'No. We can't.'

'Zara.' He snagged her wrist and tugged her down to sit on the side of the bed. 'I can't permit you to work there, not now.'

She flinched when her jean-clad hip touched his skin, then pulled back as far as his grip allowed. 'I refuse to change how I live my life because of those thugs' actions or your opinions.'

'We are lovers, Zara.'

'Do you think anything we did here tonight,' she thumped the mattress with her fist, 'gives you the right to dictate to me?'

His gaze met hers steadily but her expression altered. Her eyes now held a distance, a coldness, he'd never seen in them before.

'Is that what this,' she waved her hand along his naked body, 'was all about? You thought you could control me with sex?'

'We made love.'

'Made love.' She snorted in disbelief. 'I thought so. Until now.'

'If you'd let me explain.' He sat up and reached for her hands.

'Okay. Explain.' She wrapped her arms around her chest, tucking her fingers away from his touch.

'You made love with me, so I know you care about me. You wouldn't deliberately make me worry every night.'

'I care about you?' She repeated his words with a faint air of doubt.

'Yes.'

She looked down at the sneakers beside the bed, then bent forward. Her hair fell forward to hide her face as she shoved her feet into the shoes and laced them up.

She turned, placed one hand in the centre of his chest, and pushed. He flopped back against the pillows.

'It didn't occur to you to tell me, somewhere in this lecture, that you care about me?'

'Well, I . . .'

'You should have. Heck, you should have told me you loved me.'

'I do.'

'You do. What? Love me? Well, let me tell you, "love" doesn't give you the right to govern my life. But then you didn't actually say it, did you?'

She leaned forward until her lips almost touched his and he could see only her glittering eyes. 'You know what's really scary?'

'What?' He was tempted to lift his head the quarter inch necessary for a kiss but somehow he couldn't. And then the opportunity was gone as she jumped up and away, her long dark hair swirling across his face as she moved.

'It might have worked.' She grabbed up a sweater, then stood poised by the door. 'I'm going next door for half an hour. Don't be here when I get back.'

And then she walked out, leaving him naked in her bed.

CHAPTER 9

The next evening Rand braced both hands on the tiled wall of the shower room and leaned into the stream of hot water pounding his head and shoulders. Maybe it was just as well he'd been sent back to the changing rooms early. Heck, the team would have been better off if he'd never laced up his skates and stepped onto the ice.

He'd been trying to block the puck but instead he'd redirected it into their own damn net. Then he'd been ejected from the game for fighting.

Him!

Fighting!

He slapped his hand against the wall in frustration. This whole situation with Zara had him on edge. Why couldn't he get her out of his head? She'd been so hot and then – wham – so cold. Just because of a minor misunderstanding. What had he said that was so bad?

Women!

He scrubbed shampoo into his hair, ignoring the other men's clatter as they came into the changing area, stripped off their gear, and crowded into the shower room.

'No goals tonight, Tremayne.'

'You're wrong. He got one for the other team.'

'Has Rocket Randall lost the magic touch?'

'Talk about losing it. I think you broke that guy's nose, Rand. All for a little jostling in the corner?'

'Look, the jerk was riding me all night. I'd had enough.' Rand rinsed his hair, turned off the water, and reached for a towel. He rubbed his hair partially dry then wrapped the towel around his waist. 'Drop it, okay?'

'Oh, oh, someone's a little testy, guys.'

'Nah, I read in that national business magazine that he's having a downturn. Whatever that is.'

'I bet it's a woman who's got his knickers in a twist,' said a young man who'd been with their team for only two years. 'And because of it he cost us the game.'

'Whoa, fellas.' Walt grabbed Rand before his fist connected with the younger man's face. 'We're only allowed one broken nose a night.'

Rand stared appalled at his arm in Walt's grasp, then at the young idiot he'd almost punched. Sean was a fair hockey player and a major pain in the ass but until tonight Rand had found his antics mildly amusing.

As his muscles relaxed, Walt released him.

'Look, I'm sorry,' Rand said. 'I didn't mean . . .'

'Forget it, man.' Sean picked up a bar of soap and began scrubbing. The other men avoided Rand's gaze.

'Maybe you'd better get changed and while you're at it, make sure you've got lots of cash.' Walt stepped aside so Rand could leave the shower room. 'You owe us a round of drinks at the bar for that puck you bounced into our own net.'

Walt's comment diffused the tension and the other men resumed their usual laughing analysis of the game they'd just lost.

What the hell was happening to him? Rand snatched his street clothes off the pegs. After he'd dressed, he opened his equipment bag to put away his hockey gear and found a plain white envelope with *Tremayne* typed on the front. Where had that come from?

He tore it open. After he read it, he sat motionless for a few minutes then picked up his gear and headed for the hockey arena's office and then the car. He had calls to make and questions to ask.

Forty minutes later Rand walked into the neighbourhood pub the team always frequented after a game and was greeted by his team-mates' cheers and whistles. He sat down beside Walt and called the waitress over.

After she brought the round of drinks he tossed a handful of bills onto her tray. Because of the incident earlier at the hockey rink, he forced himself to socialize with the other guys for a while before he tried to talk to Walt.

'You get lost on the way here?' Walt rocked his chair onto its back legs.

'I have to talk to you,' Rand said in a low voice. 'Alone.'

'Now?'

'Now.' Rand picked up two of the full beer glasses and led the way to a pool table in a relatively quiet corner.

'I'll break.' Walt selected a cue, chalked the tip, and took his shot. They both watched as coloured balls ricocheted across the green felt. A yellow ball with a fat white stripe dropped into a pocket. 'What did she say?'

'What did who say?'

'Zara. When you told her you'd bought the painting.'

'It didn't come up.'

'It didn't come up? Cut the bull, Rand, it's me you're talking to.'

Knowing he couldn't avoid answering, Rand told him about Zara being attacked outside The Kicking Horse and how they'd exchanged angry words before parting.

'You dashed to the rescue at night and had a fight at dawn? And what happened during those hours in between?' Walt poked Rand's chest with the cue. 'Anything I should know about?'

'It doesn't matter what happened since at the moment she's not speaking to me. This isn't what I need to talk to you about.'

'What's up?' Walt sank another striped ball.

'Remember those papers we found on Sunday?'

'Yeah. You asked me not to mention them to anyone 'til you could do some checking.'

'I kept the papers but had the boxes delivered to ForPac yesterday. Sometime last night the boxes were ransacked. Today I asked a few quiet questions, did a little digging.' Rand watched as Walt lined up another shot. 'I found a threatening letter in my equipment bag tonight after the game. Obviously somebody objects to my interest.'

Walt cursed as the point of his cue skipped across the surface of the shiny white ball.

'Now look what you did. Couldn't you have waited for me to take my shot before you dumped that on me?' He picked up his glass and stepped back so Rand could play. 'I assume the letter's anonymous. What about the team's padlock we always put on the changing room door while we play?'

Rand chalked his cue while he walked around the table. 'The staff at the rink didn't see anything suspicious and the padlock was in place, undamaged, when I left the ice. Somebody must have come in while I was showering, before you guys got back. Either that or someone on the team hid the letter in there.'

'How would one of the guys be involved? Why would they? We're a team.'

'You should know better than anyone that being team-mates doesn't guarantee loyalty.' He bent over the table, lined up his shot, and took it. A blue ball bounced off two others and dropped into a pocket.

'That's professional sports. Big money was involved in what happened to me.'

Rand balanced one hip on the edge of the table and leaned out over the felt surface. He took the shot and sank another ball. 'Heinrich's will is about big money. Perhaps someone on the team received an offer they couldn't refuse.'

'If someone fiddled with the old man's will, we both know who must have done it or at least been aware of it. Why haven't you talked to Sheila?'

'I will. When I'm ready. I want as much information as possible before I decide how to deal with this.'

'What was in the letter?'

'About what you'd expect. Nothing explicit.' He sank two balls with one shot. 'If I don't stop, I'll be sorry. Typed envelope, computer printout, no signature.'

'It didn't mention the will specifically?' Walt studied the table over the rim of his glass. 'Maybe they're angry about something else entirely. It's not unheard of for company executives to receive threatening letters. Or perhaps your mystery jaunts triggered somebody's jealousy.'

Rand hid his grin as he sank three more balls in quick succession. Walt just wouldn't give up trying to trick Rand into revealing the nature of his weekend trips. Over the years it had become an amusing contest. 'I know. That's why I'm going to do some more checking before I instigate any action.'

'Called the cops?'

'Not until I know what I'm dealing with. Once the police get involved the media will be on it like a pack of wolves and I won't be able to control any possible repercussions for ForPac.' Only one ball left, the black eight ball. He chalked his cue as he considered his shot.

'Maybe you should call them anyway. You can't always control everything and this could be dangerous.' Walt walked around the table to stand at his side. 'Give it up, I'm going to get another turn. The eight ball's screened by three of mine. You'll never get that shot.'

'Oh?' Rand leaned forward and delivered the stroke with carefully controlled force. The cue ball banked twice before it glanced off the eight ball which rolled sideways and dropped into the pocket.

Walt shook his head. 'Lost again. I don't know why I even play pool with you any more.'

'Maybe you enjoy losing.' Rand tossed the white ball in the air and caught it. 'Another game?'

'Sure, why not.' Walt pulled balls from pockets and rolled them down the table to where Rand was setting them up for another game. 'Your lapse at the hockey rink tonight has given me hope. Even you can lose it now and then, however rarely.'

'In your dreams, Kirkpatrick. In your dreams.'

So this was how it felt to lose one's mind. Things were getting totally out of control. Over the last two weeks, since Zara had walked out on him, worry, desire and frustration had boiled into a mass of confusion that threatened to consume his life. He hadn't lived with nerves this raw since the bottom fell out of his life when he was twenty-one.

Rand held his hands under the tap and peered in the mirror at the black circles under his bloodshot eyes. Things couldn't go on this way.

'You look like hell.'

Rand splashed another handful of ice-cold water on his face. 'Did you bring him?'

'Yup. He's in your office. Catch.' Walt threw a towel which Rand snagged in mid-air.

'Is he good?'

'The best detective in the city. Are you sure this is smart? Why don't you just talk to her, tell her what's going on?'

'No.' Rand refastened his cuffs, then shrugged into his jacket before leading the way down the hall to his office.

As he walked around to sit at his desk Rand studied the rail-thin man sitting primly, hands stacked atop each other on the briefcase balanced across his bony knees.

'Hello, Mr Hoffman. I'm Rand Tremayne. Walt explained our requirements to your satisfaction?'

'Yes, sir.'

'Walt tells me you're the best.'

'My firm's ratio of success is unparalleled in Vancouver, third in the country.'

'It is crucial that our arrangement remain completely confidential.'

'Of course, Mr Tremayne. Anything less would be completely against my code.'

Rand almost smiled at the man's affronted expression but even his face muscles were too damned tired to move. 'Your career will be over if she discovers your presence.'

'I hardly think she will take any drastic action.'

'It's not her you have to worry about. It's me.'

'Oh.'

'For over a week I've worked all day and followed her at night. I'm half-dead of exhaustion. My business is suffering.'

'You have my sympathy, sir.'

'Thank you. Did you bring it?'

Hoffman opened his briefcase and lifted out a box in a white paper bag. 'The instructions are inside.'

Rand weighed it in his hand. 'It's so small and light. Is it the best available?'

'Yes, sir. We recommend this brand to all our clients. There are less expensive models, of course but I always say, it's a small price for peace of mind.'

'I agree, Hoffman.' Rand picked up a business card and a cheque from his desk. 'Here is your retainer and a phone number where you can contact me directly. If something is urgent and I am unavailable, you can talk to Walt. Since we're not sure who's writing the threatening letters, speak to no one else.'

'I understand.' He slipped the papers into his briefcase, then stood. 'I will provide weekly reports.'

'Daily. Seven a.m. at my office number.'

'We don't usually . . .' His words stopped when Rand scowled. 'Very well.'

'Start today, when she leaves the Children's Centre. Walt gave you the address?'

'Yes, he did.' The detective stood up to leave.

While Walt held the door for the detective Rand spoke again, his voice deadly soft.

'One more thing, Hoffman.'

'Yes, sir?'

'Be very careful. If you allow anything to happen to Zara Lindsey, I promise you will regret it.'

The man's adam's apple bobbed twice, then he nodded and left.

'Little hard on him, weren't you?' Walt slouched down on the chair the other man had occupied.

'I was emphatic.'

'You were an effing S.O.B.'

Rand tossed a piece of paper on the desk between them. 'That came in the mail today.'

Walt unfolded the sheet and read it aloud. '*She's a pretty songbird. Don't make me hurt her.*'

He looked up. 'I'd say this proves we were correct about the fourth note last week that threatened her. They are willing to use other people to stop your investigation.'

Rand's fist clenched on his knee and he swung around in his chair to stare out at the city. 'Yes. Zara is definitely a target. This one is more explicit than the last.'

'Who knows the two of you are . . . have been sort've involved?'

'I don't know.' A faint smile hovered on his lips. 'Other than yourself, of course.'

'Why haven't you called the cops?'

'I can't. Not until I know what we're dealing with about the will. Any mention in the press hinting at confusion in ForPac management could cost us millions.'

'When you first began checking into the discrepancy in Heinrich's will, I thought the threats might be coincidence or from a crackpot. Even if they were real, you were the target and it was your decision. The last two messages have changed my opinion.' He tossed the letter back on the desk. 'I think you should tell her. Warn her.'

'I can't tell her about the will. Not yet. But I'll keep her safe. No matter what it takes.' Rand felt the bleak certainty deep in his gut. He already knew what he had to do. He also knew that it would probably cost him any chance at a relationship with her. He glanced at his watch. 'Three o'clock. She should still be at the Centre.'

'Going to talk to her?'

'I'm going to try. After our last confrontation she'll probably tell me to go to hell but I have to find out who she might have told about . . . us. It might help me discover who has been sending these letters. I also have to tell her about the damned painting, if Neil or Sheila haven't already.'

'Remember – there's more than one way to shoot the puck. If finesse won't work, go for a slapshot from the blue line.'

'If I'm not careful the only thing likely to get slapped is my face.'

'Or you just might receive a sweet little pass and win the game.'

'Get out of here.'

'I'm going, boss.'

Downstairs Rand got in his grey company car, put on his seatbelt, turned the ignition key, then leaned back and closed his eyes.

For a few minutes he tried not to think as he listened to the rumble of the engine, the mellow tones of the radio, the tyres screeching as nearby cars took the tight turns on the coiled exit and entrance ramps. Tried not to think as he searched for the conviction, the serenity that had been so much at the centre of his life.

He wasn't sure if it was ten minutes or forever before he gave up, put the car into gear, and headed east to the Children's Centre and Zara.

The cement facade of the building was cracked and mossy, half the windows were boarded up with plywood. A leather-jacketed group of teenagers lounged on the wooden wheelchair ramp built beside the steps, watching as he left the car in the Centre's small parking lot. As he passed them, he was glad he'd driven the company car instead of the Mustang to this part of town.

Inside the Centre he blinked, dazzled by the over-bright fluorescent lights and the subdued hubbub caused by the parents and children filling the waiting room. A long hall extended to his left and right and the elevator bay directly in front of him was clogged with folded wheelchairs and stacked chairs. The air was heavy with the scent of fresh paint.

'What'cha want, man?'

He glanced at the buxom blonde girl, no older than sixteen, standing guard behind the scarred reception desk.

'I would like to speak to Zara Lindsey.'

'Sixth floor. You have to walk up. Elevator's been broken for two weeks.' Her gum snapped as she pointed to his left. 'The stairs are at the end of the hall.'

'Thank you.'

'No prob.'

After he reached the sixth floor he bent forward, trying to catch his breath and swore to get to the gym more often. Anger and frustration had taken him up the first three floors at such a fast clip that stubbornness alone had carried him up the last three.

He pushed himself away from the supporting wall. Female voices led him past what appeared to be empty classrooms to a door that was ajar an inch or two.

When he knocked the voices stopped abruptly.

A woman he'd seen once or twice with Zara opened the door. When he asked for Zara she grinned, her eyes bright with speculation.

'Please wait here.' She shut the door. When it opened again, the woman came out, followed by three other women. Each carried briefcases and wore knowing smiles.

'She's inside.'

'Thank you.'

'Our pleasure.' The door at the top of the stairs swung shut behind them, but not quick enough to block out their giggles echoing in the stairwell.

It struck him that there was something almost sinister about the sound.

'You wanted to see me?' He swung around. Zara was leaning against the open door.

'Friends of yours?' He indicated the hallway with his thumb.

'That was Billie Jones who let you in. She's in charge of the Centre's fund-raising. She and the other women are helping me organize the benefit we're hosting in a few weeks.'

'Do they always giggle like that when you have visitors?'

'No.' A grimace flashed across her face, then disappeared.

'They seemed to know who I am.'

'Yes.' She backed away, indicating he could enter.

'They know about our relationship?' He waited but she didn't elaborate. So much for adding to the list of suspects with a few adroit questions.

He closed and locked the door, determined to get through this conversation without interruptions. He didn't say anything as he studied the black sack-like dress Zara wore. Laced boots weighed down her feet and a black scarf tied back her hair.

Why didn't she wear clothes that disguised her body so efficiently when she worked at ForPac or performed at Roggo's? Of course, his peace of mind wasn't a priority for her.

'Could we sit down?' he asked.

She hesitated, then perched on the edge of the chair on the other side of the room. She folded her hands in her lap and stared at a spot beyond his left shoulder.

214

He took off his overcoat and draped it across a table as he threaded his way through the old furniture to the chairs and couch arranged in a circle in the middle of the room.

'This will have to be quick. I have to get to Roggo's.'

'I won't keep you long.' He turned the chair adjacent to hers so he could sit facing her.

'Don't you have a comment about this place or the neighbourhood?' Her tone was mocking.

'I handled things badly the other night.'

'Badly?'

'I didn't mean to offend you.'

'You didn't?'

'Of course not. I care about you.' He reached for her hands, not allowing his frustration to show when she pulled back. 'I was merely trying to show you that a prudent person would avoid the precarious nature inherent in the location of the bar, the hours you work, and the clientele that frequents Roggo's.'

'I'm not going to sit and listen to the same old refrain, no matter how many big, pompous words you use.'

'I'm trying to apologize, dammit, and you're not making it any easier.'

'Apologize? A little unclear on the concept, aren't you?' She glared at him but seemed willing to listen.

He reached up to shove his fingers through his hair but at the last minute forcibly restrained the gesture.

'I am very sorry.' When he reached for her hand this time she didn't pull away. He studied her pale face while his thumb rubbed across her knuckles. 'I care. Very much. I want . . .' Abruptly he stopped speaking.

'What were you going to say?' Zara watched his thumb massage her fingers, trying to hide the shivers his touch was sending up and down her spine. Even holding hands with Rand was never simple. His silence drew her eyes upwards to meet the fire in his.

'I want you. And, whether you accuse me of arrogance or not, I know you want me, too.'

'I don't want the man who lay in my bed and tried to manipulate me into obedience.'

'I didn't intend . . .'

She shook her head and he stopped speaking.

'Be honest, Rand. You know only one way to achieve your goals. Manipulation, either planned or instinctive, if not outright coercion. You use whatever means are necessary to persuade everyone to do things your way. It's not right.'

His brows snapped together. 'I'm right about the dangers for you at Roggo's.'

'What makes you so sure you are always right?'

'I have to be.'

The fire was gone from his eyes as if it had never been, blanked out by old torment. She knew it had to be old to be so cold.

She turned her hand in his, grasped his fingers, and leaned forward. 'Rand, tell me why you do this.'

'It's the way the world works, has always worked. Give and take, in some form, is how things get done.'

'Okay, maybe you're right at some level. But there is a vast difference between talking things over until we arrive at an answer we can both live with and expecting mindless obedience to your orders.'

'I don't . . .'

'Yes, you do.'

'Okay. I'll concede that it might appear that way from your side. Can't we work on this together?' He let her go to reach into his pocket and brought out a small parcel in a white paper bag. 'I have something for you.'

'For me?' A small smile tipped up the corners of her mouth as she turned it around in her hands. 'A present?'

'If it is,' he smiled wryly, 'it's for me.'

'What do you mean?'

'Open it.'

She opened the bag and took out a box. 'A personal alarm?' Inside the box was a yellow case about the size of a man's wallet.

'You can carry it whenever you're out at night. There's also a box of extra batteries in there.'

'I don't know what to say. This is really sweet and thoughtful.' She put it away in her purse, then leaned closer to kiss his cheek. 'Thank you.'

He cupped her face and looked into her eyes. 'I miss you so damned much, Zara.'

'I miss you, too.'

Her voice was blotted out when he growled her name, snatched her into his arms, and covered her mouth with his.

Passion surged and she responded mindlessly to his hunger and his pain, wrapping her arms around his shoulders.

The cracked leather of the old sofa dug into his skin and Rand cuddled Zara on top of himself to keep the sharp edges from scratching her. An afghan covered the sofa back and he dragged it down across their naked bodies for warmth.

Her cheek was against his chest, his lips buried in her hair.

'We must be insane.' Her warm breath tickled his skin.

'You've only just come to that conclusion?' He rubbed his hand on her back.

'The door isn't even locked, for heaven's sake. Anyone could walk in.'

'I locked it on my way in.'

'Oh. Good.'

Silence descended once again.

'This solves nothing,' she muttered.

'I really am sorry about what happened the other night. It's just . . .' His voice faded out as he tried to find a way to say the same thing in a more palatable way. 'I worry about you. I can't understand why you need to do something so imprudent when I can find you a much safer working environment.'

She stiffened in his arms and he panicked into speech.

'I'm not telling you what to do. I'm asking, trying to understand.'

'I've worked in bars like The Kicking Horse for years. Some were worse, some better. This is the first time there's been any trouble. From now on I'll walk out with the other staff. Is that why you came here today, to lecture me?'

He rubbed his hands across her shoulders and down her spine, delighting in her soft, sleek flesh, as he thought about what to say next. He knew if he wasn't very careful about his phrasing in the next few minutes, he'd risk losing her for good. 'Has Neil talked to you since the auction?'

'Neil?' He heard the surprise in her voice. He didn't blame her. Under normal circumstances this would be an absurd time and place for him to want to talk about her cousins. 'No.'

'Sheila?'

'No. Rand, what's this about?'

She tried to turn in his arms to look at his face

but he stopped her movement and pressed his lips to her tangled hair.

'I had a reason to be at Roggo's that night. I needed to talk to you.'

'I'm glad you were there.' He could hear the smile in her voice. Her lips teased his nipple.

'Yes. Well.' He cleared his throat.

This time when she tried to look at him he didn't resist. Her knee came to rest between his thighs. His heart began to beat heavily and he struggled to say what had to be said, no matter how much his body was urging him to forget talking and make love with her again.

'If you were offered a safer place to work, would you?'

'Is this why you made love to me? Hoping I'd be more persuadable after sex?' She shoved against his chest and rolled out of his arms onto the floor, taking the afghan with her.

Why did she keep doing this to him? He would be damned before he'd lie naked in front of her while she scolded him. Again. He felt anger building in his guts as he stood, grabbed the nearest garment, which happened to be his shirt, and yanked it on. He fastened the two lowest buttons, making sure the garment's hem covered his essentials.

'I am trying to have a reasonably sane conversation with a woman I care about. I am trying to tell you how I feel.'

She held the blanket against her shoulders and tried to stand up but her attempt at modesty failed. Her foot was on a fold of the afghan, she stood too quickly, and the blanket jerked from her grasp, exposing her breasts before she managed to haul it back up.

'What about my feelings?'

'It's called compromise, Zara. When two people are involved in an intimate relationship and they disagree, they negotiate.'

'Negotiate? This isn't a negotiation. This is you trying to give me orders.' She picked up her panties and whisked them under the blanket. Her gyrations to pull them on without allowing him to see her body failed miserably and he groaned as his own body responded.

The shirt was no longer sufficient to hide behind and his briefs were nowhere in sight.

She was struggling with her bra but noticed what he was looking for. 'Look under the couch.'

He thanked her gravely as he picked them up. Then he tried to shake the creases out of his slacks and pulled them on, too, being particularly careful as he slid up the zipper.

'It would be a negotiation if you would respond in a normal manner.'

'Normal?' She spat the word at him, then gave up trying to use the blanket as a shield as she dressed. She tossed it away and bent to pick up her dress. He stared helplessly at her gleaming curves until she dropped the voluminous black fabric over her head, covering her from neck to knee.

'Yes. We explain our positions, offer concessions, and come to an agreement that is mutually acceptable. You, however, have done nothing but get mad and run away.'

She had been pulling on her boots and lacing them up but at his words her hands stilled. She looked up.

'I don't run away.'

'Yes, you do.'

Her hair fell forward to hide her face, and he waited, struggling to be patient as she tied a meticulous bow at each ankle.

'Maybe you're right.' She sat down where they'd been so pleasurably stretched out a short while before. 'Okay, here I am. Negotiate. No, don't sit here. There.' She pointed at the opposite chair when he tried to join her on the sofa.

'First we have to clarify what we both want. I want to be your lover. I want you in my life.'

Zara's eyes widened at his blunt statement. She hesitated, then matched his frankness. 'And I want you in mine.'

'I worry about you working at Roggo's. The situation is making it difficult for me to concentrate and as a result my own work is suffering.' He sucked in a deep breath and expelled it slowly. 'I propose a trade.'

'A trade?'

'Yes. For my peace of mind you agree to work in a better part of town. In exchange I will give you something you want.'

'What on earth could you give me?'

'I purchased your family's portrait at the auction.'

'I see.' She wrapped her arms around her stomach and rocked forward over her knees. When she looked up again anger blazed in her eyes. 'I set myself up, didn't I? I told you all about the painting that night, how much it meant to me. Like a naive fool I told you exactly where I was most vulnerable.'

'No, I . . .'

'You planned to buy me off with my own picture.' It wasn't a question.

'Yes. No. That's not what I . . .'

'You are as despicable as my grandfather was.'

Rand watched in disbelief as she scooped up his socks from beside her purse and threw them in his direction.

'It might interest you to know that my grandfather tried to use the painting to blackmail me after my father died.'

He snatched his shoes out of the air just before they connected with his head.

'It didn't work then and it won't work now. Good bye, Rand.'

There was finality in her voice and in the quiet thud of the closing door.

Rand sagged forward, elbows on knees, and buried his face in his hands. He'd been right all along. There didn't seem to be a way for them to work things out so they could be together.

After a moment he finished dressing, put on his coat, and trudged back down six long flights. As he drove away, he thought about all the unresolved questions in his life. Only two questions seemed potentially earth-shattering at this moment.

Had he lost her for good?

What else could go wrong?

The light in the intersection blinked green. What made him turn his head as he put his foot on the gas? A flicker of movement in his peripheral vision? The look of horror he saw on the face of a pedestrian? A sixth sense?

He looked left, slammed on his brakes, and cranked the wheel right. Because he'd moved instinctively, the truck running the red light struck his car a glancing blow instead of full force into the door beside him. Just before the moment of impact he saw the driver's eyes, malevolent under the low-brimmed cap, and thought he'd seen those vicious eyes before.

He was vaguely aware of the car folding around him as it ricocheted off several parked vehicles. The truck rammed him again and his car careered toward the guard-rail along the river. Metal screamed, rubber tyres burned, smoke and dust choked the air. Within seconds everything went unnaturally still.

He lay on his side, dangling in his seatbelt and listening, from what seemed a great distance, to people shouting. He felt very peaceful, with no particular motivation to answer their questions. When a hand touched his throat, checking for a pulse, he turned his head with great effort.

'He's alive.'

Rand's last conscious thought was of the grim concern on the face of a paramedic who peered through the shattered remains of the windshield.

CHAPTER 10

'I guess this means you'll finally tell the cops what's been going on,' Walt said as he filled a glass from the carafe of filtered water. He shook two pills from the prescription bottle and carried them to where Rand had collapsed on the bed.

Rand sighed and gazed up at the ceiling, enjoying the softness of the mattress. Thankfully, because of his dogged insistence on leaving the hospital, it was his own comfortable bed in his own quiet apartment.

'Rand? Did you hear me?'

'No, I'm not ready to tell them.' Rand's eyes blinked open when a drop of icy cold water splashed on his bare chest. He couldn't hold back a groan as he propped himself up on one elbow and reached for the glass.

'At least get Hoffman to provide protection for you, too.'

'The accident could have been a coincidence.'

'Shit, man, you might've been killed in that hit and run. The car was totalled. Good thing you were in the company car instead of the Mustang. Oh boy, if that baby got wrecked . . .' He shook his head.

'Now the truth comes out. You're more worried about the car than my health.' Rand handed the empty glass to Walt, then, with infinite care, lowered his head to the pillow.

'Don't be an . . .' He was interrupted by the door buzzer. 'Just a sec. Somebody's at the door and you need more water.' He picked up the empty carafe and took it with him.

Rand couldn't make sense of the muffled voices echoing from the living room after Walt opened the door. Between his pounding head and the pain caused by the mere act of breathing, he didn't even try.

'You've got company, buddy. I'm going to blow. Phone if you need me or Marcy.'

Rand tried and failed to open his eyes but managed a slight lift of one finger in acknowledgement. The drugs were beginning to take effect at last and, combined with his recent lack of sleep, he could feel the weight of blissful unconsciousness pressing him into the pillow.

Zara followed as Walt went further into the room to put a carafe of water beside the bed, then caught her first glimpse of Rand, stretched out on his bed, eyes closed, bare chested and barefoot.

The duvet had been shoved out of the way, tumbled to the floor in a heap at the foot of the bed.

A blood-stained bandage covered his left temple. Mottled red and purple bruises marred his chest on a diagonal line from his left shoulder to his right hip. The backs of his hands were dotted with small cuts. The right leg of his trousers was tattered from knee to hem and white gauze encased his right foot.

'Oh, my God.' She covered her mouth with both hands. 'What happened?'

When the big man didn't answer immediately, looking away and fiddling with the bottles lined up on the bedside table, she touched his arm. 'Walt?'

'He was in a car accident on the way home from visiting you at the Centre. Hit'n'run. A truck tried to run him off the road into the river but a cement guard-rail kept the car from going over the edge. Damn good thing he was wearing his seatbelt. As it was the firemen had to pry his right foot out from under the dash.'

'Was anyone else hurt?'

'No. Lots of damage to other cars, though. The insurance company's not going to be happy.' He glanced at her, then away. 'When you called I told you he wouldn't be able to talk to you.'

'No. You said I had to wait a few days to talk to him. Different thing entirely.'

'Why're you here?'

Rand stirred and moaned at the sound of their voices and Walt indicated they should move their conversation to the next room.

'I needed to talk to him about some unfinished business,' she whispered, unable to drag her eyes away from Rand. Her feet felt as if they'd been anchored to the floor. 'Is he going to be okay?'

'Yeah. The emergency doctor said it was just a matter of bruised ribs and minor cuts and scrapes. He'll have a bad headache but he's so hard-headed the knock on his noggin didn't even give him a concussion. Don't worry. A few days' bed rest and he should be back in fighting form.'

She blushed. 'He told you.'

'That you two had a fight earlier today? Yeah. Not what caused it, though.'

When he again indicated the other room, she obediently turned to leave but froze when she noticed the painting leaning on the dresser.

'So now I know what caused the argument.' He chuckled. 'That's the same look Rand had on his face when he realized he'd bought the damn thing.'

'What look?'

'Stunned disbelief.'

'Stunned?'

'Yeah. One minute you rush out of there crying. Next minute his hand's in the air, giving away nineteen thousand dollars. Funniest thing I've ever seen.'

'Funny?'

'He didn't even understand what he'd done until it was too late. First time I've ever seen him do something without thinking it through first.'

'He bought it on impulse?'

'Yeah, shocked the heck outta me, too. I've never seen that man do half the things he's done since he met you. You're sure shaking things up around here, lady.'

Walt picked up his jacket and keys.

'Where are you going? Who's going to take care of Rand?'

'He's okay. He just needs to sleep it off. Tim and I are going to take turns looking in on him.'

'What about tonight? What if something . . .'

'Look, Zara, the doc said he'd be fine but if you're worried, stay. Otherwise, let's go so I can lock up.'

She didn't like the sly smile on his face but neither did she want to leave Rand alone.

'Do you have to work this evening?' he asked.

How could she stay here with Rand? How could she leave him, alone and hurting? What if something went wrong? 'I'll stay.'

'Great.' He tossed her Rand's keys. 'I'll tell Crawford you won't be in to work tomorrow. Should I tell Tim not to come over unless you phone?'

'Yes, please. I'll call and let you know how Rand is. No, wait!' She grabbed the door handle. 'Aren't you going to help him change out of those filthy clothes?'

'He told me to go to hell when I tried. Said I was making things worse.' He grinned. 'Maybe you'll have better luck getting him out of his pants than I did.'

'But –' She stared at the closed door for several seconds after Walt left, then turned and leaned back against it. The brightly lit room looked like a photograph in a furniture catalogue or hotel brochure. Perfect. Classy. Impersonal. Even the innocuous artwork was colour co-ordinated to match the furniture.

The room did not look like Rand Tremayne.

She tiptoed back down the hall, trying not to disturb Rand. The formal dining room matched the main room and the nearby kitchen was filled with enough glistening chrome to warm the heart of any professional chef. An efficient laundry room opened off the kitchen.

Giving in to curiosity, she glanced into the other rooms along the hall. Each bedroom with full bath had been decorated in the same attractive if impersonal style. Why would a single man need a four bedroom apartment?

She paused at the open door to his room. Even here there were few signs of his occupancy. A larger bed than in the other bedrooms. She could see his clothes through the open closet door, a single bottle of cologne on the adjoining bathroom's counter, and a book on the bedside table.

The portrait of her family on his dresser.

Why did he buy it? If Walt was right and he'd bought the painting on a whim, maybe she was wrong. Maybe his purpose in buying it hadn't been to bribe her into submission.

She shook her head. Forget trying to second guess Rand Tremayne, she told herself. When he wakes up, you can ask him. Until then, you're here, in his apartment. Maybe you can finally find reasons for some of the contradictions in the man.

She'd seen him driving his beautifully tended sports car only once. Usually he drove a prosaic sedan. He ran a ruthlessly efficient international corporation, yet she'd seen him greet the mail clerk by name and ask after the girl's family.

Her grandfather had commanded respect but he'd been feared, even hated, by many. Rand's employees respected him but they also seemed to like him.

Rand stirred restlessly on the bed, obviously uncomfortable in those filthy rags. Yet Walt had said that the effort involved in undressing had caused Rand pain. She thought for a while then went back to the kitchen and searched through the drawers until she found what she needed.

She'd slid his leather belt from the loops and was leaning over him when his eyelids lifted. His gaze fastened on the glittering scissors she held.

'Just how angry are you?' The wavering smile slid off his face when she held the waistband of his slacks and moved the scissors closer. 'Zara?'

'Don't be silly. You've got to get these clothes off and since the pants are already wrecked, this is the best way.'

She lifted the fabric away from his skin and began to cut. The sharp blades slid through the linen as if it were made of cobwebs. As she sliced she felt the cotton of his briefs and the heat of his skin against the back of her hand.

'Did you know this is the third suit I've had to throw away since I met you?'

'No, but I do know you'd better be quiet. I imagine it hurts to breathe, much less talk.'

He didn't say another word as she cut open the outside of his undamaged pant leg. She walked around the bed and started on the fabric that had been shredded when his leg jammed under the dashboard. After both pant legs were cut open she lay the scissors on the bedside table.

'Can you lift your hips while I pull them off?'

'I think so.'

She grasped the fabric of both pant legs inside his thighs and, when he moved, tugged downward as gently as she could. He groaned softly as he collapsed back onto the bed, now clad only in his underwear, bandages, and bruises.

She covered him with the duvet then bundled the rags into her arms and picked up the scissors to return to the kitchen. 'Are you hungry?'

'No.' He blinked, as if trying to keep his eyes

open. Obviously the pain medication was making him sleepy again. 'Thanks.'

'Maybe you will be later. I'll check on you in a little while.'

His hand lifted, then thumped back onto the mattress. 'You'll stay?'

'Yes. Just for tonight.'

His lips moved in a weak smile as his eyes closed.

'I must have rocks for brains, but I'll stay,' she whispered.

She checked on him periodically throughout the evening, trying not to look at the painting. Most people would have hung such an expensive purchase in a prominent place in their home. Why had he put it in his bedroom? Why was it still leaning against the wall amid the wrapping paper?

Why, why, why? Stop these unanswerable, stupid questions, she scolded herself. Letting the doubts run circles in her mind wasn't going to get her any answers. So why bother thinking about it? She decided to concentrate on more practical, prosaic things. Like making dinner.

Around midnight he woke up hungry so she heated a can of chicken noodle soup, only scalding the back of her hand slightly, and propped him up to eat it. Then had come the ordeal of helping him to the bathroom and hovering outside the door, worrying that he'd fall and hurt himself because the macho idiot had insisted on being alone in there.

After he'd fallen asleep again she'd curled up on the living room sofa with an extra blanket and pillow from the spare room. She began writing on a pad of paper she'd found in a desk drawer.

If she was going to be stuck here for hours taking care of Rand, she might as well take advantage of the quiet and get a little work done on some lyrics for her new songs.

Rand listened to the silence that filled the apartment, a silence he'd never noticed before tonight. Having Zara in his home for almost twenty-four hours, even if he'd only been semiconscious for most of it, made him that much more aware of her absence. An absence that he was afraid would be eternal.

Last night they'd shared little in the way of serious conversation over the midnight meal she'd prepared, a fact for which he was profoundly grateful. With his mind so muddled by physical pain and thwarted desire he was in no shape to settle their differences. Before she'd left tonight for her performance at Roggo's, at least she'd seemed to believe that he really had intended to compromise and negotiate when he told her about buying the portrait.

Negotiation! He snorted, damned glad that he wasn't facing someone like her across a boardroom table every day. She had him so tied up in knots he had no idea how they were going to resolve either the ownership of the painting or her job situation. He hadn't even dared to bring up the dangerous part of the city where the rehab centre was located.

He reached sideways for the file folder on the coffee table, flinching as his ribs complained, but determined to concentrate on the job at hand. The pain was forgotten as he compared two sheets of paper.

Sheila.

He dropped the papers into his lap and leaned back into the corner of the sofa. After Zara had left, he'd taken his mind off her by doing more work on his search for the reasons behind the discrepancies he'd discovered in Heinrich's will. Now he'd found them. Or rather, her.

How had Sheila kept that sharp old man from finding out what she'd done? Why did she do it?

Stupid question.

Money.

Greed, the oldest and most basic reason for betrayal. She'd actually changed very little of the will. A few numbers here, a paragraph there, some forged initials, and her bequest from Heinrich of the estate residuals grew from a few thousand to much, much more.

He assumed Sheila was also responsible for the threatening letters. But did she cause the hit and run? Even though he vaguely remembered that the truck driver's eyes had looked familiar, his scrambled brains couldn't put a name to the feeling. He was as sure as he could be under the circumstances that it hadn't been Sheila.

Maybe the accident was a coincidence? Forget it, he told himself. The police will let you know the identity of the driver as soon as they find the truck.

Now what? His expression was grim as he dragged the phone closer and punched out the number of a trusted friend who was also one of the city's top lawyers. Before he took any action he had to find out how Sheila's fraud would affect the rest of Heinrich's will.

Half an hour later his expression was even grimmer as he hung up the phone. More research was necessary but it looked like if he exposed Sheila's actions, Heinrich's will would be void and a much older will would come into effect.

He could lose control of ForPac. He could lose everything he'd worked for.

Again.

Or he could destroy the evidence.

The thought had crept into his mind like cancer, malignant, silent, invisible, until suddenly it was just there.

Other than the cash Sheila had arranged for herself, everything else was just as Heinrich had intended. Rand didn't know what, exactly, was in the older will. He did know that it had been written many years before. Long before he, himself, had come to Heinrich's attention and been taken under his wing.

The lawyer he'd phoned thought their discussion concerned a hypothetical situation and he didn't know enough to cause serious trouble. Walt would never mention the problem again, if he were told it had been resolved.

Sheila. His lips tightened. He wasn't worried about dealing with Sheila. The threats and violence, if she was the instigator, would stop immediately.

He lay back and pressed his fists to his eyes, hating the doubts, the memories tearing at his gut.

Could he start over? Probably. But what would happen to the people in Treville? The town's precariously balanced economy hinged on him maintaining his position as CEO at ForPac. Without his time, contacts, and money hundreds of local families would once again be thrown into poverty.

If he was forced out of Forster Pacific, what would the ensuing turmoil do to the corporation's businesses? Thousands of employees all over the country, all over the world, depended on him.

This nightmare was a million times worse than the one he'd been living with for fourteen years.

He pulled himself to his feet with a groan, a palm pressing support to his ribs. He bypassed the bottle of pills he'd ignored ever since Zara left. He needed another kind of painkiller. Scotch splashed on his fingers as he poured the amber liquid, not bothering with extras such as ice cubes or soda.

Choice.

A wicked thing to give a man caught between two demons. One demon named failure. Failure that would be measured in despair, broken hearts, and broken families, as he knew only too well. The other demon, deceit. Deceit that would maintain the status quo and make a mockery of his personal honour.

Could he live with himself if he took either road?

He looked in the mirror behind the bar at the bleak expression on his face, then poured more scotch and saluted his image before emptying the glass. A choice that was really no choice at all.

He picked up the bottle and carried it back to the sofa. At least he could get through the night with little or no pain, before he had to find a way to minimize the damage disclosure would bring.

ForPac would survive, as would Treville, if he had anything . . . He snorted. He would have little or nothing to say about it. Not for long.

'Afternoon, boss. Feeling better?' Tim's cheerful voice cut through Rand's head like a meat cleaver.

'Well enough.' Rand shrugged out of his overcoat and tossed it over the back of the chair opposite his desk. 'Not quite so loud, though, okay?'

'Sure thing. Head still aches, I guess. I didn't expect you in today.'

The boy's stage whisper was an improvement, Rand thought. Not much, but some. He probably deserved it after consuming large quantities of scotch and waking up on the living room floor, staring up at the underside of his coffee table. Life was just one new experience after another since he'd met Zara.

A weaker man would be afraid he was turning into his father.

'Wait ten minutes before you bring in the mail, please.'

'Sure thing. Oh, this was on my desk when I came in this morning.' He handed over an envelope marked confidential. It looked unpleasantly familiar.

Without opening the envelope, Rand knew what he'd find inside. Another threat. He was getting damned tired of this. Sheila's fraud needed to be proven and dealt with legally. Now that he had some proof it was time to phone the police. But when?

He had to get expert staff on-line to mitigate any panic in ForPac's many companies when the news of major changes in management hit the stock market. He tapped the unopened envelope against his lip.

'Get Sheila Bendan on the phone, please.'

'She was already here looking for you this morning. I told her about your accident and she said to tell you she was going out of town.'

'She say where?'

'No, but she'll call back tomorrow morning.'

'Damn.'

'Something wrong?'

'No. Get the legal eagles up here. Now.'

'All of them?'

Rand laughed harshly. 'Why not? All of them.'

'I didn't expect to see you in here again.' Zara dropped into the seat beside Rand.

He glanced around the shabby interior of The Kicking Horse and shrugged. 'Neither did I.'

'Especially not so soon after your accident. You should still be in bed. You looked terrible when I left the night before last and you don't appear to have slept since.'

'You really must stop flattering me, Zara. It'll go to my head.'

'Cut to the chase, Rand. Why are you here?'

'We need to talk.'

'Why don't we just take this easy for now? I'm not sure where I want to take this relationship and I don't think you do either.'

'This isn't about us. At least not directly. Come on.' Rand stood and picked up his coat. 'I'll drive you home and we can talk there.'

Zara shook her head and looked up at him. 'You just don't get it, do you?'

'What?'

'You don't *tell* me you're driving me home and coming in. You're supposed to *ask* me.'

A grimace tightened his face, then he smiled. Reluctantly. 'I'm sorry.' He bowed. 'May I see you home, madam?'

'That's more like it.' She pulled her yellow jacket around her shoulders and followed him out to his car, wading against the gale that had blown up while she performed. After they were buckled in, she tried to ask him what he wanted to talk about, but he evaded the issue, saying nothing other than he'd rather wait until they got to her house.

They drove in silence, listening to the winds buffet the car with such strength that his knuckles were white on the steering wheel.

As they neared the house, they saw the flashing lights of police and fire trucks. Spotlights on the vehicles lit the area up like a stage.

'Oh, my lord, they're at my place.' Zara leaned forward, trying to see what had happened. 'The house. What's wrong with my house?'

She stared out the window, too stunned to move as Rand pulled to a stop behind a police car and the milling crowd of neighbours.

Smoke poured from the blackened frames of what had once been the back door and kitchen windows of her home. Billie's half of the duplex seemed to have fared slightly better.

'Billie!' She scrambled with the unfamiliar seat-belt, trying to get it undone. 'Kenny! Oh, my God, where are they?'

Rand pushed her hands aside, released her seatbelt, then followed her mad dash through the crowd as she called their names.

'Zara, we're over here!' Just as Rand caught up with her, she threw her arms around Billie who was leaning on the handles of Kenny's wheelchair. The young boy began jabbering excitedly.

'You should'a been here, Zara. We were sound asleep and 'wham' the whole place shook. I thought we were having an earthquake. We got outta there pretty fast, I can tell you.'

'Zara, honey, we're okay.' Billie patted her on the back. 'We're okay. Thank heavens for insurance. The police say our half doesn't look too bad because the firemen got here so fast, mostly smoke, but . . . Oh, your place is a mess with all the fire and water damage.'

'What happened?' She held tightly to Billie's hand as she turned to look at the house.

'I think something in your furnace or hot water tank exploded. One of the firemen told me it looked like it might be an electrical or wiring problem. They said the fire was mostly in that little room and the back of the house. They also said if it wasn't for this awful wind, the damage would have been confined to a much smaller area.'

'I don't . . . I can't . . .' Zara could feel the words bubbling up inside her but couldn't make them come out. Shudders racked her. What if she'd been at home? Rand stepped up behind

243

her. When he put his hands on her shoulders, she leaned back into his embrace. At least Billie and Kenny were safe.

'I asked about your stuff in the front of the house but no one could tell me anything.'

'My music.' She looked at the front corner of her home where she'd kept all her important papers stored inside an old filing cabinet. Sheet music of the songs she'd written. Correspondence with record companies, publishing houses, and singers. She'd kept her two guitars on its top.

Her life, her future, was in that cabinet.

'Let me go.' She pulled against Rand's hold. 'I've got to check. I've got to know.'

'Not now, honey.' He wrapped his arm around her waist. 'We'll have to wait 'til we know it's safe.'

He was right. She stopped struggling and the four of them watched, a cocoon of silence amid flashing lights, scrambling firemen, and raging wind. Gradually the turmoil lessened and the firemen began putting away their equipment. Some of the neighbours stopped to commiserate as they drifted back to their own homes.

'Hi, Zara.' A tall, lanky man appeared behind Billie.

'Abe.' She introduced him to Rand and the two men shook hands. 'You got here fast.'

'Yeah, well,' he looked down, then up again and half-smiled, 'I was already here. I've been moving our cars out of the driveway. I moved yours, too, since Billie had the keys. The police asked me to park them down the block, out of the way.'

'This was an exciting night, as well as terrifying.' Billie held out her left hand. 'We're engaged.'

'It's about time.' Grateful for the normalcy of the conversation, she lifted Billie's hand for a better look. She couldn't see much more than a glitter on Billie's finger, even with all the flashing emergency lights. 'I am sure it's very beautiful. Congratulations, Abe. You're getting a wonderful family.'

'Believe me, I know. But listen, Billie, I just talked to the cops and the firemen. They're going to be a while and we can't go back in until they're done. I think you should take Kenny to my place and get out of the cold. I'll stay here, sit in the car in the driveway, and keep an eye on the place in case of looters.'

'That's not necessary.' Rand flipped open the cellular phone he'd brought from the car and began punching buttons. 'I'll get a couple of security guards down here.

'I might have known he'd take charge.' Zara knew he heard her comment to Billie but he ignored her.

'Let him. None of us can afford to hire a guard but I'd rather get Abe out of the cold, too. He's been fighting a cold all week.'

'Why don't you guys go to Abe's place right now? We'll take care of things here.'

'You sure? Can he,' Billie indicated Rand with her thumb, 'drop you off at Abe's apartment when you're done? It'll be crowded but it's cheaper than a hotel.'

Zara knew just how small Abe's place was. It would be nearly impossible for them to find even floor space for her to sleep on, much less blankets. Plus they were newly engaged.

'She's coming home with me.' Rand stepped closer. 'You're welcome to come, too, if you want.'

'No, thanks,' Billie said. 'We'll be fine at Abe's.'

Zara opened her mouth to refuse Rand's offer, then thought better of it. His apartment boasted three empty bedrooms. He had plenty of room for her. The big question was, should she go?

'We still have to talk. Tonight,' he reminded her. 'I'll find you something to sleep in and we'll stop at the all-night market to buy you a toothbrush and whatever else you need.'

She hesitated, then nodded. 'Go ahead, Billie, I'll be fine at Rand's. I'll phone you tomorrow.'

As they were saying good bye, Rand wandered over to talk to the cops standing in her driveway. While he chatted with the officers, she saw a fireman come out of her front door and decided to ask if she could check on her belongings in the front of the house.

Rand found her a few minutes later, sitting on the floor in front of what looked like an old lawyer's cabinet, stuffing papers into pillowcases. The

246

cabinet's glass fronts were filthy with rivulets of water running through the soot. Two equally dirty and damp guitar cases sat on the floor at her side, their tops flipped open.

'Any damage?'

'The cases protected the guitars. My papers are wet around the edges and the ink's beginning to run so I thought I could lay them out in your kitchen to dry.'

'Anything I can do to help?'

She rolled up one of the empty pillowcases and tossed it at his chest. 'Could you grab me some clothes? They stink of smoke and have to be cleaned but I'll need something to wear tomorrow.'

He held on to the ball of fabric. 'Anything in particular?'

'Jeans, sweatshirts, underwear, socks.' She closed one drawer and opened the other. 'Most of my things are in the dresser, just dump in a bit of everything, whatever will fit in the pillowcase. The rest can wait.'

He was almost out of the room when she said his name in a low voice.

'Rand?'

'Yes?'

'Fate's a funny thing, isn't it? Since the moment we met, I've given you a hard time about the way you handle things. And yet, if it wasn't for you and your personal rules and regulations,' she looked up

247

at the scorched and wet wall over the fireplace, 'the portrait of my family might have been hanging there tonight. It would have been destroyed.'

'Zara, I . . .'

'I should thank you.' She still hadn't looked at him. 'Events have proven you right. This time.'

'Unfortunately, the more I'm right, the more it makes you dislike me.'

'I don't dislike you.' She bent forward to scoop more papers from the cabinet. 'Could you please grab my sneakers out of the closet when you get the rest of my stuff?'

It was clear she didn't want to continue the conversation. Fine with him. He didn't know what to say about her unexpected, if welcome, announcement, so he'd rather say nothing. For now

Within two hours the last cop was gone and a couple of guards were in place, sharing a pizza inside their company van parked in front of her house.

Zara was silent on the ride to his apartment. She focused on the bulging pillowcase in her lap, hoping Rand wouldn't comment on what she'd said. She wasn't ready to do any serious talking. After they arrived, she put her guitars in the bedroom farthest from his own, dumped her clothes in his washing machine and, with his help, spread her papers to dry.

'Would you like a brandy?' he asked as they left the kitchen.

'We should go to bed.' She blushed furiously. 'I mean, get some sleep. It's late and you should still be taking things easy. I saw you wince when you put my stuff in the trunk, so I know your ribs are still bothering you. We both have to work tomorrow and Roggo's expecting me to perform tomorrow night.'

'Zara, you're babbling.' He steered her toward the sofa in front of his fireplace.

She frowned. 'I am, aren't I?'

He plucked a blanket from a chest under the window and wrapped it around her shoulders. 'Sit down.'

She sat and snuggled into the warm folds.

'Would you like me to light the fire?'

'That would be nice.'

He opened the glass doors and pushed the switch to ignite the gas. Flame burst into life and she stretched her toes out to the blaze. He walked over to the bar behind her and she could hear the clinking of glasses and bottles.

'I have to tell you something,' he said.

'Can't it wait?'

'No.' He handed her a glass of brandy and sat down next to her. 'Are you feeling better?'

'Shaky, I guess, but okay. I was really upset when we first saw the house but Billie and Kenny are safe and I didn't lose anything important in the fire so I'll be okay. What's bothering you, Rand?'

'When I talked to the cop at your place tonight, he said the arson investigator would be out to look things over in the morning.'

'Why?'

'Zara, I . . .'

She could tell something was wrong. Seriously wrong.

'He told me it looked like the wiring might have been tampered with.'

'Tampered with? As in arson or something? That's impossible. Why would he even look?'

'Because I asked him to.'

'Rand?'

He sighed and rubbed his hand over his face. 'I don't know where to start.'

'How about with telling me why you could possibly think someone would deliberately burn my house?'

CHAPTER 11

Rand sipped his brandy and slouched down to stare at the flames. 'When you were here the other day, you saw the painting in my bedroom. Why didn't you ask me about it?'

'At the time you were injured and in a mental fog from pain medication. I didn't bring it up because I knew we'd argue and it could wait 'til you were feeling better. I figured it wouldn't be fair to fight with an unarmed man.'

When he didn't even acknowledge the mild jest she clasped her glass with both hands. Where was he going with this? Her heart began to pound and she pulled the blanket tighter around her shoulders. Suddenly she felt as if she was sitting in a cool draft, even though she knew the windows were closed.

'The weekend before the auction Walt helped me bring home the boxes of Heinrich's papers from the estate office.' He gazed into the fire as he sipped. 'I'd decided to look for some proof the damned painting belonged to you before it was sold to someone else.'

'Rand, that's wonderful.'

'Save your gratitude. If that painting's mentioned in Heinrich's papers, I couldn't find it. However, I did find something else.'

'What?'

'Heinrich's rough draft for his will.'

'And?'

'There were a few significant differences between the draft and the one Sheila read to us after the memorial service.'

Her eyes opened wide.

'That, in and of itself, means little. For all I knew he could have made twenty rough drafts before he made a final decision. And I have no conclusive proof that the will inconsistencies have any connection to my car accident or the fire at your house tonight. Maybe these events were accidents. Coincidences. Maybe they weren't.'

His comment distracted her from the bombshell about her grandfather's will. 'I don't understand. You still haven't explained why you think someone would deliberately set fire to my house.'

'To stop my investigation into Heinrich's will.'

'Your . . .? What investigation?'

'I suspect Heinrich's will was changed and some signatures were forged. Someone doesn't like the fact that I've been asking questions and wants me to stop. I've received a few anonymous letters.'

'Anonymous letters? What kind of letters?'

'Warnings. Threats.'

Her hands began to shake and she leaned forward to put the glass on the table before she dropped it. 'Are you telling me it wasn't an accident when that truck hit your car?'

'I don't know. It might have been coincidence.'

'What do the police say?'

'They are investigating.' He sipped, then shrugged. 'Until the last three letters we weren't too concerned.'

'The last three? How many have there been?' Zara turned to face him and put her hand on his arm. He looked steadily into the fire, turning the glass in his hands.

'Five.'

'What's different about the last three?'

'They threatened you.'

'Me!' Her hands tightened on his arm. 'Why didn't you tell me?'

'You've had a bodyguard near you twenty-four hours a day since the second one. You haven't been in danger.'

'Until tonight. I wasn't supposed to work today. If Roggo hadn't called . . .'

'You might have been killed.' He abruptly tilted his head and tossed back the contents of his glass, hissing as if it had burned its way down his throat. 'Believe me, I haven't been able to think about anything else since I saw the damned smoke coming through the walls of your house.'

'Who's doing this, Rand?'

'The threats? I can't be sure but I do know the will had to have been changed by Sheila.'

'Sheila! She couldn't have arranged for these things to happen to us. I know you and she . . . She told me you had been, you know, involved.' She gestured vaguely.

'We dated for a while.'

'Then how could you think she would try to force your car off the road? You could have been killed in the accident. She would never do something like that to a friend.'

'It's clear you don't know Sheila. Our relationship wasn't important and she's the most hard-headed, clear-eyed, self-centred businesswoman I know. She'd weigh the risks, probably convince herself that I couldn't be permanently injured in the accident. Once she decided a certain action was absolutely necessary, she'd believe the ends justified almost any means.'

'Even if it meant threatening me or burning my home? She's my cousin. We're not friends but she wouldn't want to hurt me.'

He didn't answer.

'What now?'

'You can't go back to the house. I believe the only solution is for you to move in here until the police find Sheila and the situation is resolved.'

'Here?' Zara stopped speaking, dazzled by the offer. What if very different circumstances had led to his suggestion? What if he were asking her just because he wanted to be with her? But circumstances weren't different. She shook her head. 'No. Absolutely not.'

'You are not being logical.' He put his empty glass down on the table with such force she was surprised it didn't shatter. 'Of course you are not being logical.' He rose and began to pace in front of the fire. 'You would never base your decisions on something so reasonable.'

'Thank you.' Her smile must have looked just as bright and big and false as it felt. 'Coming from you, I know I've just been insulted.'

He stopped pacing and stared down at her for a moment, hands on hips, teeth clenched. The sound coming from his throat was perilously near a growl. Dressed in dark slacks and a thin black turtleneck that clung to his musculature, more than ever he resembled a large, dangerous cat. Hackles raised, tail twitching, he was ready to pounce.

He was a mass of naked emotion and instinct. She loved it.

He slowly, deliberately brought his palms up to cover his eyes. He dragged in a few deep breaths. Gradually, visibly, his control returned and so did the cold-blooded businessman.

'Will you listen?'

'You have five minutes.'

'Thank you. I think.'

His sarcasm stung but she managed to hide it.

'In this apartment, you will be protected by the excellent building security already in place. We will go to work together in the company limousine, which is a secure vehicle. On the nights you are scheduled to perform, the driver, with the bodyguard if I am not available, will see you safely to The Kicking Horse and the Centre. They will stay nearby, then bring you home and the guard will see you upstairs to this door.'

'You seem to have thought of everything.'

'Your desk will be moved back into my office.'

She could swear she heard his teeth grind as he spoke.

'I'm going to be spending a lot of time, weekends and my few free evenings, working with the people from the Centre. There's a lot of organizing to do and the fund-raising benefit is only a few weeks away. I have to choose costumes, sets. Meet with performers. Everything.'

'Hoffman's people will be available to escort you twenty-four hours a day. I'll give you his phone number so you can let him know your plans if I'm not around.'

'Aren't you going to tell me again that I have to quit performing at Roggo's?'

'No. You made your feelings perfectly clear on the last occasion we discussed your choice of employment.'

Zara caught a glimpse of pain in his eyes before he picked up his glass and carried it back to the bar. She twisted around so she could see him. The bottle was empty so he put down his glass to rummage through the cabinet beside the sink.

She still felt guilty over the way she'd walked out on him, several times, and never delivered an apology as she'd intended.

When she'd arrived at his apartment he'd already been suffering from the effects of the accident and painkillers. After that the time had never again seemed right. Until tonight he hadn't seemed to care.

'I am sorry, Rand. Really. Walking out like that was not nice of me.' Her hand lifted toward him, then dropped back to her lap. 'Sometimes the things you say hurt me. I get angry and react.'

One of his shoulders rose and dropped in casual dismissal. That hurt, too, until she saw the white knuckle grip he had on the cupboard door.

The man was a mass of roiling emotions, harshly controlled. It was as if he wanted to deny their very existence.

A control so rigid and long-standing could be dangerous. If he wasn't careful, someday the facade would explode and shatter into nothing. Then where would he hide?

What kind of man could he be if he ever stepped out from behind that facade? Was the real Rand Tremayne a man she could love, freely and honestly, without fear of being frozen out? Maybe she should push for that explosion?

Possibilities. As long as they were together the future held possibilities. Living together, sharing a kitchen, seeing each other with the morning blahs and late night cozies had to open up the situation. Even Rand couldn't hide all the time. All she needed was the courage to agree to the arrangement.

'I'm not comfortable staying in your apartment without paying my share of the rent and utilities.'

'It isn't "my" apartment. It's company-owned. Heinrich believed in providing a personal environment for important business guests. There are several bedrooms, each with a private bath. Heinrich asked me to live here so there would be a host on site and it suited me to agree.'

'Another way for Grandfather to make sure there were no opportunities for a rival to scoop up his clients.'

'Sound business practice.'

'Subtle manipulation. Didn't you hate having your home invaded at Heinrich's whim?'

'Why? It's a practical arrangement. The apartment is convenient to work and on-site catering is provided by the restaurant downstairs when necessary, all at no personal expense. In past years many of our out-of-town guests have preferred to stay here, rather than at the estate.'

She had to chuckle. 'I don't doubt it. Most people would appreciate time away from Grandfather.'

'So. Are you going to stay?'

'Yes. Thank you.' She decided to concede as graciously as possible under the circumstances. At least by living with Rand for a few days she would know she hadn't given up on the possibility of a relationship without trying. 'Since it's company money, I'll move in. But there are going to be a few ground rules.'

'Ground rules?' He moved several bottles and reached further back for the brandy.

'No sex.'

His hand on the brandy jerked forward, rattling bottles. His elbow knocked over the rack of bar tools, all of which banged and clattered to the floor.

Rand muttered a curse beneath his breath and began gathering the tools. 'Do you think that's realistic, given the chemistry between us?'

'Maybe not.' She allowed herself to watch the way his body moved inside his clothes. 'Probably not. I guess we can leave that decision to nature and the future. There are two things I do insist on.'

'And they are?' Rand stood and came to her side.

'No orders and no subtle attempts to manage my life.'

'Agreed.'

259

She put her fingers in his extended hand, and he tugged her to her feet. The blanket slipped to the floor.

'If we sleep together . . .'

'When,' he corrected as he slid his arms around her waist.

'*When* we sleep together, it won't be in the same room with the painting of my family.'

'I had already planned on moving it out. It's been disconcerting to have that child watching every move I make in my bedroom.' He gathered her closer into his body. She shivered at the feel of his whiskered cheek against hers. 'I'd rather spend time with the living, breathing, adult version.'

'This arrangement is strictly temporary. As soon as my house is fixed, I'm going home.'

'The police should have the situation cleared up by then.'

Even though she knew their arrangement was going to be complicated, perhaps uncomfortable, she welcomed his kiss.

Four endless days later she knew just how badly she'd underestimated the possible problems in the situation. Having a bodyguard follow her everywhere was the least of her worries.

'Thank you for taking Kenny with you yesterday when you went to meet those wheelchair athletes.' Billie pushed open the door of Glazier Formals.

She and Zara were spending the day visiting the city's costumers and second-hand stores, finding the last few wardrobe items for the benefit's production numbers and skits. Theresa Glazier was a friend of Billie's and had offered them cheap rental fees in exchange for mentioning the company in the benefit's programme.

'I was happy to have him,' Zara said as the burly young guard followed them into the store.

'He had a lot of fun and, more important, it really opened his eyes to what possibilities exist for him. He'd been a little down lately, about the wheelchair and everything.' She shuffled hangers along the rack and selected an iridescent taffeta gown. 'How about this one for the fantasy sequence? Is it Samantha's size?'

'Looks good. Here,' Zara took it out of her hands, 'Tony might as well make himself useful.' She draped it across the arms of the bodyguard.

'Kenny hasn't been so happy since he met Rick Hansen, the man who rolled his wheelchair around the world to raise money for charity.'

'I think your son was my secret weapon. Some of those athletes agreed to attend the benefit just because they couldn't say "no" to me in front of an awestruck boy.'

'Of course, now he's going to hassle me for one of the expensive, lightweight racing chairs.' Billie lay another gown across the guard's arms.

'I told him if he does all his exercises faithfully and cheerfully for six months, I'll help him get one. No.' Zara held up her hand when she saw Billie about to protest. 'This is between him and me.'

'But . . .'

'But, nothing. Let's get to work on costumes.'

'What have you two done about the portrait?'

'He tried to give it to me again but I can't take it. Not 'til things are settled. Right now it's in the dining room.'

'I don't understand you sometimes. You spend your entire adult life yearning for the darned thing. Now the guy's practically begging you to take it and you refuse.'

'You don't have to understand. I'm not even sure I understand. All I know is that I'm not making any important decisions right now. I'm taking things real easy, one step at a time.'

'Seems to me that moving in with a guy is an important decision.'

Zara couldn't think of an intelligent answer to her friend's comment so she ignored it. 'Let's get this done, okay? There are several more places we have to go today.'

Billie glanced around to make sure the guard wasn't too close.

'This is kind of weird, isn't it?' she whispered. 'Riding in a limo. Having a bodyguard with us all the time.'

Zara shrugged. This guard had been silent and stoic whether occupying the front seat of the limousine or standing nearby, as he was now, arms full of billowing clothes. His eyes moved restlessly, from door to window to the other customers, alert for potential trouble.

'*Just doing my job, Ma'am*. I can't tell you how often I've heard him or one of the other guards say that, usually when they're getting in my way.' Zara didn't bother to lower her voice as she answered. She held up a sequinned tuxedo so she could see it better. 'At least Tony is willing to help. The guy yesterday wouldn't even carry a few boxes home from the florists. Said he had to keep his hands free.'

'Ooohh, just like the movies.' Billie peeked at the guard over the rack of clothes. 'Do they wear guns under their coats?'

'I have no idea and don't sound so thrilled. Ever since the fire either Rand or Hoffman's men have told me what I can do, when I can do it, or even how to do it. My life has so many new rules I sometimes feel like screaming. He's torturing me with all this protection.'

'Where's Rand today?'

'Out of town. And don't ask me where he is, because I don't know. No one knows where he goes every Sunday and Monday. From what I've heard, his staff enjoy speculating about the mystery so much they probably wouldn't want to find out the truth.'

'Sorry I asked.'

Zara put the sequinned tuxedo back on the rack and pulled out white satin slacks and vest designed much like a tuxedo. The matching rhinestone bowtie would accentuate her bare skin under the vest. 'How about this for the Broadway segment?'

'Striking, especially with your dark hair.' Billie looked it over. 'Sexy, too. Rand seems the possessive type. Maybe he won't want you to wear it.'

'You think so?' Zara added it to the pile in Tony's arms. 'Perfect.'

'Trouble? Already? Heavens, you've only been living together a few days. Maybe you'd better come stay with me 'til the repairs on your side are finished.'

'You know I can't. Not until we know for sure what happened. I can't put you and Kenny at risk.' Because of Rand's insistence on the limousine and guards, she'd had to tell Billie about the threats.

'You're falling for him, aren't you?'

Zara glanced at Tony. This was her best chance to be alone with Billie. She needed to talk to her friend about the personal mess she was in with Rand. She certainly couldn't talk to him.

She plucked two outfits from the pile in the guard's arms. 'We're going to try these on,' she told him. 'You wait here.'

Billie followed her into the dressing rooms.

Zara went down the short hallway, looking behind the half-open drapes to make sure all the cubicles were empty, and hung the outfits in adjacent rooms at the far end, near the large mirror.

'I suppose we're in here so you can talk without an audience, right?' Billie asked. 'So why do I have to try this on?' She touched the filmy skirt.

'Like I've been telling you since we started planning this. You are introducing the acts and you need something special to wear. Now get your body into that dress. And keep your voice down, okay?'

They scowled at each other then yanked the drapes closed. Zara dropped her jacket and purse into a corner.

'Can I assume you're finding it difficult to live with Rand?' Billie's voice floated quietly across the space separating them.

'Difficult is a very mild word for this situation.' Zara yanked her bulky sweater over her head and added it to the pile of her belongings. 'He has a very strong personality. Every day's a struggle just to keep my identity from being swallowed up.'

'You've never lived with a man before, have you? Things must be even worse for you two since you're working *and* living together.'

'It's not as though he really wanted me there. We're working together because of my grandfather's will and he only suggested I move in because of the fire.' She shimmied out of her leggings, dropped them onto the pile, and stepped into the slacks.

'Zara, this is me you're talking to.' Billie's voice was muffled for a moment. 'I know you're sleeping together.'

'I admit we don't have any problems in bed. He's a terrific lover. But that's only one part of life. What about everything else?'

While they were making love, Zara thought, he was wonderful, open, receptive. In bed they were partners and he enjoyed her assertiveness. Put them in any other situation and it seemed he didn't believe she was capable of thinking for herself.

'What do you mean?'

'Every morning he reverts to a businessman I'm not sure I like very much. And he's driving me crazy with all these secrets and mysteries.'

'Mysteries?'

'He lives frugally when I know he must earn a hefty salary, not to mention bonuses and stock dividends. His suits are tailored and obviously expensive but he doesn't own many. He cooks for himself rather than eating in restaurants.'

'That sounds pretty good. I've tasted your cooking, and other than those scrumptious oatmeal cookies, it's pretty bad.'

'He lives in a company-owned apartment and drives either a company car or an old black sports car that once belonged to his grandfather. His lifestyle is spartan. In short, he is nothing like any other wealthy bachelor I have ever met or heard about.'

'Sounds like you're building molehill questions into mountain mysteries. Maybe he just has simple tastes.'

'Yeah, right. If you say so.' Zara buttoned the vest over her bra and fasten the rhinestone bowtie around her throat. 'Are you ready?'

Hooks rang along metal rods as they stepped out to face each other. They both gawked silently at each other, then turned toward the mirror.

Billie's dress oozed elegance, with its rose-coloured brocade bodice and multi-layered chiffon skirt.

Zara's satin slacks were made like any other tuxedo pant, even to the narrow stripe down the outside seam, except the stripe was rhinestones. The vest, too, was conventionally styled. Together on Zara's body, however, the look was anything but conventional.

The satin fabric clung to her hips and backside. The rhinestone stripes flowed down the outside curve of her legs, sparkling with every move she made. With a deep vee front and armholes cut high and wide, the vest was skimpier than she'd expected, exposing her shoulders and both sides of her breasts.

They stared at the images in the mirror.

'You look absolutely stunning,' Zara said. 'Abe's eyes are going to pop out.'

'Talk about popping out, you won't be able to wear a bra under that,' Billie said.

'I noticed.'

'Rand's pretty conservative, isn't he?'

'Yup.'

'He's going to hate that outfit, isn't he?'

'Yup.'

'You're going to wear it, aren't you?'

'Yup.'

'Is that smart? Especially if you're already having problems.'

'The benefit's next weekend and we have no more time to waste looking around. It's the perfect costume for the segment and that's all that matters.'

'One question. Are you going to model it for him when he gets home tomorrow night or wait to spring it on him at the benefit?'

'I think I'll wait. Let's see how Rand likes surprises.'

'There was a good turnout. They must have raised a lot of money,' Walt said. When Rand didn't respond he glanced at his wife, Marcy. She shrugged.

Rand knew he was making them uncomfortable but he couldn't seem to help it. He'd been such a fool.

The benefit was over and they were sharing a cab for the short ride between the Queen Elizabeth Theatre and the Children's Rehab Centre. All three were invited to a cocktail party for performers, regular patrons of the charity, and those who'd paid two hundred dollars for a seat in the front of the theatre.

'That Broadway medley Zara did at the end was wonderful, a real show-stopper. Right, Marcy?'

'Yes, dear. And the man who sang and danced with her was very good, too. I saw him perform on Broadway when I visited my sister in New York last year. Did you know he's from Vancouver? It was really nice of him to do this for Zara, wasn't it? It's really important to have the help of your friends when you're trying to do something like this benefit.'

'Yes, she is well thought of in the music world.' Rand smiled grimly. Evidently that was a gross understatement, if what he'd overheard was the truth. He'd enjoyed her singing but he'd never taken it seriously or seen it as a threat to their relationship. Why would he? After ten years of trying, she was back in Vancouver, singing four or more nights a week in a ramshackle bar.

'That was quite a getup she wore at the end.' Walt winked. 'Too bad Marcy doesn't have one just like it.'

'Walt, grow up. That kind of thing can only be worn on stage.' She glanced out as the cab stopped in front of the Centre. 'We're here.'

Rand paid the driver, stepped out, and opened the back door to help her out.

'Thank you, Rand.' They stepped up on the sidewalk and waited for her husband. 'Zara's encore was truly lovely. Brought tears to my eyes. Someone told me she wrote that song herself.'

'Yes. So I heard during the intermission.' Two men in suits had stood directly behind him in the line for drinks. One had been a music producer from New York, the other from Nashville.

Their conversation made it clear that Zara's songs were in demand by performers whose names even he recognized. When the two men argued about which town would be better for Zara's career, he'd realized that her music could, and probably would, take her away from him.

Her reckless impulses were driving him crazy with worry. Her suggestions on how to run ForPac were charitable, plentiful, and would drive the entire corporation into bankruptcy within six months if she were ever given free rein.

Right now he couldn't seem to care. Her sweetness made him happy and her tartness made life exciting. Making love with her was a revelation, sleeping with her in his arms was devastating. The flavours of the woman were rapidly spoiling him for any other kind of life.

What in hell was he going to do when she left?

CHAPTER 12

Zara pretended to be asleep as Rand kissed her cheek and got out of bed. Wouldn't be long now, she told herself.

After he was safely in his bathroom she rolled onto her side and thought about the night just past. A standing ovation. Two contract offers, one from a New York producer, the other from one in Nashville. Finally, her work was receiving the recognition she'd hoped for. Obviously her decision to move back to Vancouver and concentrate on writing rather than performing had been the right one.

After the party following the benefit they'd returned here, where Rand had made love to her with a hunger, a desperation, she'd never experienced from him before. Afterward she'd tried to find out what was wrong but he'd shushed her with a kiss, pulled her into his arms, and claimed he was too tired to talk.

She'd woken twice in the night and he lay unmoving, one hand resting possessively on her hip as he stared up at the ceiling.

Both times she'd been tempted to ask him what was on his mind, but somehow she knew that pushing him now would be a mistake. Coward, her inner voice scolded. No, she answered. Smart. This was not the right time to push him. With any luck, that would come later today.

She listened as he turned on the shower, then crawled across the wide bed so she could look at the clock.

Five-thirty. Her face dropped into his pillow. She couldn't believe that she was actually awake at five-thirty in the morning. Hopefully Billie hadn't had any trouble with her part of the plan.

She rolled over, swung her legs to dangle over the edge of the bed, then stopped moving. Lord, this had better be worth it.

She heaved herself off the bed and staggered down the hall to the bedroom where she kept her clothes. Though Rand thought it whimsical, she still wasn't ready to share his closet though she shared his bed.

Right now she needed a quick shower and several cups of coffee if she was going to pull this off. By the time Rand was ready to go, so was she, a bulky terry robe covering her tee shirt and rolled-up jeans. The man wasn't stupid; if he knew she was dressed so early he'd wonder why. If he asked questions she might have to change the plan.

This had to work. It had to. She didn't know how much longer she could survive this emotional seesaw.

If only he had different priorities.

Sometimes she didn't really like the man she feared she was coming to love.

He was rigid and demanding with his staff and based all his decisions on the profit factor. Then something would happen and she would see the caring man he was inside, the man he could be if only he wanted to try.

She was tired of trying to cope, tired of living with all the secrets and uncertainties in their relationship. It was time for action.

In the dining room she blew a kiss to the smiling face in the portrait. 'Wish me luck, Mama,' she whispered.

She followed him into the kitchen and poured herself a cup of coffee while he poured milk on his cereal. The man was a morning person, darn him. Although today he looked unusually glum.

'Six in the morning is an uncivilized time of day to be eating breakfast.' Zara sipped her coffee and blinked sleepily. 'It's been almost two weeks, Rand. Why can't they find Sheila?'

'The lieutenant told me they were working on it. Understaffed as the police are, he tells me we can't expect miracles. Especially on a case where there have been no more incidents.'

'What about that guy you hired, the private security guy, Hoffman?' She reached into the fridge for the last piece of pizza left from lunch the day before. 'Why hasn't he found her?'

'He's got someone on it. You shouldn't have given him such a hard time last Monday. The poor guy was only following orders.'

'It was bad enough when he stood outside my dressing room at Roggo's. He shouldn't have insisted on standing beside the stage, staring out into the audience while I performed. Ruined my rapport with the audience for the whole evening.' She knew she looked as petulant as she felt as her teeth tore the pizza crust.

'Congealed pizza is uncivilized at any time, especially for breakfast.' He shook his head and almost smiled. 'You knew Hoffman had no choice when you made your plans. He works for me. He has to do whatever it takes to keep you safe.'

'You're right. I was going to buy some new underwear today but I'll save that for his day off when you're in charge. Then I can drag you through all the lingerie shops in town.'

'Sounds good to me.' He winked, then got up to rinse out the mug and bowl and set them in the dishwasher.

'Speaking of shopping, you never said anything about the outfit I wore last night.'

'You looked lovely.'

So much for a jealous reaction. Obviously he didn't care how daring her stage clothes were.

He picked up his leather jacket and dropped a kiss on her forehead as he passed. 'I'll see you tomorrow night. Be careful and don't drive the poor man into quitting, okay? He's the best at his job.'

She sulked. As much as she hated the feeling, there was no other word for her behaviour and she couldn't seem to act any other way. She was starting to hate Sundays. 'I'm going to walk down Granville Street, have lunch on Davie Street, then rent a bike and spend the day in Stanley Park. And that's just today.'

'Zara, be reasonable. None of those activities are safe right now.'

'Then play hooky with me. We won't leave the apartment, I swear.'

His hand withdrew from her shoulder. 'You know I have to work. We've talked about this before.'

'Fine. I'll stay here and write songs. You can tell Hoffman's guy he has the day off.'

'No.'

'I can't stand having him here all the time. It's hard to write any music when I can feel him watching me.'

Rand lifted her to her feet and then he wrapped his arms around her from behind as he nuzzled her neck. 'Fine. I'll tell him to stay outside.'

'Outside the building?'

'Nice try. Outside the apartment door.'

She twisted around so she could look into his eyes. 'Where are you going, Rand?'

He answered her with a mind-numbing kiss. Her knees melted, her eyes closed . . . then he was gone with no explanation. Again.

That man seemed to think a kiss would put an end to any unwelcome line of conversation she started. Too bad it worked.

Well, this time she was ready. Two minutes later she had whipped off the terry robe, rolled down the legs of her jeans, grabbed a jacket, and slipped on her shoes. She fidgeted while she waited by the door, watching through the peep hole as Rand said a few words to Hoffman's employee.

The security man sat down on the upholstered bench beside the elevator and Rand left. She shifted impatiently. Where was Billie?

The other elevator opened and she had to smile. Billie looked adorable in uniform. The 'new' female concierge beckoned the guard over. After a few whispered sentences they both entered the elevator. Good, he'd fallen for the 'mysterious lurker' ruse. Now to get out of here.

She ran and arrived breathless, dishevelled, and sweaty but in time to drive Billie's car out of the parking garage only seconds behind Rand.

She hadn't expected him to leave the city core and almost lost him on the freeway. The traffic this far out in the suburbs was thin this early in the morning so she hung back and nearly missed following him onto the connection to the Trans Canada Highway.

Forget downtown. He seemed to be going out of town. No wonder he arrived home so late on Monday nights that she was usually asleep.

Zara checked she had a full tank of gas, selected a cassette tape from the ones Kenny had left between the seats, and settled back to see where Rand led her.

'What do you want me to do with this, Mr Main?' The young man stood at Rand's elbow with a roll of blueprints in his hands.

'Round file it, Bob. That contractor's suggestions are always too expensive and too ambitious. We'll go with Keating's plans.'

'Yes, sir.' He crumpled the blueprints into a makeshift ball and slam-dunked them into the trash can through the basketball hoop they'd hung over it, then sat down at the other battered desk.

Bob Chong had changed considerably from the scared teenager of a few years ago who'd pretended so hard to be a tough son of a bitch. He'd barrelled into the old store where Rand had established his Treville office and demanded a job.

Once a highschool dropout with a pregnant girlfriend, now he was a husband and doting father. He helped Rand with the Treville paperwork, taking care of things around the office five days every week while Rand was away in Vancouver. If there were any problems he left a message on the phone line Rand kept for that purpose. Last year he'd taken his highschool equivalency exam and passed with high marks.

Rand glanced around the premises of what had once been a women's clothing store. Thanks to Bob, it looked very good, considering Rand hadn't wanted to spend much money turning it into an office. Luckily the boy had considerable talent with a saw, hammer, and paint brush. He'd even sanded down and repainted the rusty old filing cabinets Rand had brought over from the offices of the closed mill. Now they were lined up in the area that had once been dressing rooms.

Bob was probably going to tackle the wide front window next. It still bore the gold-lettered legend *Minette's Ladies Wear for All Occasions* on the glass and he resented the occasional teasing the sign generated among his friends.

Rand pushed back his chair and walked over to file some papers. While he was standing there he glanced out the window and caught a glimpse of long black hair on the woman getting out of a car across the street. Could it be . . .?

Damn, he was easily distracted these last few weeks. He was so besotted he was seeing Zara everywhere, even one hundred and fifty miles from Vancouver.

Then the woman swung a yellow jacket around her shoulders and slammed the car door. The resemblance was eerie but it couldn't be Zara. That wasn't her car.

The woman glanced down the street to her left, then headed right, straight for Millie's Place, the cafe directly across from his office. The cafe where he ate all his meals when he was in town.

As she drew closer, he caught a clear look at her face. She *was* Zara.

How the devil did she get here? Clearly he'd underestimated her determination, curiosity, and ingenuity and so had Hoffman's employee.

He cursed again and leaped for the door. If he knew Zara, she intended to ask the women working in the cafe where she could find Rand Tremayne. Just mentioning his real name would draw a storm, he knew.

Of course, they wouldn't be able to direct her to him because he used the name Dal Main in Treville. But her questions would bring on a flood of information he couldn't allow her to hear.

The door banged open into the wall, glass panes rattling, as he sprinted out. 'Zara!'

Before she could open her mouth he waved at the two ladies avidly peering through the cafe windows, grabbed her elbow, and escorted her forcibly back to his office.

Bob stood behind his desk, questions hovering on his lips.

'Excuse me, Bob, but could you go now and get those documents photocopied at City Hall? Thanks.' Rand kept on walking, his hand on Zara's arm.

She dragged against his hold, smiling at the younger man. 'Hello, I'm Zara Lindsey.' She held out her hand to shake Bob's but Rand kept walking. He didn't want to be forced into introductions because introductions led to conversation. Conversation led to people using other people's names. The wrong names.

'I'd appreciate it if you went immediately. And while you're out, could you bring me back something to eat? Thanks.'

Rand pushed Zara ahead of him into what had been the storage area behind the shop. Now it served as a make-shift bedroom for the one night a week he slept in Treville. He shut the door and stood there until he heard the rattle of glass indicating Bob had left.

'Sit down.' He waited until she'd settled onto the only chair in the room, an old vinyl dinette chair, before he sat on the edge of his cot.

Great. Not only was Zara here in Treville, his actions outside would have attracted attention from Millie and her daughter, Sally, the two biggest gossips in town. And, even more newsworthy, no woman from out-of-town had ever visited him here. Millie and her staff would be sure to pump Bob for information when he arrived to order Rand's meal.

'What was that all about, Rand? Who was that young man?'

'My assistant, Bob Chong.' He heard the bite in his voice but was too angry to temper his tone. 'Why the hell did you follow me?'

'Why did I have to?' She jerked her arms free of the yellow jacket and placed it across her lap.

'There was no need for this.'

'There was every need. Every time I asked you about your mysterious venture,' she waved her hand in circles, indicating the storefront office, the packing crate bedside table, and the rest of the third- or fourth-hand furniture, 'you either refused to answer or kissed me senseless.'

'Senseless, is right.'

'Well, pardon me. Is honesty too much to ask?'

'Is privacy to much to expect?'

'I thought sleeping in your bed almost every night gave me some rights. I guess not.'

'Dammit, you know it does.' The damned tap was dripping again. He jumped to his feet, stalked to the yellowed porcelain sink, and tightened the handles. He opened the door and looked through the office, through the plate glass window, to the cafe across the street.

Millie and Sally were still watching. He smacked his fist against the crumbling plaster wall then spun around on his heel. 'Just not . . .'

'Just not what, Rand? Not this town? Do there

281

have to be secrets? What are you hiding? What's her name?'

'Her name?'

'I noticed how quick you were to keep me from talking to the residents of the town. I assume you're hiding something. Your employees all think it's a woman.'

'Another woman?' He slid his hands up over his face and buried his fingers in his hair, leaving them there with the heels of his hands covering his eyes. 'Give me strength.'

As a prayer for deliverance, it was obviously weak because it wasn't answered.

'I need to know, Rand.'

His arms dropped to his sides, suddenly as heavy as his heart.

'Why would you assume there was another woman in my life? Have I said or done anything to make you believe I didn't care deeply for you?'

'Nothing, except disappear for two days, once a week, and refuse to tell me why.'

He walked slowly back to the cot and sat down.

'Why did you follow me?'

'I am tired of the secrets, Rand. Tired of wondering where you are, who you're with. I'm living with a man I don't even know. You won't let me.'

'You know me. Probably better than anyone else.'

'No, I don't.'

Her mistrust was like a blow to his chest. He could feel himself shutting down. It was a painful process. The emotions her warmth had thawed were screaming in agony as they froze over again.

The room was silent so long, Zara felt her anger begin to turn to nervousness. She clenched the strap of her purse between her fingers, waiting for Rand to look at her again. When he did, she almost cried out at the dead look in his eyes.

'Until the repairs are complete on your home, I'll arrange to stay somewhere else. I'll call Walt and ask him to pack up my clothes. By the time you get back to Vancouver, everything will be arranged.' He stood and waited politely for her to precede him from the room.

Reluctantly, she got to her feet.

'He'll make sure Hoffman gets one of his men over to protect you immediately. Under the circumstances, it would be best if you fulfilled the terms of Heinrich's will at one of ForPac's subsidiaries. It won't be for long.'

'Rand . . .'

'Walt will notify you about your new employment by eight a.m. Tuesday.'

She grabbed his sleeve and dragged him to a stop. 'Listen to me.'

He nodded once but didn't look at her.

'Why are you doing this?'

'I fail to see your point. Our association is over and I am making arrangements for a civil conclusion.'

283

'Civil? This isn't even close to civilized. We're in the middle of an argument and you shut me out? I ask to get to know you and you refuse?'

When he looked at her, his eyes seemed to burn with emotion. The fire in his gaze seared her skin but anything was better than the deadness that had been there before.

'You want to know me? Fine. Come with me.' He snatched up the leather jacket from a hook beside the sink. He took one step toward the front of the store, then turned and opened the back door. 'After you.'

Outside in the alley, he reached for her arm, once an automatic gesture when they'd walked, one she'd barely noticed until today when he jerked back and shoved his fists into his pockets. At the end of the alley they turned onto the street, half a block beyond the restaurant.

'Where are we going?'

'To show you what kind of man I am.' He strode off down the cracked sidewalk. She had to scramble to catch up. By the time they'd travelled two blocks of business premises, half of them derelict, they'd left what must once have been a bustling shopping area.

His expression grew grimmer and he still didn't speak as they passed a crumbling school with a rusty playground and a deserted bandstand. The sports field was tended but the grandstand had tumbled down. Here and there among neglected or abandoned homes she saw a few decorated with bright new paint. Some of the occupied homes had a car in their driveway, none had two.

They met a handful of people, most of whom smiled and nodded but none stopped for introductions or a chat. They obviously knew Rand but for some reason didn't speak. How odd for a small town.

This place on a Sunday afternoon was nothing like any of the small towns she knew or had heard of. Where were the neighbours gossiping over the fence while their children rode bikes in the road?

The town seemed half dead.

'Seen enough?'

'I don't understand. What did you want me to see?'

They had walked in a full circle and were once again passing the abandoned school. She was exhausted after the long drive from Vancouver and tired of Rand's ambiguity. She didn't know which was worse.

She did know she wasn't going another step without an explanation. In the playground, under the spreading branches of an ancient oak tree, sat a weather-stained bench that must have once been a place for weary mothers to rest while their children played.

'Let's sit there.'

'You've seen everything. It's time for you to start back to Vancouver.'

'What are you afraid of?' She glared at him, daring him to talk to her, then went to the bench, praying he wouldn't walk away from her.

She sat at one end and waited, barely breathing, until finally he sat down as far away from her as was physically possible. His fists were still deep in his pockets and as he leaned back the bench's supports creaked in protest. He ignored both the sound and her, stretching out his legs, negligently propping one ankle on the other as he stared into the distance.

'I don't understand why we're doing this.'

'Look around. What do you see?'

'A town.'

'A dead town. A ghost town.' His voice was so low as he spoke that she almost didn't hear his last sentence.

'This isn't a ghost town. I've seen several families, a few businesses.'

'For every operating company you saw, there are two out of business. For every family in town, three had to move away. This town used to have a population of over three thousand. Now there are barely eight hundred, most of them women and children living alone while the fathers travel, looking for work. Believe me, even if you can't see them, there are plenty of ghosts.'

'I still don't understand.'

'Did you notice the name of the town as you drove in?'

'Not really. I was too busy trying not to lose sight of you on the highway.'

'Treville. Named after my ancestor who moved here more than a hundred and fifty years ago to start up a mill. For four generations Tremayne's was the biggest employer in the area. Fourteen years ago Tremayne's closed down and the town died.'

'It happens, Rand. People have been building towns and cities for centuries. Things change and some are abandoned. I don't understand what that's got to do with us.'

'It's an interesting sensation to know you are responsible for killing a town and destroying so many lives.'

'That's absurd. One person can't kill an entire town.'

'When I was twenty-one my parents died in a car accident and I inherited Tremayne's. Within eight months the company was forced into receivership. Everyone lost their jobs and I left town with all I had left – my clothes and my grandfather's Mustang.'

'That's all they let you keep? A car?'

'I was lucky to get that, even though it belonged to me, not the company. When some of the people who lost their jobs threatened to wreck the Mustang, I hid it until I could leave.'

'Sounds like you feel about that Mustang just like I feel about a certain painting.'

He ignored her comment. 'Treville's death has been slow and painful but there is no doubt; it was my failure and I am responsible.'

'So speaks the oracle.' Zara jumped up and stretched out her arms in the air like an old-time revival preacher. 'Let no man or woman dare to disagree.'

'This is no joke.'

'Yes, it is. A bad one. At least this proves you've always had this ridiculously immense sense of responsibility and it isn't just my competency you question.' She sat down at his side and placed her hand on his arm. 'How old did you say you were you when your parents died? Twenty?'

'Twenty-one.'

'And your father left you a company that was solvent and thriving?'

Slowly his head turned until he met her gaze. 'What are you saying?'

'I'm saying that even at twenty-one you must have had some of the same skills that convinced Heinrich to name you his CEO. Even that young, there is no way you could have destroyed a successful company in only a few months.'

'My father was a drunk whose management style was chaotic at best.' Rand pulled his hands from his pockets and sat up straighter. 'Tremayne's had decayed steadily for most of the four years since my grandfather's death.'

'I told you so.'

'That changes nothing. My father had the support of the bank and our creditors. I lasted eight months. Tremayne's would have operated for years, maybe for decades, even with him in charge.'

'You don't know that. No one knows that. The bank wasn't into charity, no bank is. They would have dealt with your father the same way.'

He pulled away from her touch and stood up. 'You don't know what you're talking about.' He walked over to the broken seesaw and nudged the wooden plank with his foot. It fell apart at his touch.

She hated the lack of emotion that was deadening both his voice and expression. At least angry, she'd felt he was within reach. This coldness was a shield she couldn't allow to come between them. She wasn't sure she had to strength or ability break through it again.

'Yes, I do. I have dealt with quite a few banks in my life and no bank manager gives away money without a chance of recouping the principal. Plus interest.'

'This manager would have. Jack Hudson seemed to be willing to support my father forever. Within reason.'

'Why?'

'Probably because Hudson was my mother's lover and my father wasn't above blackmail.'

'Blackmail? Because of an adulterous relationship?'

'Hudson was the black sheep son of one of the richest banking families in the States. Treville Savings and Loan was the toy they gave him to stay in Canada and out of their hair. My father knew Hudson didn't want to give up access to his family's money, which would have happened if there were a scandal.'

'And because your mother died, he no longer had a reason to support Tremayne's.'

'Though he preferred my mother, there were other willing women in town. I doubt he cared if she were dead or not but he'd probably have kept paying my father for years, to keep his mouth shut.'

'Then why did he . . .'

'The day my parents died, we'd had a fight. I'd had enough. Enough of my mother's greed and promiscuity. Enough of my father's drunken stupidity. Enough of his rages. In the usual asinine fashion of young men I'd decided to make them pay for my "suffering".'

Rand wandered over to the sandbox and crouched down. He yanked out a handful of the weeds that choked its sandy surface.

'What did you do?'

'What I did isn't as important as what happened because of it. I was arrested, the cops called my parents and told them to get down to the jail. My father, drunk as usual, compelled my mother to get in the car and they headed for the courthouse.

They didn't travel four blocks before he ran a stop sign and hit a car full of kids.'

Zara gasped.

'Because of me, my parents and six teenagers died, one of them Jack Hudson's only daughter. He decided that someone had to pay for Katie's death and I was the only Tremayne left.

'I got dumped into running Tremayne's with little experience and he let me drown in financial deep water. Because of his rage and grief, the entire town suffered. They all hated me, with good reason, especially the families of the kids who died.'

'When are you going to learn? Everything that goes wrong isn't your fault. You weren't even in the car.' She slapped her palms together in frustration. 'This guilt you insist on carrying for the rest of the world's faults is driving me crazy. Rand, your father was drunk. He shouldn't have been driving.'

'He wouldn't have been on the road that day if I hadn't screwed up.'

'The actions of your father and Jack Hudson closed down the business. It wasn't you.' She knelt on the ground beside him and cupped her hands on his jaw, turning his face so he had to look directly at her. 'You have to let this go.'

His hand rose, as if to touch her lips, then dropped. He closed his eyes, then pulled away.

He stood up and put one hand under her elbow to lift her to her feet.

'The worst part was watching fear and despair tear families apart while their livelihood disappeared. No more jobs at Tremayne's because it was almost done for, and no chance of jobs anywhere else because most of the secondary industry depended on their wages. Have you ever seen what happens to people who are hopeless? They turn on each other, even those they love.'

'Rand . . .'

'And they hated me.' He stared around the dilapidated town square. She had to strain to hear his whisper when he spoke again. 'Almost as much as I hated myself.'

'Is that why you come here every week. To wallow in guilt?'

His head turned sharply and he glared at her. 'No.'

'I saw a factory on my way into town that looked like it was thriving. What do they produce?'

'Wood specialty products.'

'And that cafe across from your office. I didn't see much of the interior, but it looked newly decorated and more than half the tables were occupied by people buying meals.'

'Where are you going with this?'

'Give me a minute, okay?' She stood toe to toe with him, hands propped on her hips as she stared him down. 'Sure there are empty buildings in this town. But there are a few busy ones, and we passed more than a few smiling faces. That proves they don't hate you now, if they ever did.'

'They don't know who I am. I've changed physically over the years and I use the name Dal Main when I'm here.' He turned away from her and strode away.

'You're hiding behind a pseudonym?' She shook her head. 'Never mind, we're getting off the point.'

'What is the point?'

'Granted I wasn't in your decrepit little storefront office for very long, but I saw rolled blueprints stacked in a box, ledgers piled on the floor, and what looked like more than a dozen business proposals on the desks.' She poked him in the chest. 'Ever since I met you I've wondered where all your money was going. Now I know. You're pouring it into Treville, aren't you?'

'Zara . . .'

She poked him harder. 'You don't own a big fancy house or a hot car or talk about playing with your stocks and bonds like every other man in your position. No, that's not good enough for Mr Randall "shoot-me-I'm-guilty" Tremayne, is it? You decided you have to be responsible for a whole damn town.'

293

He grabbed her hand. 'That's enough.'

'I agree. Enough is enough. Grow up, Rand, and let the rest of the world do the same.'

'It's time for you to leave.' He didn't release her hand as he strode down the sidewalk, heading back toward his office and towing her behind him.

She knew she couldn't let his anger stop her from saying what had to be said.

'You should tell these people who you are and what you are doing. They have the right to know you for the person you've become, rather than be taken care of like a bunch of little kids by a man who can't see straight on this issue. I bet you're wrong about them, anyway. Wrong about how they'd feel if they knew who you really are.'

Her voice had risen as he'd increased his pace and people were turning to watch the show.

He stopped so abruptly that she slammed into his back. He spun around and grabbed her shoulders, pulling her up onto her toes.

'Will . . . you . . . be . . . quiet.' His nose was practically touching hers when he spoke.

She looked around at their interested spectators. As much as she wanted him to tell these people the truth, she couldn't let it come out because she was arguing with him in the middle of the street. 'I'm sorry.'

He didn't answer but when he started walking

294

again he held her more gently and adjusted his stride to hers.

He didn't speak to her again until she was in her car and the door shut. She wound down the window, determined to try one more time.

'Think about it, okay?'

He looked at her as if he doubted her sanity. 'You have no idea what these people went through. You cannot grasp the depth and breadth of the hatred I lived with until I couldn't stand it any longer and walked away. Who am I kidding? I ran, just as far and as fast as I possibly could.'

'Not that far. You stayed close enough to do all this.' She pointed out some of the recent improvements around them.

'Good bye, Zara. Make sure you get the gas tank filled up on the way out of town.'

'Just can't resist telling people what to do, can you? Always so sure you know what's best for them.'

He turned his back and was walking away when she shouted after him. 'Don't bother calling Walt about picking up your stuff from the apartment. You're not moving out. I'm not done with you or this conversation.'

He froze, then continued into his office without acknowledging her threat. Or was it a promise? She wasn't sure herself.

The only thing she did know was that the next

few days were going to be painful and life-altering. For both of them. Rand's guilt was too old, too deeply ingrained in his personality for him to change easily. And she loved him too much to let him continue the way he was going.

CHAPTER 13

Rand's phone rang and Zara glanced at him. Today the sun streamed in through the office windows, casting a puddle of light around his desk. He'd shed his jacket and rolled up his sleeves but her desk sat in shadow and she was glad of the heavy sweater she'd worn for the season's first wintry day.

Sharing this office and the apartment day after day was every bit as painful as she'd feared. Their personal relationship seemed to be over. Since the day she followed him to Treville he hadn't talked much beyond the basics necessary to any two people sharing work or living space

As imperfect as it was, she missed what they'd had together. Sleeping alone at night was mighty lonely and Sunday morning was looming closer every day. She missed him now. How would she feel when he left for Treville again?

'Of course. Would you send her up, please?' Rand replaced the phone and stood to don his jacket.

'Are you having guests? Do you want me to leave?'

'No. Helen Parker is downstairs and asked to see us both.'

'Mrs Parker? Did she say what she wanted?' She put down the papers she'd been feeding through the scanner and went to stand beside his desk.

Before Rand could answer, Tim poked his head around the door, pulled a sour face, and announced Heinrich's former employee. Zara blinked in awe when the other woman swept into the room.

Mrs Parker had always been perfectly and precisely groomed but with Heinrich's gift of a home and annuity, she had moved uptown and so, obviously, had her style. With expensively refined make-up, hair, and clothes she appeared more likely to hire a housekeeper than to be one.

'Good afternoon, Randall. Margaret.' She allowed Rand to help her out of her full-length fur coat and then sat in one of the chairs facing his desk as if it were a throne. 'Please sit down.'

Zara obediently took the seat beside her while Rand returned to the chair behind his desk. At least she could enjoy the warmth of the sun for the duration of Mrs Parker's visit.

'That young man should be dismissed immediately.' The older woman settled her purse on her lap. 'He is disrespectful.'

'I'm sure you didn't come here to discuss my staff, Helen. What can we do for you?'

'I understand you have a detective searching for Sheila Bendan,' Helen said.

Zara felt her mouth drop open in shock.

'How did you . . .' Rand didn't get to finish his question.

'How I know is neither here nor there. Please tell me if the information is correct.'

Rand was silent for a moment while he considered. 'I see no reason to hide the fact we are trying to locate her. Why do you ask?'

'Tell me why you are looking for her. Please.'

Zara could tell the last word was an afterthought.

'That information is confidential,' he said.

'Does it have something to do with the legal work she did for Heinrich?'

This time Zara managed to keep her mouth shut. Barely.

'And if it did?'

'Heinrich was a good man, misunderstood by many, even one who owed him her love and obedience.' She glowered at Zara.

'I didn't owe him my entire life!' she exclaimed hotly.

'You are an adult now, Margaret. No need to fly off the handle when a person points out your faults for your own good.' She looked Zara up and down.

'You don't dress properly and I imagine you are as stubborn as ever. Though you persisted in a career of which Heinrich disapproved, I have been told you are a very successful songwriter and I believe you have grown up to be an honourable person. Your grandfather would be pleased.'

Words of repudiation tangled in Zara's throat but Mrs Parker majestically ignored her stuttering attempts to speak.

'Randall, my duty to Heinrich's memory obliges me to ensure his estate is settled as he intended. I am aware you removed several boxes of his papers from the estate some weeks past. Did you find anything interesting?'

'Why do you ask?' Rand leaned forward, resting his linked fingers on his desk.

'Because you are not a stupid man. You would have recognized the significance of the information I placed there for you to find. I was very pleased how quickly you became aware there were . . . discrepancies . . . and took steps to search for answers.'

'*You* put that file there?'

'Of course. I extracted it from that girl's brief-case and hid it before she could have it destroyed. She thought she'd misplaced it.'

'You knew she intended to falsify portions of Heinrich's will?' Rand jerked to his feet, planted his hands on the desktop, and loomed closer. 'And you did nothing to prevent her?'

'What could a mere housekeeper do?'

Mrs Parker shook her head disapprovingly when Zara snorted in laughter.

'You could have told me, Mrs Parker,' he said. 'The company lawyers . . .'

'I am not here to debate what might have been or not been my best action. We must concern ourselves with the present situation. What action do you intend to pursue from this point forward?'

'Our lawyers want to interview her. The police want to talk to her. Until then, we can make no definite plans.'

'And you, Randall? What would you like to do to her?'

'I would like to . . .' Rand's hands curled into fists as rage glimmered in his eyes. Within moments he'd masked the anger. 'What I want is of no significance.'

'Mrs Parker, why did you come here today?' Zara asked.

'I know where she is.'

Rand was putting away his wallet when another cab screeched to a stop behind his. Zara tossed some money at her cabbie and leaped out onto the sidewalk. Damn. He shut his cab's door, and walked toward the rental cottage owned by Neil's wife.

'Rand, wait.' She was breathless when she reached his side. 'That was fun.'

'Fun?'

'I've always wanted to jump in a cab and tell the driver to "follow that car". We lost you once but luckily I remembered the name of this street.'

'I told you to stay at the office. The police and I can handle this.'

'And I told you I was coming. We might not have anything in common but she is my cousin and you're incensed enough you might do something you'd regret.'

'I won't.' He'd learned his lesson at an early age. He didn't need any more regrets to live with.

Zara practically trod on his heels as she followed him up the cracked and weed-choked driveway. 'Weren't you supposed to wait out front for the police?'

'They made a suggestion. I didn't agree.'

'No, you didn't. But I suspect the cops aren't going to accept your interpretation of their orders.' She looked around and shuddered theatrically. 'This looks like the witch's cottage in *Hansel and Gretel*.'

'The house is very small and appears abandoned. The grass has gone to seed and there are rotting leaves, dead branches and other garden debris from more than one autumn. It was probably long empty before Sheila needed a place to hide.'

'What if she isn't here?'

'If she isn't, we'll wait.'

'Where? In the bushes?'

He looked at her, not quite believing what he'd heard her say.

'Okay, okay.' She held up her hands. 'I agree you're not exactly the type to lurk in the bushes.

You don't think she's going to open the door just because we ring the doorbell, do you?'

'I don't know. Let's give it a try, shall we?' He pushed aside the ivy on both sides of the door until he found a button embedded in the stucco wall. When he pressed it they heard a discordant tinkling in the distance.

They waited a few moments before he pressed it again.

'See I told you . . .'

She was interrupted when the door swung open, hinges squawking a protest.

'It's about time . . .' Sheila hung onto the door jamb, swaying slightly, the voluminous folds of her colourful caftan drifting around her ankles. She stopped and blinked when she recognized them. 'Oh, it's you. I thought you were Neil. You might as well come in.' She disappeared from sight.

Rand couldn't resist. He quirked an eyebrow at Zara and smiled.

'You needn't look so superior.' She swept by him and led the way into the cottage.

Inside proved to be as small as it looked from the outside. A mattress set directly on the floor and a card table with one chair were the only pieces of furniture. Every available surface, except the mattress, was stacked with cardboard cake boxes and tin pie plates – all empty.

A galley kitchen was wedged in one corner of the room. Sheila leaned inside an old refrigerator, one hand propped on the lever handle, the other holding an empty glass.

'Want something to eat? There's plenty. You can help me with my research. I'm starting a brilliant new career, you know.'

She took out a slab of chocolate cheesecake and hip-checked the door closed. As she crossed the bare wooden floor she tripped on an empty champagne bottle, losing her grip on the cake. It flew out of her hands, heading directly for Rand's chest.

He snagged it neatly in mid-air, getting only a small amount of the chocolate on his fingers.

'Oops,' she said. 'Just put it down on the table. There's a good boy.' She scooped up a corkscrew and another wine bottle, a full one, and collapsed onto the mattress. 'You can help with the research. Neil's such a wimp. He couldn't stick it out.'

'Sheila, we came to talk to you.' Rand put down the cake and wiped his fingers on a tissue from his pocket.

'Said it was making him sick. I ask you . . . Ooopsy.' She fell backward as the cork pulled free from the neck of the wine bottle. She struggled upright again and poured a full glass, then thumped the bottle down on the floor beside her.

'Cheers.' The wine slopped over the edge of the glass onto the sheets when she toasted them and drank.

'We notified the police where you were. They should be here soon.'

'What was I saying?' She swirled a finger in her glass and licked it off.

'Is Neil coming back, Sheila? When you opened the door, did you think we were him?'

'Oh. Yes. Research. I can't be a lawyer any more, you know that? Once the Bar Association finds out what I did,' she sliced a finger across her throat, looking very solemn.

An instant later she grinned. 'I'm going to open a dessert bar. The Chocolate Tort. Don't you think I'm clever? I'll serve only wine and desserts.'

Zara couldn't stand it any longer. She crouched down beside Sheila. 'Why'd you do it?'

'Do it? Why'd I do it?' Sheila suddenly looked sober. 'The old bastard owed me. He worked me damn hard. Dangled the chance at my own practice in front of me like a carrot and I fell for it, didn't I? Well, I showed him. Almost.' She drained the glass.

'Sheila, you're going to make yourself ill.' Zara took away the wine bottle before her cousin could refill the glass.

'So? Thanks to his nosiness,' she pointed a wavering finger at Rand, 'everyone is going to find out what I did. And I probably won't have any damn money, either.'

'Is that why you sent me those letters?' Rand asked.

'Letters?' Her forehead wrinkled in thought.

'I warned you, Sis,' Neil said from the open door, a bakery box in his hands. 'I said Tremayne wouldn't be swayed by anonymous threats.'

Rand swung on his heel to confront the unexpected addition to their gathering but Zara noticed a peculiar expression cross Sheila's face while her brother talked. Sheila stared at him for a moment, then fell back on the pillow and closed her eyes.

'Bendan. We didn't hear you come in.'

'I won't allow you to browbeat my sister, Tremayne. No matter what she's done.'

'That's enough, gentlemen. We'll take over from here.' A police officer stepped into the room behind Neil.

Within minutes Rand and Zara were outside the cottage waiting for a cab. Two police officers were inside with Sheila and the door was firmly shut. Neil had been allowed to stay because he was her brother.

'I've never seen her like that, have you?' Zara asked Rand.

'No.'

'You know, when Neil was talking, she looked . . . I don't know. Puzzled, maybe. What do you think?'

'She looked drunk.' Rand took her elbow and escorted her to the cab that had just pulled up in front.

'No. Well, yes, she was drunk. But there was something more going on.'

'Yes, with all that sweet stuff and alcohol she's been living on, she was probably about to be sick. Now, please get in the cab. I have to get back to the office.'

'You *have to get back to the office?*' She braced her hand on the open car door and resisted his urging to climb inside. 'My cousin, a woman you were involved with and presumably cared about, is in deep trouble with the police, and that's all you can say?'

He met her gaze straight on and she saw the shadows in his eyes. 'Yes. Now, if you want to come with me, get in the cab.'

She got in. 'So, I've been wondering about something. Why didn't you tell Mrs Parker how you only found the problems with the will by accident when you were looking for something else?'

He looked at her and raised one eyebrow. 'Would you?'

'No. I don't think I would.'

They didn't speak again during the drive back to the Forster Pacific building. They rode up in the elevator together. While she was hanging up her jacket, she heard Rand asking Tim to send for the lawyers and to set up a board of directors meeting for the beginning of next week.

She knew he was seriously distracted when he

suggested she spend the rest of the work day helping Walt's staff. Before she could respond, he went into his office and shut the door.

'Well, little cousin, looks like you'll be the big shot around here now. I'm surprised the old man wrote even one will leaving everything to you. I bet he's spinning in his grave.'

Zara winced when Neil's sarcastic laughter roared beside her ear. She didn't, couldn't, look at the head of the table that occupied the centre of Forster Pacific's largest boardroom.

Rand sat with his back to the room, looking out the wall of windows at a city obscured by threatening rain clouds. The rest of ForPac's major shareholders and executives listened to Mr Faber, the company's senior lawyer, take away everything he'd achieved.

Rand must have known about this for days. He saw her at the apartment every morning and evening. Why hadn't he warned her?

Other than the lawyer's dispassionate words and Neil's laughter, the two dozen people around the table were absolutely silent, the expressions on their faces varying from shock to fear. Except Walt. He was furious.

Zara stumbled into speech. 'I don't understand. Sheila changed Heinrich's will, and forged the witness' signatures? And that makes the entire will void?'

'That is a very much simplified version of events but essentially accurate.'

'Because she made sure there is no written, signed copy of the correct version of the will, now the one Heinrich wrote seven years ago, shortly after my aunt Lucy's death, comes into effect? A will where he left everything to me?'

'That is also correct.'

'Hey, I just thought of something.' Neil grabbed her hand. 'Now you don't have to work here every day to get the million dollars. And you don't have to give it to some blasted charity, either. All you have to do is order Rand to write you a cheque. Fran and I will even help you spend it, little cousin. Just say the word.'

She squirmed her hand free of Neil's grip. 'Mr Faber, could you please explain Rand's plan again?'

'If you approve, he will remain as chief executive officer until such a time as the situation is resolved. This provides continuity in the executive offices and reassures those business associates who are understandably nervous about the co-operative ventures Forster Pacific is currently involved with. The details are in front of each of you.'

He indicated the black file folders that were placed around the table.

She opened one and stared at the neat rows of figures, pie charts, graphs, and long pages of single-spaced paragraphs.

'Ms Lindsey?'

'Yes?' She looked up and realized they were all waiting for her to speak. 'Oh. Yes, of course Rand must remain in charge.'

'Kick the bastard out, Margaret. Show him who's boss.'

'Be quiet, Neil,' she said, then nodded to the lawyer. 'Please continue.'

'Now, with a show of hands, the board and company executives must indicate their vote of confidence in Mr Tremayne's leadership.'

Each person around the table raised a hand, except for Neil who was still grinning ferociously in the seat beside her. 'I'll never vote for that bastard.'

Everyone in the room ignored Neil.

'It will,' Mr Faber continued, 'be some time before this case is finalized by the courts, but Mr Tremayne feels this strategy must be placed in effect immediately to mitigate any unfavourable repercussions in Forster Pacific's many business ventures.'

'What is going to happen to Sheila?'

Zara couldn't tell who'd asked the question, but she was glad someone had.

'Ms Bendan's actions were fraudulent,' the lawyer said. 'The Law Society has suspended her from practising law and an injunction has been filed so she cannot abscond with the funds. Forster Pacific has instigated a civil case and the police are determining if they will proceed with criminal charges.'

'Where is Sheila?' Walt asked.

'The police questioned her last night but she was released, since it has not been determined whether or not she is responsible for the anonymous threats against Mr Tremayne and Ms Lindsey. There is as yet no evidence of her guilt in the apparent accidents that have occurred.'

Walt thumped the table. 'We'll get the evidence.'

The lawyer blinked, then turned back to Zara. 'Do you have any further questions?'

'No, thank you.'

She looked down at the contents of the folder again while the lawyer adjourned the meeting and everyone filed out. Neil started to laugh again but he quieted immediately when Walt put a heavy hand on his shoulder to escort him from the room.

Eventually she was left alone with Rand who had not acknowledged the events of the board meeting. Even now he appeared engrossed by the low clouds pressing closer against the glass.

'Have you found out any more about why she did it?'

'You now own everything I've worked for and all you can ask is why Sheila played games with the paperwork?' His voice was cool and reserved, just as it had been ever since he returned from Treville

311

and found her still determined to share his apartment. He didn't turn to look at her.

'Rand?'

He propped his feet on the windowsill and relaxed deeper in the leather armchair that had been Heinrich's for so many years.

'Have you talked to her again? Do you know why she did it?'

'Supposedly she felt that her years as Heinrich's personal lawyer ruined her practice. It seems he was so demanding she was never able to develop a client base sufficient to support a private practice. She resented the small amount of cash left to her in the will and felt it proved how little he felt her services were worth.'

'And . . .?'

'She changed the will to substantially increase the percentage she would receive in the residuals. Heinrich signed the original will with Mrs Parker and the chauffeur as witnesses. Their signatures on the altered will were forged.'

'How could Heinrich not have known how resentful she was?'

'He trusted someone without using enough cash to ensure their loyalty, always a mistake.'

'That's pretty cynical.'

He shrugged.

'The letters. Did she send them?'

'She admits to using them as a tactic to protect herself, hoping the threat of violence to you would stop me. Presumably she knew nothing else would. However, she insists the "accidents" were a coincidence which lent authenticity to the warnings.'

'Do you believe her?'

Again he shrugged. 'The police are investigating.'

'Damn you, Rand.' She shoved away her chair, stood up and planted her hands on the table. 'You ignore me at the apartment, you ignore me at work, and now you won't even look at me.'

He didn't move or respond.

Enough was enough. Two nights ago when she'd finally got up enough courage to hint at how much she missed his touch and his kisses, he had walked away without comment, leaving the apartment entirely. She hadn't seen him since. If he thought he would end their relationship this way, he could think again.

She rose and walked around the table to stand directly behind his left shoulder.

'Why are you doing this to us?'

Obviously he hadn't heard her move because her quiet voice, so near, startled him. His feet struck the floor as he jerked upright.

He glanced over his shoulder at her, then spun the chair around.

'I don't know what you mean.' He leaned over the table and began stacking papers and placing them inside his briefcase. 'I thought you'd be glad you no longer have to come to work at the office every day.'

'I would never have picked you for a coward, Rand.'

'Fine.' He snapped the locks on the briefcase and picked it up. 'You're the boss. I have an important meeting but I can give you two minutes.'

Her hand lifted, then fell.

'No. I will not allow you to do this.'

'Do what?'

'Demean my feelings by dismissing them as unimportant compared to your work. My grandfather and my father did that to me. I will never again permit anyone to do so, not even you.'

Her lashes were damp as she stared into his eyes for a very long two seconds.

He looked away first.

'If you change your mind, you know where to find me.' She sighed, then walked quickly away.

How had it happened?

Friday night and instead of standing on a stage she was slaving over dinner. Zara shook her head. Weird how a person's priorities changed, she thought.

She savoured the aromas of cheese, garlic, and tomato sauce as she slid the foil-covered tray into the pre-warmed oven as directed by the restaurant's kitchen staff. While the vermicelli boiled she sliced the warm French bread, uncorked the bottle of wine, and tossed the crisp spinach with the prepared dressing.

She set crystal and china for two at one end of the dining room table, then glanced at her watch as she dimmed the overhead lights.

Seven o'clock. He'd be home any minute now. She pressed a hand to her stomach, trying to calm the butterflies that had taken up semi-permanent residence ever since she'd had this idiotic brainwave.

A simple little dinner. Alone together. Hah!

The last few days had fumbled by with neither of them quite sure what should happen next. On the rare occasions they saw each other in the apartment, it seemed they were both careful to say nothing personal.

Rand's hours at Forster Pacific and his trips to Treville kept him even busier than usual, so busy she suspected he was avoiding her. She slept late, wrote all day, and worked at Roggo's every night. She tried to spend all her free days and evenings at the Centre, where there could be no chance meetings.

On the nights she performed or worked at the Centre, one of Hoffman's men waited for her inside the building, escorted her to her car, then followed her home. He stayed nearby until she was safely inside the apartment building's elevator, proving that at some level Rand still cared even if he wasn't willing to say or show it.

315

She kept telling herself that life wasn't all bad. Thanks to her new circumstances she never again needed to worry about money. No more exhaustion from working all day and performing at night. All the time she needed for songwriting. But the price was heartache. Heartache that was changing the songs she wrote. Gone were the love songs; in their place were lyrics of pain and loss.

Last night's performance had been a rock'n'roll tour de force, an exercise in pretending nothing was wrong.

Tomorrow the final repairs on her home would be complete and by the time he returned from Treville on Monday, she'd be gone from Rand's apartment. Odd as it seemed, the worst part was not knowing if he felt anything for her or for what they'd had together.

Tonight would be their last dinner together. Everything would be over, no more pretending she was fine. Perhaps she should call the last few weeks an insane interlude and try to put them behind her. At least now she had the money the Centre needed at her fingertips. Or she would soon.

Last night when she left for Roggo's, she'd left a message taped to the coffee pot, inviting Rand to eat dinner with her tonight and asking him to bring the cheque. Though everything else had changed, the Centre still needed Heinrich's million dollars.

Returning to the silent apartment at three this morning, she'd checked the coffee pot. He'd replaced her note with one of his own, accepting the invitation. No mention of a cheque but she knew he'd bring it. She was his boss now, wasn't she?

Right now it would feel really good to give Heinrich's money to charity even if it meant asking Rand to go against his profit-oriented instincts.

She stopped in front of the portrait of her family. 'What do you think, Mama? Is this going to work?' She kissed her fingertips, then reached up to press them against her mother's painted cheek. 'Wish me luck, Mama.'

The scent of sulphur was strong as she struck a match to light the fat white candle she'd encircled with daisies and carnations for a table centre. When she heard Rand's key in the lock, she sneaked one last peek at her reflection in the window pane to check her appearance, then pulled the drapes closed, shutting out the night.

Show time.

When she went out into the hall, he was hanging his overcoat in the front closet.

'Hi. You're home.' Great, she thought, when you don't know what to say, state the obvious.

Rand's hand faltered, then continued the motion of placing the hanger on the closet rod. 'Traffic was bad. I thought I'd be late.'

'Dinner's ready.'

'It smells delicious. I'll just wash up.'

She went back into the kitchen to arrange the drained pasta on a serving platter she'd found in the cupboard. While she was scooping the primavera sauce over the pasta, Rand came back and he helped her carry the food into the dining room.

While they were occupied with the bustle of settling at the table and serving food she began to think the evening might go well. By the time they were sitting opposite each other with a full plate in front of them, it was beginning to dawn on her that she might have made a big mistake.

She hadn't realized how much it was going to hurt to be in the same room with him.

'Can I pour you some wine?'

She looked up from the dessert fork she was fiddling with. 'Yes. Thank you.'

They watched as the deep-red liquid swirled into her glass, then into his.

After several more minutes of tense silence they both spoke at the same time. 'The police . . .' 'Have you . . .'

'I'm sorry. What were you saying?' she asked.

'No, please, you go first.' With his fork he speared a wedge of tomato from his salad bowl.

'I was wondering if you'd heard from the fire department today, too. The woman who's been

318

investigating the fire at my house called today. It definitely started because of some faulty wiring in the old hot water tank.'

'So it wasn't arson.'

'She lectured me on storing flammables so near the furnace.' She twirled some noodles onto her fork. 'So now we know it wasn't caused by Sheila, even if she did send the letters.'

'I did hear from the police earlier this week. They've found the vehicle that hit my car. It was stolen only a few minutes before the accident and abandoned later that day on an old logging road in the mountains near Hope.'

'Do they know who was driving it?'

'Not yet. The officer said there are a few leads to follow up and he'll call when, or if, they find anything. He gave me the impression they don't expect to discover any proof of the driver's identity.'

Zara had been avoiding looking at Rand, but when he stopped speaking she looked up and for a long moment they stared into each other's eyes over the candle's light. A minute later they both averted their gaze and began busily wielding their forks.

Conversation languished at that point, except for a compliment from him on her cooking and her comment that she'd had most of the food delivered from the restaurant downstairs. Once upon a time they'd had no trouble talking for hours, Zara thought as she cast about for something, anything, to say.

'Tomorrow . . .' 'Which day . . .'

She smiled. 'You go first this time.'

'Which day would be convenient for you to come in to the office on a weekly basis?'

'Why? For what?'

'Under the new circumstances, there will occasionally be paperwork for you to sign, meetings you must attend.'

'There will?'

'It would be most efficient if you chose one morning or afternoon of the week for your regular visit to the office. The staff would always know when to expect you and could plan accordingly.'

'But why once *every* week? Couldn't you just have someone phone me when I'm needed?'

For the first time since she'd met him Rand appeared flustered, but only for a moment. 'Regular visits would be more efficient.'

'I don't think . . .'

'I had planned for you to use an office near mine but,' he smiled, 'you could use Heinrich's. It's still empty and he had a swivel chair exactly like the one at the estate. I guarantee no one will say a word if you spend the entire time spinning it around.'

She had to smile, too. He'd remembered, even though it seemed like forever since their talk that day in the estate's library and her comments about growing up with her grandfather and Mrs Parker as guardians.

'That one spin was enough to sweeten a bad memory. It would probably be better if I were closer to you.' She could feel her cheeks redden at the unintentional double entendre. 'Your office, I mean.'

'Would Tuesday mornings be acceptable for you?'

'Sounds okay.' He refilled her glass but not his own. 'Don't you like the wine?'

'It's delicious but two glasses is my limit to-night. Remember, it's Sunday and I have an early start in the morning.' He put his fork down on the plate and patted his lean stomach. 'Thanks for a wonderful meal. Now, your turn. What were you going to say?'

'My house is ready. I can move home tomorrow.' Maybe now he would beg her to stay, tell her he was sorry he'd been so stubborn lately, that it was stupid to let the problems with Heinrich's will ruin something as important as their relationship.

She lifted her glass and tilted it to study the wine. If she held it just so, in front of the candle, the liquid glowed blood red.

As his silence lengthened she blinked rapidly, fighting back tears she refused to shed. Eventually she won the battle and put down her glass.

'Did you bring the cheque for the Centre?' The candle's flame danced and she leaned forward to snuff it out. Enough of this romantic fantasy, she thought.

'I arranged to have the money transferred to their bank on Tuesday.'

'That's very efficient. Thank you.' She pushed back her chair and picked up their plates.

'Zara, I don't know what to say.'

'Then say nothing at all.' She pushed open the swinging door with her hip. 'I'll be gone by the time you get back from Treville.' The door swung closed behind her.

She'd rinsed off the plates and was stacking them in the dishwasher when the door swung open again. Rand carried in the platter with the remains of their pasta.

'If you'll wait a couple days, I'll be able to help you move.' He put the dishes down on the counter.

'That's not necessary. I don't have much stuff and Billie said she and Abe would help me pack it up and move it back to the house.'

'I'll call Bob and tell him I won't be coming to Treville this weekend.'

'No, I don't think that's a good idea. I'll leave the apartment keys with the concierge.' She reached for the platters but he put out his hand to stop her, catching her fingers to tug her around to face him.

'Zara, please . . .'

'You don't want me here.' She pulled free and backed away. 'You don't want me at all, now. Fine, I can accept that. But don't pretend to care, okay? It hurts too much.'

'Don't do this, Zara. I'm not ready for this conversation but I do care.'

'Not enough.' She pushed him away and went back to get the rest of the dishes. 'And not the way I want you to.'

He followed her back into the dining room where he took the salad bowls out of her hands. 'You made dinner. I'll clean up.'

'Fine.' She was almost out of the room when he spoke again.

'I'll re-wrap the painting for you before I leave. It's heavy so I'll ask the concierge to help carry it down.'

The despised tears filled her eyes again. This time they would not be denied so she didn't turn to face him. 'No, don't. It's not mine any more.'

She got ready for bed and lay there, knowing she wouldn't sleep, listening as he moved around the apartment. Eventually all noise ceased and she lay there, listening to the silence and thinking about all the different ways, maybe better ways, she could have handled the evening.

At last it was almost dawn and she heard him showering and getting ready for his trip. When he left for Treville, he paused outside her bedroom door. She held her breath but eventually she heard his footsteps again as he moved away. His keys jingled as he locked the apartment door.

Finally, she slept.

CHAPTER 14

When Rand came home Monday evening he sensed the emptiness of the apartment as soon as he walked through the door.

So. She'd really left him.

As he wandered through the rest of the apartment he thought it strange how, until she was gone, he hadn't noticed the way her things had filled and changed his home.

The bedroom and closet she'd used were empty of everything except her scent lingering in the air. The guitars and scattered sheet music were gone from the corner of the living room. In the kitchen there was no junk food in the cupboards, no oven-warm cookies in a bowl, no left-over pizza in the fridge.

He did find one reminder of her: another note taped to the coffee pot.

After everything changed, she'd begun leaving him notes, telling him about meals, phone calls, or meetings. Rand tugged this note off the pot and unfolded the paper. Its message was painfully blunt. 'Good bye'.

He crumpled it up and hurled it across the room.

Enough of this, he thought, and pushed through the door to the dining room. So she was gone. Why should he allow that fact to send him reeling?

He stopped short in the doorway, realizing she'd left him one last unpalatable surprise.

Saturday night, after he'd cleaned up their dinner, he'd packaged the portrait of her family and propped it in the front hall, ready for her to take when, if, she left. While he was in Treville someone had unwrapped and rehung it on the dining room wall.

He was all alone and the little black-haired girl still laughed at him.

'What made you think this would work? It's crazy.' Billie shouted in Zara's ear, trying to be heard over the deafening music and boisterous kids. The walls of the dimly lit auditorium were practically vibrating.

'Just look at your son, Billie!' Zara shouted back. 'He's having a wonderful time.'

Kenny sat behind a console on the tiny stage, bouncing in his wheelchair as he listened to the CD he was playing for the gyrating teenagers. The song ended and he chatted into the microphone as he changed the music, just like a professional disc jockey.

'But a dance? It was a crazy idea. I don't know how you convinced the Centre's directors to let you organize this. Last I heard they were adamantly opposed.'

'The turning point might have been when I told them we'd be responsible for any mess the kids make. More likely they decided to be amenable after Rand deposited Heinrich's money in the Centre's bank account. I don't know why they gave me such a hard time about this. "Physically challenged" or not, these are still kids. Look over there.'

She pointed at a young couple in the middle of the dance floor. A young man in a wheelchair held a pretty girl on his lap. Her arms were wrapped around his neck and they were both laughing as he spun them circles.

'That's very nice, of course, but can you explain to me how Abe and I ended up as chaperones for this shindig?'

'Now, Billie, you and I both know you're here for your son. Kenny's so proud to be in charge of the music and you wouldn't have it any other way, would you?'

'No, darn you, but I still blame you for this headache that's mushrooming behind my eyes.'

For the next two hours they didn't try to make themselves heard over the noise. Abe and two of the Centre's counsellors circulated around the darker corners of the room, shooing kids back into the light. Zara and Billie hovered over the buffet, restocking the goodies and cans of pop from supplies Zara had persuaded a local grocery chain to donate below cost.

At eleven o'clock Kenny put on the last piece of music. When it was over the lights were all switched on and the party-goers streamed outside to where their parents waited. Abe helped Kenny pack away the music and took him home, since they both had school the next day. The two counsellors who'd volunteered to help were checking the rest of the building to make sure everyone had left.

Zara and Billie stood alone in the middle of the big room, trash bags and broom in hand.

'You said it would be fun. You said I wouldn't regret it.' Billie spun slowly in a circle, surveying the party debris. Napkins, paper plates and empty pop cans were scattered in the bleachers and piled around overflowing trash and recycling containers. Tattered decorations hung limply from the walls. 'Well, Zara, I have to tell you I *am* regretting this.'

'This won't take us long to clean up. You'll be home in bed within an hour, I promise.' Zara's nose wrinkled when she lifted out the plastic lining from the trash cans and tied each top into a tight double knot. 'Whew, what a stink.'

'At least it's finally quiet enough to hear ourselves think.' Billie took a large clear plastic bag into the bleachers and began collecting pop cans.

'So where'd you get that shiny new briefcase I saw you carrying earlier this week?'

'From the staff at the Centre. There was a novel, an apple, and a crossword book inside when they gave it to me. I guess they find it hilarious to think of me as a business person.'

'You don't exactly fit the image, do you?' Billie put the bag full of cans near the exit and picked up another empty one before heading back into the bleachers. 'I thought you were only going to work Tuesday mornings?'

'I've been going in as much as two or three mornings a week, depending on what's happening. After all, I'm responsible for the company now. I have to keep an eye on things.' Zara didn't feel it necessary to mention she'd also been half-hoping she'd run into Rand.

'Keep an eye on things?' Billie asked. 'What things?'

'Don't sound so surprised. There are lots of things for me to do. I go to board meetings. I sign cheques, write letters, and read contracts.'

'You? Read contracts?'

'When I told Rand I wanted to be part of the decision-making process he put me in charge of any requests they receive for charity.' She hefted two bags of trash and puffed her way across the room to where she'd been arranging the bulging sacks near the exit.

'So, are you seeing much of Rand?'

'No, not really. He's a very busy man.'

'What's going on, Zara? I thought you two were a hot item but, as far as I can tell, he hasn't been to your place since you moved home.'

'No. For a while I thought . . . Things just didn't work out, okay? It happens. We can't all be as lucky as you and Abe.' Zara dropped another load of trash beside the first. 'How are you doing with the recycling?'

'That's the last, thank heavens.' Billie placed the bags of pop cans near the stack of trash bags, then came to help Zara finish sweeping the hardwood floor. 'You don't see him at all?'

'Not at the office. Once or twice I thought I saw him in the audience at The Kicking Horse. I almost asked Doris or Roggo if they'd seen him there but in the end I didn't.'

'Why not? Then at least you'd know he wants to see you. There's no other reason for him to go to a place like that.'

'It doesn't matter. I've known for days that it was over.'

'Are you okay?' Billie put her hand on Zara's shoulder.

'I miss him.' Actually she missed him terribly and it was getting worse but she wasn't about to admit it out loud. That would give it a reality she didn't think she was ready to cope with.

'Oh, honey.' Billie wrapped her arms around Zara and patted her back.

Zara returned the hug and blinked back the stupid tears brought on by her friend's warm sympathy. 'It's over and that's that.'

'Don't give him another thought. Men are jerks.'

She had to chuckle as she wiped her eyes. 'Even Abe?'

'Abe is a prince among frogs.'

'Right. So have you and Abe set a date for the wedding?'

Zara was grateful when the subject changed to Billie's life. She couldn't fool either Billie or herself that the next few weeks were going to be easy but neither was she willing to wallow in pain. That wouldn't change anything.

Besides, one recent development because of her involvement with Rand and Forster Pacific had turned out well. She'd never realized how many letters a big corporation received from organisations or individuals asking for money. It was really rewarding to be able to make things easier for people who had more and worse troubles than hers.

Rand drew in a deep breath, held it for the count of three, then exhaled slowly. He had to do it two more times before his heartbeat slowed to normal. When he had his body under control, and felt sure he could maintain that control for the length of a meeting, he leaned forward and picked up the phone to buzz Tim.

'Please ask Zara to come in.'

He brushed a fleck of lint from his sleeve. When he looked up, she was there. Immediately his pulse began to race, as it had for every one of their Tuesday morning meetings. So much for being prepared. He stood up and gestured to the chair opposite his desk.

'Please. Sit down.' Yes, and please do it quickly. At least then most of her body would be obscured by his desk. Why, oh why, did she wear clothing to these meetings that seemed specifically designed to drive him crazy?

The suit she wore today, teal blue and clinging to every curve, the skirt flipping around her thighs as she walked, was enough to cloud the mind of a man made of iron.

'Thank you.' She placed the ridiculously large briefcase on the floor at her feet.

'How are you?' he asked. Did she miss him? Did she ever think about the time they'd shared? 'How's the music business?'

'Wonderful. Terrific. I heard from a producer in Nashville and one in Los Angeles. Two of country music's biggest stars are going to record one of my songs as a duet plus a brand new jazz trio are going to perform it for a movie sound track.'

'Very exciting.' Enough polite chitchat. He could handle only a basic amount of knowledge about her other life. Too many details made it too real. 'You wanted to talk to me?'

'Yes.' She leaned forward, snapped open her briefcase, and searched through its contents.

He blinked and quickly averted his eyes. He didn't think she was wearing anything except a scrap of black lace under that jacket. He focused on the pen in his hands, concentrating on reading the manufacturer's name scripted in very fine print on its pocket clip.

When she sat back he looked up again.

'Before we begin I have some news for you,' he said.

He heard the whisper of stockings as she crossed her legs. 'Yes?'

'The police discovered the identity of the driver who hit my car. Remember the young man who was arrested for attacking you?'

'The mayor's nephew?'

'The fingerprints they found in the stolen truck were his. When they brought him in for questioning, he told them he was actually looking for you but when he saw me go into the Centre that day, he stole the truck and waited for me to come out. If I hadn't been there that day, it would have been you he tried to kill.'

'This was about revenge?'

'Seems his buddies found out how I stopped him with a toy gun. Because of this and the fire department's report on your house, the police now feel positive the accidents were coincidental.'

'I'm really happy that's over. At least now we don't need to wonder if my cousin was really trying to hurt us. Any news about Sheila?'

'She's staying with Neil until the hearing.'

'I phoned but she won't talk to me.'

'She's not talking to anyone at the moment, on the advice of her lawyer. She will never be able to practise law again but she probably won't go to jail. They have asked their lawyer to petition the court for a portion of Heinrich's estate.'

'That's one of the things I wanted to ask you about today. Would you please arrange for them each to get one third of the cash realized from the auction?'

'One third? Each?'

'For years Heinrich promised them money in his will and I intend to make his word good. Sheila will probably need some to pay her lawyer.'

'Fine. Anything else?'

'This is a list of charities which have approached me for funding.' She handed him the piece of paper to which clung the subtle aroma of her perfume.

His nostrils flared and he remembered waking in the night with her asleep in his arms, nights when he would bury his nose in her hair and just breathe.

It was a struggle but he managed to direct his attention to the actual words written on the paper. As he read the list, his frustration and anger flared hotter.

'I haven't heard of even one of these organisations. The "Hoot Owl Rescue Squad"? The

"League for Neglected Mothers"? The "Preservation of Good Music Society"?' He tossed the paper onto his desk. 'Where are you finding these people? My staff researched the last list you gave me and only one group on it was even a registered charity.'

'I don't find them. They find me. It seems to be a word of mouth thing.'

'Word of mouth? I agree. Word of an easy mark has probably circulated in the con artist community.'

'I resent being called an easy mark. I don't ask you to give anything to any group unless we are able to substantiate their claims and they prove to be truly needy.'

Needy. He needed, probably more than any other person she knew. He craved her smile, her kisses, her loving. The hunger was relentless.

He inhaled slowly, through his mouth to avoid her scent as much as was humanly possible, then exhaled carefully so she wouldn't notice, silently counting as he did so. After two repetitions he was able to ignore his body's unruly demands.

He couldn't do this any more.

'It's up to you.' He pushed the paper back to her side of his desk.

She looked at him, surprised, and he knew why. He had capitulated too easily. Until today, he'd refused her requests until she was forced to use her status as company owner and his titular boss to pull rank. The worst part was he could tell she secretly enjoyed forcing him to do as she asked.

'I've appointed two staff members and one of the junior lawyers to work with you on your charitable requests. They'll do the research, reporting back to you. From now on you can deal directly with our accountants. They've been given a dollar figure for your total annual budget but you will ultimately decide on the recipients.'

'I get to decide?'

'Yes, but once you've spent the budget there won't be any more, no matter how deserving or needy the cause, until next year, so choose wisely. If you need any further information, you can call Tim.'

Just for a minute he thought he saw pain in her eyes, but then it was gone. She said nothing but he knew what she was thinking. They both knew he was doing this to avoid her.

'Well. I guess I'd better be going. I know how busy you are.' She leaned forward again to close and pick up her briefcase.

She stood and waited. Usually he showed her to the door. Before today he hadn't been able to resist the opportunity to touch her back as he walked her across his office.

Today he couldn't stand up without embarrassing himself. He couldn't let her know how weak he was in her presence. Next time things would be better. If there had to be a next time.

Calm. Cool. Collected. Controlled.

Things would happen his way from this point forward.

Zara sat across from Rand and waited for the explosion she expected, even hoped was coming.

Today she'd gone too far and she knew it. She'd deliberately prodded the lion in a desperate effort to shake things up.

After choosing her witnesses carefully, she'd countermanded one of his orders in front of his staff.

Walt and Tim were both intensely loyal to Rand and neither would ever say something outside this office that would be detrimental to his authority. Rand would be annoyed, even embarrassed, but there would be no lasting damage.

For two weeks she had obediently dealt with lawyers and accountants about her charity work. She'd accepted messages relayed through Tim when her signature was necessary on a document. She'd even stopped complaining about the guards he still insisted on sending to escort her home at night from Roggo's.

Enough was enough.

Her emotions were in such a tangle she'd developed writer's block, a new experience. She hadn't created a decent song in the weeks since she'd moved back to the duplex. Weeks that felt like months or maybe years.

'Walt and Tim? Would you please excuse us?' Rand's expression revealed nothing.

The other two men finally managed to close their mouths, which had fallen open in shock, and hurried out.

He leaned back in his chair and tapped the file he still held against his chin as he contemplated her face.

She felt like squirming under his examination but managed to control the movement.

'So . . . you know better than myself how this deal should be handled.'

'Galway has a proven track record and is better equipped to fulfil this contract. Their company has fewer employee rights violations registered with the union.'

'You've done some research.'

'Yes, I have. Besides, I don't like the way Thomas Brother treats his secretary.'

'I assume this means you feel you are ready to run Forster Pacific.'

Zara watched, bewildered, as he stood up and stepped to one side.

'Come here.'

'I never intended . . .'

'Come here!' Something in his tone had her on her feet and moving around to his side of the desk. 'Sit down.'

'I only wanted . . .'

His hand closed on her shoulder and pressed downward relentlessly, his fingers stopping short of causing her pain, until she was seated in his chair. The leather was warm from his body.

Once she was seated he dropped the file in front of her. 'Here you go.'

He opened a desk drawer, removed some papers which he placed in his briefcase, then strolled across the room to the closet where he took out his overcoat.

'What are you doing?'

'I'm going on holiday. A novel concept but I'm sure if I try hard enough I'll get the hang of it.'

She watched helplessly as he donned the coat and straightened the lapels.

'But what about the business?'

'I'm sure everything will be fine. After all, you will be at the helm, won't you?'

'This has gone far enough.' She jumped up.

'Sit down!' His words thundered in the room. Finally she heard frustration in his voice, saw storms in his eyes, and realized just how angry he was. She sat.

'You push me so hard every time you walk in this door that I don't know if I'm coming or going. Well, now you've got your wish. I'm going.'

She could swear she felt her heart splintering. She wasn't sure because it was difficult to hear anything over the roaring in her ears.

'No!' She shook her head in disbelief.

'Yes.'

'But I don't know how to run the company.'

'You'll learn. I did.'

'When will you be back?'

He looked away and put his hand on the door knob. 'I don't know.'

She ignored the tears that filled her eyes and ran down her cheeks. 'Rand.' She whimpered his name. She knew it and didn't care. She was about to beg and didn't care. 'Don't leave me.'

His expression softened for an instant, then all the emotions on his face were ruthlessly wiped away, anger included. 'I must.'

'What about Sheila's hearing next week?'

'I've discussed everything with the lawyers and they know how to handle the situation. I won't be needed until that day.'

'What if something goes wrong? What if there are more threats?'

'There won't be.' He opened the door. 'I'll talk to Tim and Walt on the way out and tell them I'm leaving. Tim will help you around here and Walt will know where to find me, if absolutely necessary.' He left without looking back.

He was gone. Was he gone for good?

Zara crossed her arms on Rand's desk, put her head down, and cried until there were no tears left. Then she used the small bathroom off Rand's office to splash cold water on her face and tidy her hair. She dragged his comb through her hair and eyed herself in the mirror.

340

Maybe she should try positive affirmations. Billie said she looked in the mirror every morning and told herself she was a great mother, a valued employee, and a good friend, adding in anything appropriate to get herself through a difficult day. She claimed that if a person did it every day pretty soon she would feel good about herself, and that if that person really believed, the things came true.

It was worth a try, wasn't it?

'You can do this,' she told her reflection. 'It's only for a short while. He won't be able to stay away for long.'

No. Not positive enough.

'You are a smart woman. You can handle everything that happens and if a problem arises, you will delegate it to the correct expert.' She braced herself on the counter and leaned forward to stare at her own eyes. 'You can do this!'

She stood tall, straightened her blouse, and nodded to her reflection. That felt pretty good, if a little silly.

Maybe Billie had something with this.

Back at the desk she buzzed her own office to talk to the staff she'd left working on the charity requests. Might as well start with something she knew she could do right and then work her way up to running the rest of Forster Pacific.

Zara's hands fell to her lap and she stared open mouthed at the television screen. Up until this point she and Billie had been enjoying a comfortable evening relaxing after a terrific meal the three of them had cooked together. She was watching the evening news, Billie was reading a book, and Kenny was in his room, quiet for the first time this evening while he did homework.

She tried to say her friend's name but nothing came out past the ball of panic blocking her throat. She tried again.

'Billie,' she croaked.

'Yeah?' Her friend turned a page and kept reading.

'Is there a big letter "M" on my forehead?'

'What did you say?' She lowered the book slightly until her face appeared over the top edge.

'Is there an "M" tattooed on my forehead and I'm the only one who can't see it?'

'Is there some point to this?'

'Rand said I was an easy mark for con artists.'

'Well, you are generous but I don't think it's that bad.'

'I'll phone. Maybe it's not too late.' She jumped to her feet and raced to where Billie usually kept her portable phone. The base was there but no phone receiver. 'Where's the phone, Billie?'

'I don't know. Maybe Kenny left it in the kitchen.'

Zara leaped for the doorway and saw it on the counter. She grabbed it and punched out Tim's phone number.

'What's going on?'

Tim's line was busy. She disconnected and pushed the redial button. Still busy. She did it again.

'Answer me, Zara.'

'There was an item on the news about some people who were arrested this afternoon.' Still busy. She tried again. 'They were running a charity scam.'

'And?'

'I recognized one of the men in the picture. He came to pick up a cheque from me today. This afternoon.' Still busy.

'Oh, shoot.'

'You can say that again.' This time it began to ring. 'Shush, it's ringing. Hello? Tim? It's Zara.'

Billie plopped down at the kitchen table to listen.

'Did you see tonight's news? The part about the people who were arrested today? I think that was the guy who came to my office this afternoon. Yes, I gave him the cheque. Yes, my staff investigated him first.' She began to pace in circles around the kitchen table.

'According to the report, he must have been arrested almost immediately after he left my office. I want you to call the television station and track down the reporter who did the story. Find out the name and phone number of the detective who made the arrests. Maybe the jerk still had the cheque on him.'

Zara listened for a minute. 'Sounds good. Phone me back at Billie's as soon as you know anything. In the meantime, I'll phone the company accountant and tell him what happened. He can stop payment on the cheque first thing in the morning.'

Billie made tea while Zara talked to accountants and lawyers. Then they sat in tense silence and waited for Tim's call.

Zara picked the phone up on the first ring. 'Hello? You talked to the detective? He won't? Why? You've got to be kidding! Give me his name and number.' She scribbled on the pad of paper she'd borrowed from Billie.

'How is that spelled? O,u,e,l,l,e,t,t,e. One more thing, who's in charge of the Vancouver police force? And the name of the mayor? Thanks. Yes, I'll let you know what happens.'

'What did he say?' Billie asked.

'The detective wouldn't give Tim any information about the arrest we saw on the news. He also refused to tell Tim if the man had the cheque on him when he was picked up.' Zara started dialling the detective's number. 'Something about not having time because he's going to a party and we can call back in the morning.'

'What are you going to do?'

'I'm going to talk to Officer Ouellette and explain to him, politely but firmly, that I need that information immediately.'

'And if he still refuses to tell you anything?'

Zara bared her teeth in a ferocious smile. 'I guess I'll find out how much of Heinrich's blood really does flow through my veins.'

Twenty minutes and three calls later Zara put down the phone and leaned back in her chair.

'Wow,' Billie said. 'Maybe I should start calling you Heinrichetta?'

'I don't think so.' Zara held up her hands. They were trembling. 'I was scared to death. I hope I never have to do anything like that again.'

'But you did it.' Billie got up to pour them each another cup of tea. 'You found out that guy didn't get a chance to cash ForPac's cheque and Ouellette probably wishes he'd never heard of you. You should be pleased.'

Zara wrapped her arms around her chest, tucking her fingers under her arms, trying to stop the shaking. She felt so cold. How did Rand do this every day? She much preferred the adrenaline rush from performing. There was considerable difference between being scared she might sing badly and terrified that she'd lost fifty thousand of Forster Pacific's dollars.

'I have to convince Rand to come back.'

'Why don't you phone him?'

'No. I need to see him.' Zara gratefully accepted the hot cup from Billie and cradled it in her hands. 'There's a meeting on Thursday between Sheila, her lawyers, ForPac's lawyers, and the rest of the family. He'll be there.'

'Good. You can talk to him after the meeting. Maybe you should take him out to dinner.'

'No. Not dinner. But I will talk to him after the meeting.' No matter how scared she was. After all, hadn't she just won a difficult confrontation? Maybe if she had a little moral support . . .

'Billie? Can I buy you lunch on Thursday? And then, maybe, you could stick around for a few hours?'

'Are you bribing me to come with you to the meeting?'

'Yes, I am, all right? I admit it, I'm scared and I need some moral support from my best friend.'

'I'll have to get an afternoon off work.' Billie looked thoughtful. 'Which restaurant?'

'Your favourite, The William Tell. I'll even buy the pizza for dinner with Kenny that evening.'

'Okay, you convinced me. I'll go with you to the meeting but if it's really boring I'll expect a bottle of wine with the pizza.'

Zara shivered and pulled her jacket tighter across her chest. Thank goodness she'd told Billie they should bring their jackets to the meeting so they didn't need to go back upstairs.

They'd been sitting on uncomfortable wooden chairs and listening to the lawyers talk for over an hour in a chilly meeting room on the ground floor of Forster Pacific's head office. She didn't know which was worse, the cold or her numb bottom but

346

Billie, who sat to her left, didn't seem bothered by either.

Maybe it's the drab wintry afternoon, Zara thought as she glanced out the wall of windows to her right. The sun had never really showed its face today and it was so cold the rain drops on the panes had hardened into rivulets of ice.

Raised voices drew her attention back inside. The large space was set up much like a courtroom, with rows of chairs separated by a centre aisle and facing two tables. Between the tables a raised dais held a single chair which a psychologist currently occupied.

At one table Sheila, elegant and composed, appeared to be ignoring her lawyer's low-voiced comments. Opposite them, ForPac's team of lawyers watched carefully while their boss asked questions.

The police officer in charge of the case observed quietly from immediately behind Zara and Billie. Neil and Fran sat alone in the front row on the other side of the centre aisle. A gaggle of reporters, barred from the building, waited outside for the participants to emerge. One enterprising photographer snapped shots through the windows.

Mrs Parker had swept into the room on Uncle Crawford's arm, which was surprising considering he'd always been so critical of her relationship with Heinrich. He'd tenderly settled her into a seat then sat down beside her. After placing her purse on her lap, Mrs Parker smiled benignly at everyone else in the room.

The grin of pride and possession on Uncle Crawford's face made Zara wonder if the former housekeeper had found a new companion.

She supposed Mrs Parker was here to see the results of her meddling. Why, finally free after years of obeying Heinrich's orders, was she determined to keep an eye on what she perceived to be his interests?

Ever since Zara could remember, whatever their private relationship, in public he'd treated her like a servant rather than as the woman who shared his bed. As she grew older Zara had often questioned Mrs Parker's motives, her seemingly endless patience with the old man's foibles. Now she wondered – all these years, had the housekeeper loved Heinrich?

Zara had only caught a glimpse of Rand because he arrived just before the lawyers opened the proceedings. He'd remained standing at the back of the room, and she would have had to turn completely around in her seat to see him, but she thought he looked tired.

'Have you read these anonymous letters, Doctor Towne?' Mr Faber, ForPac's lawyer, put one hand on the sheaf of papers stacked on the corner of a table.

'I have,' answered the psychologist. Mr Faber had already established Doctor Towne as an acknowledged expert in criminal behaviour. The doctor's list of credentials had been impressive and they'd been told that all the court cases at which he'd testified for the prosecution resulted in convictions.

'In your professional opinion, was Randall Tremayne justified in seeing them as a serious indication of danger? To believe Zara Lindsey and himself were in jeopardy?'

'Yes, sir.'

'In your experience are such threatening letters the act of a coward?'

'I wouldn't word it exactly that way.'

'In layman's terms, Doctor Towne?'

'Yes, sir.'

Zara noticed the doctor wasn't looking at Faber. He was staring at something beyond the lawyer's left shoulder. She turned around, trying to decide who or what he was looking at. Only four people occupied that side of the quasi-courtroom. Several empty rows separated Neil and Fran from Hoffman, who sat at the back with Tony, one of the bodyguards hired by Rand to escort her.

Strange that they'd sit so far back when the whole section was empty. Come to think of it, hadn't Hoffman been accompanied by two of his men? When she scanned the room she discovered that his burly employee was stationed near the only other exit.

Was Rand expecting trouble?

'This kind of behaviour is often accompanied by other anti-social actions and personal deficiencies,' Doctor Towne continued.

'Can you explain?'

'They are usually incompetent and unable to hold a job. They blame others when they don't get promoted, claiming to be victims of a plot. They have one or more failed relationships. They see all advice as criticism and can be paranoid, perhaps delusional.'

Zara realized he was staring pointedly at Neil or Fran. She leaned forward so she could look around Billie to see her cousin and his wife more clearly. Neil was red-faced and fidgeting. Fran whispered in his ear and gripped his knee tightly with one gloved hand.

'Are there any other personality or physical traits common to this type?'

'Such men are often impotent.'

'I am not!' Neil yelled and jumped to his feet. Fran grabbed his arm and tried to drag him down again but he shook her off. 'You're full of it.'

'Sit down, you fool, and shut up!' Sheila shouted at her brother.

Neil's face went white when he realized what he'd revealed. He turned to run but Hoffman's men moved to stand directly in front of the closed doors.

Billie leaned over and whispered to Zara, 'You don't have to buy the bottle of wine.'

'Do you have something to add to the proceedings, Mr Bendan?' asked Faber.

'No, he doesn't.' Sheila rose to her feet and directed a menacing look at her brother. 'Sit down, Neil. You must be quiet and let me handle this.'

'Don't you think you've been quiet long enough, Bendan?' Rand sauntered down the centre aisle to stand beside Neil. 'Or are you going to hide behind your sister all your life?'

The next few minutes were rough and tumble. Rand ducked Neil's fist, then side-stepped his lunge. By the time Neil regained his feet, Tony and his partner had a firm grip on his upper arms.

'I'll take over now, gentlemen.' The police officer, who'd been silent and motionless to that point, snapped handcuffs on Neil's wrists then looked at Rand. 'Are you going to swear out a complaint?'

'Yes.' Rand picked up his overcoat which he'd dropped while getting out of Neil's way.

'Come down later this afternoon and we'll do the necessary paperwork.' The officer took hold of Neil's elbow.

'Fran? Will you come bail me out?' At Neil's plaintive question his wife picked up the purse which had been knocked out of her hands at the beginning of the melee.

'Did *you* write those horrible, nasty letters, Neil?' she asked.

'Was that so terrible? I never even knew Rand had been in a car accident 'til Sheila told me. I wouldn't have actually hurt Zara or Rand, no matter how treacherous and greedy they are. I just wanted what Heinrich promised me, you know that, honey.'

'How could you embarrass me like this?'

'But, honey, I did it for you.'

'What good is the money if we're shunned? What if my friends think I knew about it, or even helped you? For all I care, you can rot in jail. You'll hear from my lawyer tomorrow about a divorce. I want my share of Heinrich's money before you spend it all on defence lawyers.'

She tilted up her nose and swept by Neil, ignoring his pleas for forgiveness.

He stumbled after her, followed by the policeman and Hoffman's men.

'Why couldn't you just leave it alone, Rand?' Sheila asked quietly, her face weary and grey. 'I'm going to lose my career anyway for altering Heinrich's will. I'd claimed responsibility for writing the letters. You had someone to punish. You didn't need both of us.'

'He frightened Zara, Sheila, and for that he has to pay the consequences. It would be wrong to let you take the blame for him.'

'Who gives a damn about what's wrong? Neil's my little brother.'

'I'm sorry you feel that way, Sheila.'

352

'And I feel sorry for you, Rand.' She took her lawyer's arm and left.

Within moments everyone else in the room had gone except Rand, Zara, and Billie. The two women hadn't left their seats during the confrontation.

'Hello, Zara.' He donned the overcoat and shoved his hands into the pockets.

'Hi.' She couldn't think of anything to say. She didn't feel brave enough to ask the really important questions like, when was he coming back? Did he love her at all?

'Stand up,' Billie whispered and jabbed her elbow into Zara's ribs. Zara leaped to her feet but still said nothing.

'Oh, jeez,' Billie said, then she stood too. 'Well, that was exciting. I'm glad Zara invited me along. I was wondering, did you plan that whole thing or did you just get lucky?'

'A person can't wait for luck if he wants to get things done. Faber suggested to Sheila's lawyer that we might agree to an out-of-court settlement if everyone involved attended a meeting.'

'Setting the furniture up like a courtroom was a nifty idea,' Billie said.

'I can't take credit for that. It was Faber's idea.'

Zara felt Billie's hand pushing against the middle of her back and allowed herself to be propelled toward where Rand stood in the centre aisle. As soon as she was beside him, Billie's shove changed to a grip on her jacket as she hauled Zara to a stop.

'Sheila was really upset,' Zara commented.

He shrugged. 'I'm sorry for that but I couldn't allow her to take the blame for Neil's actions. She's got enough problems of her own.'

She jerked free of Billie's hand and edged around him, intent on escaping. 'We've got to go now. We promised Kenny we'd go out for pizza tonight.'

'Hey, Rand, do you want to . . . Ouch!' Billie glared at Zara, who'd deliberately stepped on her toe to prevent the looming invitation to join them for pizza.

'Bye, Rand.' She grabbed Billie's hand and dragged her out the door. She hadn't gone far when she changed her mind and rushed back alone. What would it hurt to ask at least one of the questions? The worst he could say was 'no'. What could it hurt?

He was still standing in the same place though now he seemed sort of droopy and sad as he looked at his feet.

'Rand?'

His spine straightened with a jerk and his expression cleared.

'Yes?'

'Does this mean you'll be back here in the office tomorrow?'

'No, Zara.'

It hurt. She spun on her heel and hurried back to Billie.

'What was that all about?' she asked.

'I asked him if he was coming back to work tomorrow.'

'And?'

'He said no.'

'You should have let me ask him out for pizza. We could have worked on him over dinner.'

'I doubt we'd have succeeded.'

'How about I send him an anonymous letter that threatens you? It worked before, maybe it will again.'

'Do you have any idea how petty that sounds?'

'You already thought of it, didn't you?'

Zara nodded miserably. 'I can't do something that dishonest.'

'What do you care, as long as it gets results? But if you've changed your mind . . .' She shrugged.

'He's got to come back, Billie, but not because of a lie. Oh, no!' Zara saw there were still a few reporters lingering outside. She pulled her hood as far down over her face as it would go. 'Keep your head down. Maybe they won't notice us.'

'Yeah, that's going to work,' Billie said, sarcasm vibrating in every word. 'You're wearing a lemon yellow jacket and my raincoat is cherry red. As if they won't notice us. Isn't there a back way out of here?'

'I don't know. Let's ask.' She pushed back her hood and led the way over to the security guard standing beside the elevators. She followed his instructions carefully and eventually they found their way out of the building through a maintenance room.

They flagged down a taxi in the next block and breathed a sigh of relief once they were seated safely inside and heading for home.

'I can't do this, Billie.'

'Pay for the cab? My treat.'

'No. I don't have or want the skills necessary to run any business, much less one the size of Forster Pacific. I never knew how efficiently Rand tempered the pursuit of profit with caring for his staff. I never gave him enough credit for how hard he worked.'

'Why the heck didn't you tell *him* all this good stuff back there when you had the chance?'

'I couldn't today. I have something to prove to myself first.'

'Won't hurt to give him a little more time to miss you.'

'Hope not.'

'Let's get the cab to stop at the liquor store on the way home. I think after showing me such an exciting day, I owe *you* that bottle of wine.'

She couldn't go through with it. She didn't want to do this.

But she had to.

Zara could feel the sweat of panic forming and resisted the cowardly impulse to cancel the meeting. She had to calm down or she'd have to change her blouse – again. Only one more hour to get through and it would be over.

Rand had been gone for twenty days and she was about to chair her first board meeting. Twenty days of hell and, if she couldn't convince him to come back, there was no end in sight.

While Rand was on 'holiday' his staff had been competent, professional, and supportive during crisis after crisis. Things might have gone worse for her if Walt and Tim had told anyone the truth about what had happened to make Rand leave.

Even the two men had done their best to help ForPac survive her ineptitude and hopefully they'd also managed to prevent any expensive disasters. When it came to business, she'd been sent to school and knew without doubt she'd come close to failing.

On the other hand, she'd learned a lot. She'd given orders, made decisions, studied proposals. She was a master at delegating.

She'd even had to fire someone, a nightmare experience, the memory of which made her cringe when she recalled how she'd taunted Rand. Never again.

She glanced at her watch. Ten o'clock. It was time to go.

When she entered the boardroom, every place at the table was taken. She saw a mixture of annoyance, doubt and curiosity on every face, even those few who were clearly reserving judgement.

She glanced at her watch again. Two minutes after ten. She just had to get through the next hour. Sixty measly minutes until she could walk out of this room and out of this building.

She was going to look for Rand, apologize, and then beg him to come back to ForPac, if not to her. Running ForPac entailed taking risks. She didn't like the potential for causing so many people to lose their jobs if she made a bad mistake. She wanted to make people happy with her music, something she knew she was good at.

One day there'd been so many problems she'd briefly reconsidered telling Walt she'd received another anonymous threat, knowing that if Rand believed her to be in danger he'd come back.

She couldn't do it. Playing silly games had driven him away. Only a straightforward approach from her would bring him home. She had to go to Treville.

CHAPTER 15

Zara thought about turning the car around several times as she drove to Treville but after having a stern word with herself, she kept going.

As she neared a faded sign on the outskirts of town that read 'W LCOM TO TR VI LE' she pulled off the highway, intending to go back to Vancouver, but a van stopped in front of her, blocking the narrow space. Thinking they were turning around, too, she decided to wait for them to pull forward so she could turn her car.

The van's side door opened and half a dozen teenagers piled out, laughing and pushing each other around while they unloaded brushes, cans of paint and two ladders. She could have man-oeuvred the car around their vehicle but she was curious about what they were doing.

Soon she realized they had come to re-paint the town's welcome sign. She watched for a while, vicariously enjoying their fun, while they got as much of the bright paint on themselves as on the sign.

The young man who'd driven the van seemed to be in charge. He was directing the others, chiding them whenever the silliness seemed about to get out of hand, while he did most of the work himself. When they shook their brushes at him in retaliation, splattering all the different colours on his coveralls, he laughed as much as they did.

He was tall and dark and bossed everyone around. He was an attractive boy and someday he'd be a very handsome man. Rand must have been a lot like that boy once, she thought. He would have been about that young man's age when his world fell apart.

As a child and teenager, Rand must have had friends though he hadn't mentioned any when he related his tale. How had they reacted after the car accident? Had they turned away from him, too?

Her mind made up, Zara shifted the car into gear, pulled back onto the highway and turned right, for Treville. When she parked the car in front of Rand's storefront office she noticed his assistant, Bob, was scraping away the gilt letters on the inside surface of the large glass window.

She stepped out of her car and breathed deeply of the clear air, so different from the light smog that seemed to be part of nearly every day in the city.

He noticed her and came to open the door for her.

'Hello. You're Ms Lindsey, right?' He wiped off his fingers and shook her hand. 'Mr Main's not here right now.'

'Do you know where I can find him?'

'I think he's . . .'

The door swung open and banged into Zara, who was still standing just inside and hadn't seen the woman approaching the storefront.

'Oh, my dear! I'm so sorry. Are you okay?'

The elderly woman's eyes were bright with curiosity, her white curls bouncing around her head almost like miniature Slinky toys run amok.

'Yes, I'm fine, thank you.' While Zara rubbed her numb elbow she couldn't help staring at the woman.

She didn't stop moving, or so it appeared. She fidgeted around Zara and Bob, touching this, patting that. Even if she stood still for a moment, her hair continued to spring back and forth. Before the bounce in her curls had completely subsided she was moving, starting the reciprocal motion all over again.

'I saw you drive up and I just *had* come over and say hello. You're Dal's friend, aren't you?'

Zara drew breath to respond but the woman was talking again.

'I just knew it. Just the other day I told Sally . . . Sally's my daughter, the best cook in the whole province except for her biscuits. I said it then and I'll say it now – Jack Tremings would have married her except for those biscuits. Where was I? Oh, yes. Just the other day I told Sally that, mark my words, we would soon be hearing interesting news about that boy.'

Her gyrations paused and she whispered in Zara's ear. 'He's not been himself lately. Downright moody. He's never spent so much time in town before. It's always been here today and gone tomorrow for that boy.'

'Millie!' Bob said. 'You know Mr Main doesn't like you to gossip about him.'

'Why, Bob, as if I would. The very idea! I'm just concerned about that boy's troubles and, as his friend I want to help. And I'm sure Miss . . . What did you say your name was, dear?'

'She didn't,' Bob said. He shook his head but smiled and shrugged at Zara, as if to say he was sorry but helpless. She understood. Who could resist such relentless enthusiasm?

'My name is Zara Lindsey.'

'Zara? Such an unusual name, dear, but very nice. You have a beautiful, melodious voice. I bet you're a wonderful singer.'

'As a matter of fact . . .'

'Are you two engaged?'

'Engaged?' Zara felt dizzy, as if she were trapped in the eye of a verbal hurricane.

'I've said it before and I'll say it again – that boy should be married with a wife and little ones to care for. He works too hard, it's always business, business, business. Worry, worry, worry.

I've said it before and I'll say it again – no matter what happened in the past, a person has to make sure . . .'

'You'd better hurry back to the restaurant, Millie.' Bob interrupted with a sideways glance at Zara. He put his arm around the older woman and hustled her toward the door.

'I can see several customers lined up at the restaurant's counter and you know Sally can't cope without you.'

He shut the door behind her and when he turned back to Zara he was smiling ruefully. 'I'm sorry, Ms Lindsey. She has a good heart but she will talk.'

'I didn't mind. Do you know where . . . Dal is?'

'Mr Main said he intended to check out the old mill over on the north side of town. Stay on this street for five blocks, then turn left and go straight. You can't miss it.'

'Thanks.' When Zara went out to her car Millie was standing outside her restaurant with a middle-aged woman. The brown spiral curls, bouncing as she waved a greeting, made it clear they were mother and daughter.

She smiled and waved, then followed Bob's directions. Finally, on the outskirts of town, she saw an abandoned building with 'Tremayne's' painted in faded red letters on its side. Crossing her fingers, she drove around the back to the parking lot and saw his car.

She pulled up beside the Mustang, then thought for a minute before reversing and parking behind his car, blocking it between hers and the wall. She had to keep him in one place long enough to listen. This way he couldn't try to leave until she was finished, not unless he wanted to risk scraping that car.

The big gates that had once been the main entrance to the mill were chained and padlocked but on the far side of the parking lot she found a smaller door. An open padlock hung from the hasp and the door was ajar an inch or two. She pushed it open and tiptoed inside.

'Rand?' Her voice echoed and re-echoed weakly through the mostly empty building, bouncing back at her from the lofty roof. Sunlight shone through translucent panels near the high ceiling. She peered at the vague, ghostly shapes of machinery in the distance, trying to find him. 'Rand?'

'Why are you here?' his voice boomed out of the shadows.

She jumped and spun on her heel. Behind her lay an area that had obviously been an office. Metal rods hanging from the much higher roof supported more of the translucent ceiling panels. When she stepped closer, through an empty doorway, she realized that the wooden frames on either side must have once held glass panels to separate the clerical area from the dust and noise of the work floor.

Inside, a dozen desks of the same vintage as the two he and Bob used in the storefront were arranged in rows. Several held some very old office equipment. On the nearest desk she recognized a cumbersome adding machine, its pull handle snapped off in the middle. An old manual typewriter with missing keys sat nearby.

She scanned the shadows at the back of the office and saw him. Or rather, she saw his long legs.

Though the area where she stood was relatively well lit by stray sun beams, he was sitting in a patch of shadow at the back of the office.

His face and upper body were obscured but she could tell he was slouched in a large wooden swivel chair, his feet propped on an open desk drawer.

'I asked why you came here.'

'To beg. Why are you here?'

She couldn't read his reaction to her admission. Or if he reacted at all.

It was a few minutes before he answered her.

'The bank asked me to have a look at it for someone who's considering moving their business to Treville. I'm supposed to decide whether to fix up the place or tear it down. Perhaps I should consult a management expert, since there's one handy. What do you suggest?'

'I don't have any idea what you should do about this building.'

'Good Lord, she admits she doesn't know all the answers.'

She stepped closer, trying to see his face, but he lifted his feet off the drawer and rolled the chair back further into shadow.

'I'm willing to admit I don't know the answers to any number of questions, and I'll even throw in a truck load of doubts, if only you will come back to Vancouver with me.'

'I think she meant it when she said she was going to beg. This should prove interesting.'

'Rand, would you stop being silly?'

'Silly?' He stood so abruptly the chair rolled back and banged into the wall, shaking loose several boards and a cloud of dust. The boards slammed into the floor with enough force to start a chain reaction of vibrations. She looked up, horrified, as several of the suspended ceiling panels began to sway. They banged together spilling out more dust which thickened the air.

'Let's get out of here,' he said.

He followed her out of the building. They both collapsed against the wall, coughing and choking for a few minutes after they'd gained the clear air.

'Are you okay?' he asked.

'Yeah. I think so.' She grabbed a tissue from her pocket and wiped the tears from her eyes. 'That place is dangerous. No matter what you decide . . .' She broke off.

For the first time she could see him clearly and his appearance shocked her. He hadn't shaved in days and his eyes were bloodshot, though that might have been a reaction to the filth in the mill. She'd never before seen him in scruffy jeans and a torn sweatshirt but at least his clothes were clean.

What had happened to the compulsively immaculate man who not so long ago would not have dreamed of being seen in public without a freshly polished pair of shoes? Even in jeans at midnight, when he'd thought he was alone and she'd slipped in through the basement of the estate, he'd looked clean and pressed.

Today he looked as neglected and depressed as the building he'd been sitting in.

He noticed almost immediately how she'd parked her car.

'Making sure I don't get away?'

'Let's sit down together some place quiet, okay? We need to talk.'

He looked down in silence at the hand she'd placed on his arm but he didn't pull away. 'I had recently come to the same conclusion.'

'Do you want to drive into town? We can go to the cafe or your office.'

'No.' Finally he stepped back. 'Let's walk. I have a decision to make and there are more things I have to see first.' He studied the area behind the parking lot where machinery sat rusting away to reddish silt then looked down at her feet.

'Are you going to be okay in those shoes?'

She looked down at her feet, too, determined to

hide the love she knew would likely be visible in her eyes. His question proved he still felt the need to take care of her. She felt comforted by the knowledge.

'These have rubber soles, good for anything short of climbing a mountain,' she said, fighting the urge to say more, to ask him if he felt anything at all for her, other than the normal concern he would for any person visiting him here.

Before coming here today, she'd decided to ask him to come back for the sake of the company. Trying to force the issue of their relationship was how she got into trouble in the first place. She might wonder if he loved her but she wouldn't ask.

'Be careful where you put your feet. This place could be dangerous for the unwary.'

She walked silently at his side as he checked over the old equipment. 'What are you looking for?'

'Rust. Corrosion. Rot. How old the machinery is. If any of it is still viable for use with today's technology. I'm not sure exactly what's been put out here over the years. I need to know if any of this is salvageable before I can determine the cost of start-up.'

'They're going to re-open Tremayne's?'

'No. That type of business is no longer viable here and even if I tried to run this as a mill, automation has taken many of the jobs these people once held. They want to know if this space would be suitable to do fine carpentry. There are still skilled craftsmen in the area and they could pass on their talent, teach the younger people.' 'Isn't that going in the opposite direction of everyone else?' She helped him shift a large metal bar, then brushed the rust residue off her hands. 'I hear all the time about businesses getting more high-tech machinery, removing people from the creation process.'

'I think it will succeed. I've discovered there is a small but very rich market for top quality work. The really wealthy will pay the price to have the best.'

'Rand.' She looked at him over the roll of wire they were moving so he could examine the engine beneath. When he ignored the plea in her voice she tugged slightly, forcing him to look at her. 'ForPac needs the very best. Come back.'

'You can hire a paper pusher anywhere. Have Walt retain a head-hunter to steal the best from another firm.'

'They need you.'

'No one is irreplaceable.'

'You are.'

'Drop it, Zara.'

In the shock at hearing him actually say her name, her fingers loosened and the awkward roll of wire slipped from her grip.

'I didn't mean for you to take me quite so literally.' He chuckled.

It sounded as rusty from disuse as the metal all around them, but it was real.

'I came here today to ask you to come back with me.' She swallowed nervously and looked around for some place to sit down. She stepped carefully over to a pick-up truck that had been gutted for parts and perched on its tailgate.

She patted the metal beside her. 'Sit down, Rand. Please.'

He slowly placed the tangled wire to one side and studied her face. She didn't know what he thought he saw there, but couldn't repress a niggle of relief when he nodded and sat down.

'I am so sorry for the things I said to you. I allowed my personal,' she hesitated, searching for the correct word, then finally choosing one as innocuous as possible, 'agenda to affect our business relationship.' She waited in vain for some response, any response.

'I'm not totally incompetent but several of the deals you set up might be in trouble. Some of these guys won't deal with me. At first I thought it was because I was a woman. I soon learned that it's because I'm not *you*.'

'You're exaggerating the situation. Walt told me you're not doing too badly.'

'Ha! So Walt *has* been reporting to you. I knew it.' She jumped to her feet. 'You had no intention of walking away from ForPac. Just teaching the interfering woman a little lesson, huh? How long were you going to let me grovel? Ooohh, you make me so mad.'

She threw her hands up in frustration and whirled to leave.

Her foot slipped and her arms flailed as she felt herself begin to fall. Rand grabbed her and hauled her back onto the tailgate and into his arms.

'I warned you to be careful. Look at that, damn you.'

He pointed to the business end of a forklift, right where she would have landed if he hadn't caught her.

She looked at the rusty spikes and shivered. Then she felt his arms tighten around her. When she met his gaze there was heat in his eyes. She shivered again, this time from anticipation rather than fear.

'Rand?'

His answer was a kiss with a depth and passion she'd feared she'd have to live without forever. Because she'd feared she'd have to live without him.

When he lifted his head at last, she was curled in his lap. He leaned back against one side of the pickup and shifted so he could see her face.

'Why did you walk out on us?' she asked.

'I'm still not sure,' he said.

'You must have had a reason. You always have a logical reason for what you do.'

'You want the real reason?' he asked.

She nodded.

'I was angry. Angry at you and angry at myself. Oh, I told myself I was leaving because there was a crisis here in Treville and business had to come first. But I was lying to myself. I didn't know where we were going. Our personal life was a mess. We were at loggerheads at the office.' He shook his head. 'I don't handle that kind of confusion well.'

'I didn't think you were coming back. I was sure you didn't love me.'

'I'm sorry, honey. Walt told me you were upset but I really thought you could hold the fort while I straightened things out here. I knew if I managed to convince you to take me back, if we ever got together, I couldn't spend every weekend in Treville. It wouldn't be fair to you.'

'No. It wouldn't. Not the way things are right now.' She slanted him a look from beneath her lashes and was relieved to see his smile. She lifted her hand and rasped her fingernail across his unshaven jaw. 'But if you told them who you really are, then we could spend our weekends here together.'

He stiffened and his smile faded.

'I'm setting up the businesses with managers I've hired from Vancouver. They will run things here in town with the stipulation that my name is never revealed. Eventually, if they don't want to relocate to Treville permanently, they will train someone local as their replacement.'

'You're still determined not to tell anyone the truth?'

'Yes.'

'You are underestimating these people. I think your bad memories and your guilt are colouring your judgement.'

'If we're going to try to make this thing between us work, Zara, you have to understand that this issue is dead and as far as Treville is concerned, Randall Tremayne no longer exists. This will not change.' He lifted her off his lap and stood up. 'Maybe you should make up your mind right now.'

She looked at him and knew he was telling the truth. If she insisted on pursuing this discussion she would lose him.

But could she let it drop, when she knew that leaving it unresolved would affect all his decisions and probably their relationship in the future?

What about any children they might be lucky enough to have? What would he tell them when they asked about his childhood? Would he lie?

He'd crossed his arms over his chest and waited, staring steadily, calmly at her while she tried to think clearly through the doubts tearing at her.

The necessity for an immediate answer was taken away by a distant crash and children screaming.

Rand's head lifted. A minute later he was moving as quickly as possible through the maze of equipment, Zara close on his heels as they followed the sounds.

They found a gaggle of children huddled around a hole in the ground, peering down. Several were crying, all were scared.

'Get away from there, that's dangerous,' Rand shouted. He grabbed several by their jackets and hauled them away from the edge. The rest sidled backward on their own.

'What happened?' he asked.

When several kids all started talking and crying at once the two adults couldn't understand a word.

'Wait, wait.' Zara shushed them. 'One at a time.'

'You.' Rand pointed to one of the older children, a raw-boned girl with untidy corkscrew curls who looked about twelve or thirteen. 'Tell us what happened.'

She gulped back her sobs and tried to talk.

'We . . . we didn't mean any harm, Mr Main. Honest. We was just playing robbers and Benji fell down the hole.'

'He's down there?'

Rand and Zara both looked at the jagged hole in the ground just beyond the edge of a paved area, with dirt and loose sod on its other three sides. While they watched several clumps of dirt broke loose and fell into the hole.

'What is it?' she asked.

'I don't know,' he said. 'It could be almost anything. In the old days if they wanted to get rid of anything like scrap or garbage, they just dug

374

a hole and buried it. Maybe over the years it rotted or compressed and a sink-hole opened up.'

Two rusty girders lay across from one edge to the other. Massive cement blocks used for building retaining walls were stacked nearby. Dangerously near. If much more of the dirt broke loose on that side they could topple over into the hole, crushing everything in their path.

'Some big boys went across those pole things and they dared Benji to do it. He was scared but he did it anyways. He . . . he got part way across and he . . .' She began to sob and one of the boys took up the tale.

'He lost his balance and felled in, Mr Main, and then the big boys ran away.'

'What should we do, Rand?' Neither of them noticed that Zara had used his real name.

'First I'd better have a look.'

Moving very carefully, he went to the end of the nearest girder and stepped onto its surface. It shifted slightly under his weight as he inched out far enough to see down into the hole.

'Benji?' he called.

No answer.

'Can you hear him, Rand? Can you see him?'

Rand shook his head and inched further out onto the girder.

The other kids began to wail and Zara shushed them so Rand would be able to hear anything, even the smallest noise, from the hole.

'Benji, can you hear me?'

Just then they all heard the boy whimper and Zara sagged in relief. He was alive.

'Benji, you just lie still. We'll get you out as soon as we can.' Rand edged backward until he was on firm land again.

'What's your name, honey?' He put his hand on the sobbing girl's shoulder.

'Be . . . eth.'

'Do you know how to use a cellular phone?'

'Yes.'

'Here.' He handed her the keys to the Mustang. 'You know where my car's parked?'

'The black one? It's near the gap in the fence by the gate.'

'Use the silver key to unlock my car, then get the phone from the glove compartment and call the police. Tell them what's happened. Tell them to bring an ambulance, just in case. Can you do all that?'

'Yes.' She stood straighter. The other kids' sobs had quieted while Rand talked.

'Good girl. Hurry but be careful. Benji's counting on you. Come back as soon as you talk to them so I know they're coming.'

Before she was out of sight he turned to four of the boys. 'In the factory, near the office, is a big box. There's some rope inside and I want you guys to bring me all of it. Just be careful, okay? We don't want another accident.'

376

They nodded strenuously and took to their heels.

Rand turned to the last three littlest ones who were looking up at him with hope in their eyes.

'Okay, I want the rest of you to go down to the main gate and wait for the police. Your job is to show them where we are. Okay?'

They leaped to their feet and two ran past him. One little girl wrapped her arms around his leg in a hug, the only part of Rand she could reach, before she chased after the others.

Rand roamed the immediate area, studying the abandoned equipment.

'What do you want me to do?' she asked.

'I might need your help if the kids don't manage to bring someone else.' He stooped to study a machine's support structure.

'What are you looking for?'

'I need to find something that's heavy enough and strong enough to support my weight. Some of the pieces have been here so long the metal has disintegrated.' He squeezed a bar she thought looked solid and it fell apart in his fingers.

When the boys came back with the rope he tied one end around the axle of a tractor. Then he hung the loops of rope over his shoulder and walked toward the hole, feeding it out as he went. When he dropped the other end of the rope over the edge of the pit he was careful to avoid the side where he'd heard the boy crying.

'Keep the boys with you, Zara. I'm going down to have a look.'

'Wait! He might be bleeding and these would be better than nothing.' Zara kissed him when she gave him the tissues from her purse. 'Be careful.'

'I will, honey.' He put the tissues into his pocket.

He slowly lowered himself into the hole and Zara prayed the old rope would hold his weight. It felt like forever before she heard his voice.

'He's still alive.'

'Thank God,' she whispered.

Just then Beth ran back. 'They're coming,' she gasped and then they all heard the sirens.

Zara walked as close to the edge as she dared and called down to Rand. 'They're almost here.'

'Tell them I'll need some help down here. He's wedged in.'

Within seconds the area was swarming with police officers and volunteer firemen. Zara recognized Bob under one of the volunteer firemen's helmets.

She told one of the officers everything she knew then gathered all the children around her out of the way. Within minutes agitated parents arrived to collect their missing children, along with what seemed like more than half the town.

A policeman climbed down Rand's rope into the hole and, on his signal, two others lowered a stretcher. Then the rest of the men on the surface pulled together, hoisting the loaded stretcher carefully until they were able to swing it up and over the edge.

Then Rand and the officer climbed out and they all waited anxiously as the town's doctor bent over Benji.

Eventually he straightened up and smiled. 'He's going to be okay.' A woman who'd been hovering nearby, obviously Benji's mother, fell to her knees and began to weep.

Everybody crowded around Rand to thank him for his actions. The ambulance took Benji, his mother, and the doctor away. When the parents began scolding the rest of the children Zara discovered that they were supposed to be at a function in the community centre Rand built, not playing robbers in the abandoned mill.

She was enjoying the general jubilation of the people around her when she noticed Rand standing by himself away from the crowd, staring into the distance. She walked up behind him, put her arms around his waist, and rested her cheek on his shoulder.

'You're wonderful.'

'This was Tremayne property. I'm responsible for what happened here today, for that boy's injuries.'

Frustrated, she let him go and whacked him on the shoulder. 'You listen to me, Rand Tremayne. The bank repossessed this years ago, right? You don't own this any more, so what happened here today is not your responsibility. It's the whole town's.'

'Tremayne?'

They both went still, then slowly turned to face the same police officer who'd climbed down into the hole with Rand. The man looked bewildered. A deathly hush fell over the crowd.

'You're Randall Tremayne?'

Zara moved closer to Rand's side and slipped her hand into his. For years they'd known him as Dal Main, their elusive benefactor. Now almost the whole town knew he was Rand Tremayne and it was her fault.

CHAPTER 16

Zara almost wept with relief when Rand didn't push her away. Instead, his fingers tightened around hers.

'He sure as tootin' is.' Millie pushed through the crowd. Sally followed closely on her heels, with her arm around Beth. Now they were together, Zara could see the resemblance in all three generations.

'Me and Sally have known about him for years.' When they stopped in front of Rand, Millie grabbed his hand and shook it exuberantly. 'Thanks, boy, for saving Benji. Our Beth was just telling me all you did.'

'I knew who he really was, too.' Bob walked up and held out his hand to Rand. 'Thanks, Mr Tremayne, for my job and everything else you've done for this town.'

'How did you know?' Rand asked.

'Heck, you might have taught me everything I know about business but I was never stupid. I knew almost from the beginning but I needed the job so I kept my mouth shut. And once I got to know you the old gossip didn't matter any more.'

There were a few low-voiced mutters from the crowd.

'Who said that? I can't see a blasted thing. Get me up there, boy.' Millie poked at Rand until he and Bob helped her to stand on the tractor. She kept her hand on Rand's shoulder and surveyed the crowd.

'That's better. Now, who here doesn't owe this boy? Why, we wouldn't even have our own doctor if he hadn't fixed up the clinic and paid the doctor's wages that first year. He brought jobs back to Treville and for that you should all be darned grateful.'

'It was his fault we lost 'em,' shouted a voice from the crowd.

'No, it wasn't, Chuck,' shouted someone else. 'The mill was in trouble for years and you know it.'

'I agree it was a mortal blow to the town when the mill closed and this boy's parents, may they rest in peace, have to take most of the blame. But what about us?' Millie asked. 'What did we do to save our town? Nothing, that's what.

'We all prayed for those poor children and their families. A lot of you sat on your duff and whined about how unfair it was for you to lose your jobs. Some of you made this boy's life hell and I've been ashamed ever since that I didn't put a stop to it then.'

382

Sally climbed up beside her mother. 'The future's always been in our own hands and in our grief and despair wc let it go. Now, thanks to Mr Tremayne, we have another chance and if we're willing to work hard we *will* rebuild our town.'

'I say we should be grateful for his help,' Bob said, 'but whether this town survives or not will be up to us, with or without Mr Tremayne. Though I, for one, want him to stick around.'

A few voices were raised in a ragged cheer.

Rand pulled Zara closer.

'My brother died in that car,' a woman cried out.

'So did my cousin and his death hurt my family . . .' Bob said.

Zara felt Rand jerk in surprise. Obviously he hadn't known that fact.

'. . . but they never blamed Mr Tremayne because they knew he wasn't driving that car, his father was.'

'Mr Tremayne backed my new business,' one man yelled from the back, 'and now I can pay my mortgage. As far as I'm concerned, he's got my vote.'

'And mine,' echoed many more voices.

'It's getting cold out here and some of these little ones need to get home,' Millie said. 'Anyone here who wants to come to Millie's Place and continue this discussion, the first cup of coffee's on the house. Now get me down from here, boy.'

Rand obeyed her order while Bob helped Sally. As the crowd dispersed several people came up to shake his hand and thank him. Since they had to wait for everyone who parked in the mill's yard to drive away, he and Zara were the last to leave.

'I'll follow you to Millie's.' Zara was about to unlock her car when Rand spun her into his arms. His arms tightened around her in an almost painful squeeze. When he spoke, his voice was muffled against her neck.

'Do you think today was real?'

She let her purse and keys fall at their feet and buried her fingers in his hair. 'Yes, this was very real.'

'Let's go home.' He pressed her up against the door and kissed her until she was breathless.

'Millie's expecting us.'

'I owe Millie a lot but right now . . . to hell with her. I need you.'

She began to laugh. 'Fine with me, but you're the one who's going to have to face her next weekend.'

He groaned.

'Not to mention all those other people who are probably waiting in her restaurant to talk to you.'

'I hate it when you're right.' He kissed her again and slowly, reluctantly, set her away from him. He stooped to pick up her purse and keys, then kissed

384

her again before he gave them to her. 'We'll go to Millie's. For a *very* short visit.'

'I told you so,' Zara whispered, a sound barely audible over the soft music coming from the radio beside the bed. 'You could have told them a long time ago.'

Rand smiled and caressed her bare shoulder. 'Just couldn't resist rubbing it in, could you?'

She smiled, nuzzled her nose into the hair on his chest, happy to be back in what she'd always considered 'their' bed in his apartment. 'Nope.'

'You have to admit, if it hadn't been for Millie and Bob things could have easily become very unpleasant.'

'Absolutely not. I don't have to admit any such thing. A lot of people in that town like you.'

He ran his free hand down her side under the blanket. She yelped when he pinched her bottom.

'Hey, buster. You'd better behave or I'm outta here.'

'You don't really mean that.'

'Probably not.' She rubbed her hand low on his stomach, enjoying the way his breath caught. 'Before we left Treville that gathering at Millie's Place had turned into quite a party. We should have fun like that more often.'

'Mmmm,' Rand murmured, half-asleep.

She snuggled closer and they listened to the radio station, enjoying the warm afterglow, the pleasure of being skin to skin. The station played a commercial and she was thinking about turning it off when a new song came on. She jerked upright.

'Hey! Turn it up.' She scrambled across his body to reach the radio's volume control, ignoring his grunt of pain when her knee bumped his ribs.

'That's my song.' She flung her arms around his neck and kissed him. 'That's my song! It's on the radio already!' She flopped over on her back at his side and grinned up at the ceiling. 'Doesn't it sound wonderful?'

'Congratulations. I know you've worked really hard for a long time. You deserve this success.'

Slowly the odd tone in his voice penetrated her euphoria. She rolled over onto her side and propped her head up on one hand so she could see his face. 'Rand? What's the matter?'

'When are you leaving?' He didn't look at her.

'Leaving? Who said I was leaving?'

'Have you decided on New York, Nashville, or Los Angeles?'

'Rand,' she cupped his chin and turned his face toward her, 'what are you talking about?'

'Your career,' he answered, his expression bleak. He still wouldn't look at her. 'I do understand. You deserve to pursue this chance at success but I'll miss you.'

'You're talking crazy. I'm not going anywhere.'

His gaze met hers for the first time since her song began to play on the radio. 'You're not?'

'Why would I? I moved back to Vancouver to get away from the business end of things and I hated all the travelling. I can write better songs right here with you. I love you.'

He grinned, leaned over, and kissed the breath from her body.

'Wow,' she said as she cuddled into his side, her cheek on his shoulder. 'If that's the reaction I'll get every time I tell you I love you, you're going to be hearing it constantly.'

'We'll get married as soon as possible.'

She froze, then slowly lifted her head.

'Is that a question? It sounded more like an order. I thought we'd talked about this bad habit of yours, Rand.'

'I'll rephrase that.' He slipped his hands under her arms and dragged her up and over his body until she was stretched out on top of him. He kissed her chin. 'I think we should get married.'

'Well, it still needs a little work, but it's getting – oh! – better.' He'd flexed his hips while she was talking and the delicious reactions in her body were making it difficult to think.

'Stop that. You are not going to distract me from this. If you want me to marry you, you are going to have to come up with a proper proposal.'

'If you say "yes" now, I'll give you the portrait.'

'Rand! How many times are you going to try bribing me with that thing? It's never going to work.'

He laughed and tipped her off his body. Then he slid off the bed and knelt on the floor. He grasped her waist and pulled her to sit on the edge of the mattress.

'Zara Lindsey, will you marry me?'

'Rand, we're naked.'

'Stop scolding, woman, and answer me.'

'I told you I wanted a *proper* proposal. We're supposed to be dressed in elegant clothes, sitting in a beautiful garden. There's supposed to be music playing, birds singing, and the sun shining.'

'Zara.' His hands slid to her inner thighs and his thumbs moved in small circles, gradually moving higher and higher. 'This is as proper as I intend to get.'

'Oh. Well, in that case . . .'

THE EXCITING NEW NAME
IN WOMEN'S FICTION!

PLEASE HELP ME TO HELP YOU!

Dear *Scarlet* Reader,

As Editor of *Scarlet* Books I want to make sure that the books I offer you every month are up to the high standards *Scarlet* readers expect. And to do that I need to know a little more about you and your reading likes and dislikes. So please spare a few minutes to fill in the short questionnaire on the following pages and send it to me.

Looking forward to hearing from you,

Sally Cooper

Editor-in-Chief, *Scarlet*

QUESTIONNAIRE

Please tick the appropriate boxes to indicate your answers

1 Where did you get this Scarlet title?
Bought in supermarket ☐
Bought at my local bookstore ☐ Bought at chain bookstore ☐
Bought at book exchange or used bookstore ☐
Borrowed from a friend ☐
Other (please indicate) _____

2 Did you enjoy reading it?
A lot ☐   A little ☐   Not at all ☐

3 What did you particularly like about this book?
Believable characters ☐   Easy to read ☐
Good value for money ☐   Enjoyable locations ☐
Interesting story ☐   Modern setting ☐
Other _____

4 What did you particularly dislike about this book?
_____

5 Would you buy another Scarlet book?
Yes ☐   No ☐

6 What other kinds of book do you enjoy reading?
Horror ☐   Puzzle books ☐   Historical fiction ☐
General fiction ☐   Crime/Detective ☐   Cookery ☐
Other (please indicate) _____

7 Which magazines do you enjoy reading?
1. _____
2. _____
3. _____

And now a little about you –
8 How old are you?
Under 25 ☐   25–34 ☐   35–44 ☐
45–54 ☐   55–64 ☐   over 65 ☐

cont.

9 What is your marital status?

Single ☐   Married/living with partner ☐

Widowed ☐   Separated/divorced ☐

10 What is your current occupation?

Employed full-time ☐   Employed part-time ☐

Student ☐   Housewife full-time ☐

Unemployed ☐   Retired ☐

11 Do you have children? If so, how many and how old are they?

_____

_____

12 What is your annual household income?

under $15,000	☐	or	£10,000	☐
$15–25,000	☐	or	£10–20,000	☐
$25–35,000	☐	or	£20–30,000	☐
$35–50,000	☐	or	£30–40,000	☐
over $50,000	☐	or	£40,000	☐

Miss/Mrs/Ms _____

Address _____

_____

_____

Thank you for completing this questionnaire. Now tear it out – put it in an envelope and send it before 31 January 1998, to:

Sally Cooper, Editor-in-Chief

USA/Can. address
SCARLET c/o London Bridge
85 River Rock Drive
Suite 202
Buffalo
NY 14207
USA

UK address/No stamp required
SCARLET
FREEPOST LON 3335
LONDON W8 4BR
Please use block capitals for address

OUCON/7/97

Scarlet **titles coming next month:**

THE MARRIAGE CONTRACT Alexandra Jones
Olivia's decided: she's not a person any more . . . she's a wife! She's a partner who's suddenly *not* a full partner because of a contract and a wedding ring. Well it's time her husband, Stuart, wised up, for Olivia's determined to be his equal . . . in *every* way from now on!

SECRET SINS Tina Leonard
When they were children, Kiran and Steve were best friends, but they drifted apart as they grew up. Now they meet again and Kiran realizes how much she's missed Steve . . . and how much she loves him. But before they can look to the future, she and Steve must unravel a mystery from the past . . .

A GAMBLING MAN Jean Saunders
Judy Hale has secured the job of a lifetime . . . working in glamorous Las Vegas! Trouble is, Judy disapproves of gambling *and* of Blake Adams, her new boss. Then Judy has to turn to Blake for help, and finds herself gambling on marriage!

THE ERRANT BRIDE Stacy Brown
What can be worse than being stranded on a dark road in the dead of night? Karina believes it's being rescued by a mysterious stranger, whom she ends up sharing a bed with! But better *or* worse is to come, when Karina finds herself married to Alex, her dark stranger.